FINAL SLAUGHTER

SERGIO GOMEZ

Copyright © 2024 Sergio Gomez

All rights reserved. No part of this publication may be reproduced, distributed, or transmitted in any form or by any means, including photocopying, recording, or other electronic or mechanical methods, without the prior written permission of the publisher, except in the case of brief quotations embodied in critical reviews and certain other noncommercial uses permitted by copyright law.

This is a work of fiction. Names, characters, places, and incidents either are the product of the author's imagination or are used fictitiously. Any resemblance to actual persons, living or dead, events, or locales is entirely coincidental.

Cover Design: Teddi Black
Interior Design: Megan McCullough

I.

CHAPTER 1

Somewhere in North Pennsylvania
November 1st 3:30am

DEBBIE DROPPED ANOTHER piece of newspaper into the firepit. The flames in it latched onto the crumpled-up paper and started burning through it, turning it black and into ashes. But it wasn't enough to make the fire bigger. Next to her, Larry, her boyfriend, tried to use the stick in his hand to stoke the flames, but his attempt was just as fruitless.

The campfire they had going was beginning to dwindle, and the smaller it got, the more the group was reminded they were camping in northern Pennsylvania with winter right around the corner.

"Well, this turned out to be a stupid fucking idea, didn't it?" Ray complained, sitting on a log on the other side of the fire.

"I don't see you trying to help," Debbie fired back.

"Stop, Ray." Kelly, his girlfriend and Debbie's best friend, said as she lightly slapped him on the shoulder. "Try to have fun."

Ray held up his can of PBR and shook it. The liquid inside sloshed against the metal. Out here, in the quiet remoteness of where the couples were tent camping, the sound was loud enough that all four of them heard it.

"I'm gonna need a few more of these for that to happen." Ray said, standing up.

"There ya go," Larry said to him, still focused on moving the kindling around to liven up the campfire. "That's the right idea. Mind getting me one, too?"

"I got you." Ray said. "Anyone else?"

The girls shook their heads.

"Alright. I'll be back in a few. I gotta take a shit, too." Ray started heading toward the coolers, which were sitting in front of their two tents.

Behind him, he heard one of the girls groan and the other say "Ew."

He laughed to himself as he made it to his and Kelly's tent. He grabbed a roll of toilet paper and a flashlight and then went out behind the tents to find a spot to do his business.

Ray shined the light down at his feet as he walked through the woods, watching the dead grass brush against the side of his Jordans. The soles of his shoes left behind a slight imprint in the dirt that was damp from the few showers that had been coming here and there all night.

After walking a few paces past the tents, he looked over his shoulder and could see the glow of the campfire and smoke rising out from the pit. He had the flashlight, but even still, the darkness between him and where the others were made the distance seem much more significant than it was.

"Debbie and her boyfriend want us to go on a camping trip for Halloween." Kelly had said to him, trying to convince him it would be spooky fun because it would feel like danger could be lurking anywhere this deep in the woods.

It certainly felt like that for damn sure. But the "fun" part he had yet to experience.

Ray turned away from the campfire, shining his flashlight through the woods to find a good spot to relieve himself. It wasn't like there could necessarily be a *bad* spot, but still he wanted to make sure he wasn't going to be hovering his ass over a rat's nest or a snake pit or something.

As he swept his beam through the woods, something reflecting the light back at him in an odd way caught his eye.

A few paces away, he saw something hanging from a tree. His first thought was that it was a mobile, like something that would hang over a child's crib. Whatever it was, it seemed to be made of various parts that were long and pearly white.

"What the fuck…" Ray said under his breath, and before he realized he was doing it, he was stepping closer to the tree the object was hanging from.

Ray kept the light concentrated on the object, watching it sway in the wind. The sound it made was different than the tree branches hitting one another—but only just barely. From their campsite it would've sounded like nothing more than just the clattering of branches to their ears. But the closer he got to it, the more he could hear the subtly, musical rhythm the object produced.

This was no mobile. It was a windchime.

Ray stopped in his tracks. He stood close enough to it now to tell it was made of bones. Bones that belonged to a bird or some other small animal, Ray wasn't sure. He wasn't a fucking nature expert.

Ray swept the flashlight to another tree and saw another windchime. He brought the flashlight down to ground level, shining it through the trees. Or rather, shining it through the clearing of trees he'd stumbled upon.

In the middle of the clearing was a large, stone firepit with some kindling still in it. The kindling was scorched black and covered in ashes, the flames that had produced this may have been extinguished hours ago or this site may have been abandoned long ago. He wasn't too sure about this, either.

He inspected more of the area, and the rest of what he saw reminded him he needed to take a crap.

"Yo!" Ray screamed, turning around and heading back to the others. "Yo! We gotta get outta here!"

CHAPTER 2

"YOU GUYS EVER hear of any of the legends about this place?" Larry said, giving up on stoking the flames and putting the stick down on the ground. He stood up, wiping his dirt-covered hands on the lap of his pants.

"Which?" Kelly asked. She looked over in the direction Ray had left to make sure he wasn't on his way back. She had an idea of what Larry was about to bring up, but she'd conveniently left out those rumors when trying to convince Ray to come out on this trip.

"There's one about how this place is supposedly haunted. Or that people will randomly go missing."

"Shut the fuck up." Debbie said, looking over at him, scanning his face to see if he was joking. Of course, he had his stupid grin. "You're making shit up, right?"

"No," Larry said, shaking his head. He settled into the camper chair behind him and grabbed the PBR sitting in the cupholder, noticing he was running low and hoping Ray would come back with another one for him soon.

"It's true. Everyone in the towns around here knows about these legends." Larry continued.

"We're from fucking Mayfair, how would you know about rumors all the way up here?" Debbie challenged him.

She looked across the fire at Kelly, to see if she was on her side, but to her chagrin, the color had drained from Kelly's face, suggesting she was buying Larry's shit. She'd even moved to the edge of the log she was sitting on and was leaned over now.

Larry laughed and took a swig of his beer, finishing it off. "I use something called the internet, babe."

"Yeah, yeah, right." Debbie said, taking another sheet of the newspaper from the plastic bag next to her, crumpling it, and throwing it into the fire. The flames raged, and a piece of the wood started glowing red as it caught on fire.

"Yes!" Debbie jumped up, pumping her fist into the air.

"Good job. I knew you'd get it," Larry cheered on. "Anyway, my favorite rumor is the one about the cannibal."

Debbie turned to him, her celebratory expression disappearing from her face. "You're still going on about this?"

"The one that supposedly lives in an abandoned campground in these woods?" Kelly asked him, keeping the conversation on track before the couple had a chance to get into a squabble.

"Yeah, that's it!" Larry said, excited someone else knew about this. "Supposedly he wears skinsuits made out of his victims."

"Oh, you know about this too, Kelly?" Debbie said, turning to Kelly, her arms crossed.

"Yeah, I read a little bit about it." She admitted, her face flushing red, knowing Debbie would be annoyed she was kind of on Larry's side. "I didn't hear about the skinsuits, though."

"Yeah, I saw something about it on some old forum. Real sick shit, huh?" Larry said, his grin growing.

"You didn't know about that part of the story because Larry is just making shit up now." Debbie said, turning to him with a chastising look. "He's just ripping off that movie. The scary one that takes place in Texas. What's it called again?"

"*The Texas—*" Larry started, but before he could finish what he was saying, they heard screaming in the distance.

"What the fuck?" Debbie said, her eyes getting big. Instinctively, she bent down and picked up the long stick Larry had been using to try to stoke the flames, holding it like a sword. "What was that?"

"Sounded like Ray." Kelly said, jumping up to her feet and looking in the direction of their tents.

Much to her relief, they saw her boyfriend come stumbling out of the woods a few seconds later. He rushed over to them and stopped in front of them.

"We have to go." He panted as he stopped in front of the group.

"Whoa, relax, honey. What's going on?" Kelly asked, swooping over to him. She put her arm around his waist and fixed the Scully cap on his head, which was leaning off to one side.

"I saw some weird shit in the woods." Ray said, gently pulling himself way from Kelly's hold.

"What?" Larry asked, on the verge of laughing. "An animal or something?"

"No, no." Ray shook his head. "No, man. There's another campsite. With bones hanging from the trees and shit."

Debbie looked at all three of their faces, feeling a bubble of anger starting to swell in her. "Are you guys all just fuckin' with me right now? Did Larry put you guys up to this?"

"What?" Ray said, shaking his head. "What's she talking about?"

"Nothing." Larry said. "What do you mean bones hanging from trees?"

"Yeah, what do you mean?" Kelly asked.

"I don't know. It was weird shit. But there was a firepit, too. And some owl statues—and when I saw those, I scrammed out of there."

"You serious?" Larry asked.

"Why would I make this shit up?" Ray said, scrunching up his face.

"Because he makes shit up like this all the time." Debbie said, pointing at Larry.

"Well, I'm not." Ray said, turning away from the group. "Come on, let's pack up and get the fuck out of here."

"Wait! Hold on. Was there a fire in the pit?" Larry asked.

"No."

"And you didn't see anyone?"

"No."

"Then what's so scary about this?"

"Did you not hear the part about the bones hanging in the trees?"

"It's probably just stuff someone put there to prank other campers." Larry suggested. "I kinda wanna see it."

"Are you serious?" Debbie said, stepping closer to Larry.

"Yeah," he said. "Come on, babe. Thought you wanted to come out here to do spooky shit."

"Yeah, like Goosebumps book scary. Not, actual scary shit."

"It was that way?" Larry said, pointing into the part of the woods Ray had come out of.

"Yeah." Ray said.

"Alright. I'm going. Who's in?" Larry said, marching in the direction of the other campsite. He glanced at Kelly, hoping she'd be in because he knew it would mean Debbie would come along.

"Fine." Debbie said behind him, beating her friend to the punch. "Kels, you coming?"

"Let me go talk to Ray really quick," Kelly said, hurrying after her boyfriend, who'd retreated into the tent by now. She could see his silhouette through the canvas, sitting on the ground hunched over like a child on timeout.

Larry and Debbie grabbed some flashlights from their tents and then waited for Kelly outside the tent. They could hear a few murmurs coming from the tent, and then about a minute or so later, both Kelly and Ray emerged from it carrying flashlights.

In one hand, Ray had one of the kitchen knives he'd used to cut up the steaks they had for dinner earlier in the night.

"I'm only going because Kelly wants me to." Ray said to the couple as he and Kelly came up to join them. "But you guys are fuckin' crazy."

"We've already been out here for a few hours, anyway." Larry said, starting to lead the group into the woods. "May as well see what we can find."

"If we see a skinsuit, I'm booking it." Debbie said, trailing close behind him.

As the darkness of the woods began to swallow them, she grabbed onto the bottom of Larry's windbreaker and drew in closer to him.

"Skinsuit? What's she talking about?" Ray asked, turning to Kelly and shining his light in her face.

"Babe, please." Kelly said, putting her arm up to shield her face from it.

"Oh, shit. Sorry." Ray swept it away but kept Kelly's face in the glow of the beam.

"Some story Larry was telling us over the campfire." It was Debbie who answered for him. "Just local myths, though. Right, Larry?"

Larry didn't answer right away because he was too busy concentrating on what was ahead of them and making sure none of them would step on anything perilous. The woods were rather uncharted territory here. They were camping at an unofficial site, probably a part of these woods they weren't even supposed to have ventured into it, but there was no chance anyone would find them out here. Something told Larry the park rangers didn't come out this deep into the woods.

And no one in their party knew this tidbit besides him, either.

"Right, Larry?" Debbie repeated.

"Right." Larry said, stopping as the end of his beam revealed the break in the trees a few paces away.

"This is the spot I was going to take a shit. I remember because I was thinking of shitting on those big ass mushrooms right there in case I lost my balance—"

"We found it." Larry said, keeping his eyes on the campsite, which seemed to be abandoned.

"Yeah, so you can spare us the details of your shit." Debbie said, coming up next to Larry.

They were standing on the edge of the woods and what could be considered the campsite, staring at it with a mixture of wonderment and weariness as they swept their flashlights through it.

Without a word, Ray and Kelly walked up next to them. The wild grass and dry leaves crunching underneath their feet was the loudest sound until a small gust blew by them. The windchimes Ray had described began to clatter against one another, making a macabre rhythmic sound, like an auditorium full of people snapping their fingers one after the other.

"You still think it's just a prank?" Ray asked Larry, with a flair of arrogance to his question.

Larry had his flashlight focused on an owl statue carved out of wood. It was about the size of a toddler, and even from this distance, he could tell the patterns on it were intricate. This was no cheapo decoration from a department store; no, this was made by a delicate hand and an eye keen on details. The individual feathers on its chest and wings were meticulously carved out. Its feet had deep lines of separation between the toes and nails, and the owl's big eyes somehow looked animated. As if the bird were alive and watching them.

But to make matters even more interesting, there were other owl statues placed around the abandoned campsite. Some smaller than this one but just as detailed. Some of the bird statues were in different positions, made to look like the owl was soaring or sleeping.

It was all much too elaborate to be just a "prank" the way Larry had been theorizing.

They continued to sweep their flashlight beams across the site in silent awe. Awe, mixed in with nervousness and wonderment. As people who'd lived most of their lives in the city or suburbs, they'd never actually seen anything like this.

"You think it's abandoned?" Kelly asked.

"Look." He said, pointing across the campsite to where a rundown tent was nestled by the trees on the other side of the clearing.

The others followed his beam, their lights joining his, revealing more of the tent. The massive tent was old and worn, with a striped patch in the top corner of one of its front flaps. The thing was covered in wet dirt.

"Okay, I've seen enough." Ray said, taking a few steps back, waiting to see if anyone else would join him.

To his surprise and dismay, the other three stayed put.

"You think someone's staying here?" Kelly asked. It was the same question as before, just reworded.

"Not sure. But if I had to guess, I would say no. It looks like this place was abandoned… a while ago." Larry said, reaching up and scratching the bridge of his nose.

"I'm not staying to find out." Ray said, making this announcement even louder than his first one, hoping his volume would convince the others to come with him.

The others ignored him. Larry turned to the girls, shining his flashlight on them to get a read of their expressions. They both looked intrigued, though nervous, and Debbie was somehow paler than usual.

He reached out and grabbed her hand with his free hand. She turned to look at him, trying to force a smile on her face and act like she wasn't as scared as she was.

"It's just some dumb statues and an old ass tent," Larry said, smiling at her. "Come on, let's get closer and snap some pics."

"You really want to?" Debbie asked, squeezing his hand tighter.

"Yeah, we'll be in and out before you know it." He said, his smile getting bigger. "And if there's any trouble, I'll protect you."

"Man, fuck this." Ray said, turning around and booking it through the patch of woods that connected the two campsites.

Kelly turned to watch her boyfriend running through the trees, her flashlight concentrated on him. Her stomach began to knot with worry.

"You going with him?" Debbie asked Kelly, jotting her heard toward Ray.

"Or are you brave enough to come with us?" Larry asked before she could answer.

Kelly watched her boyfriend disappear into the woods, seemingly swallowed up by the darkness between the two campsites.

"I think he'll be alright." Kelly said, turning back to Debbie and Ray. "We're just going to be there for a few minutes anyway, right?"

"Yeah," Debbie said.

Larry regripped Debbie's hand and then without another word, he started pulling her out of the trees. She followed behind him, dragging her feet on the ground. Behind them, Kelly shadowed them.

She took a second to peer over her shoulder at the patch of dark woods behind them, trying her best to gauge how far they were from their campsite and from their vehicles.

Not like it mattered much anyway.

CHAPTER 3

Larry was hunched over the firepit, pointing his flashlight into it with his other one. He could hear the girls walking around him, staying close, but inspecting whatever parts of this site interested them. Dead leaves crunched underneath their steps, almost as a reminder of how quiet and isolated it was out here.

"Huh… This is kind of weird." Larry said to the girls without taking his eyes off the firepit.

"What is?" Debbie asked, stopping to look over at him, seeing him reaching into the firepit with his free hand. She pointed her light at him and saw her boyfriend's face was contorted into worry.

Larry felt his veins fill with ice water and his lips go dry in an instant. He wanted to answer Debbie, but the realization that the kindling was still warm had him frozen with sudden terror.

By now, Kelly was looking over at him, standing underneath one of the windchimes she'd had her light concentrated on. The girls watched Larry's Adam's Apple bob up and down like a buoy out in the ocean before he turned to them, his eyes big.

"The kindling… it's… it's still… it's still warm."

"What's that mean?" Debbie asked, but she had an idea of what it meant. She'd just said the words to make noise, to drown out the deafening silence surrounding them.

Larry stood up, putting his free hand on his hip, and shaking his head. "I guess whoever was here left this place more recently than I thought."

"What if someone's still here?" Debbie said, taking a few steps closer to him.

Larry started walking across the campsite, walking past Debbie and Kelly, his light concentrated on the tent as he walked toward it.

"I doubt it." He said, shining the light up and down the tent, inspecting it from a foot away. "Someone would've come out and said something by now—"

The last of his words were cut off by a sudden glow coming from the tent. The silhouette of a person moved about inside.

Larry was too stricken with terror to move; all he could do was follow the zipper track with his light beam as it came undone.

A hand, as white as a sheet of paper and covered in a web of dark green veins, emerged from the open tent flaps.

"Get away from my home!" The person whose hand this belonged to shrieked, as she reached between the tent flaps and pushed Larry in the center of his chest.

Instinctively, Larry jumped back, slapping the arm away from him.

An old woman with long silver hair came charging out of the tent. One hand stretched out to push at Larry, the other swinging a lantern at him.

The flame inside the lantern went out as it arced through the air and smashed into the side of Larry's head. He heard a metal clang, followed by his legs turning to rubber, then he was falling backward on his ass.

Behind him, the girls screamed and started running out of the campsite into the trees.

"Get away from me!" The old woman shrieked. "Get away from my home!"

Through blurry vision, Larry watched the old woman reach underneath her knit sweater and pull out a large knife. The sight of the weapon, and the imminent danger, sent a blast of adrenaline coursing through him.

He turned, determined to get away from this loon. The old woman slashed at him. The knife sliced Larry across the back, opening up a four-inch wound just above the waistline of his jeans.

"Ah, fuck!" He screamed as the sudden flash of pain caused him to stumble.

Before he could find his footing, the old woman stabbed the knife into the back of his thigh, the blade almost coming out the other side. This new pain made him completely lose his balance.

Larry fell forward, his momentum moving him too fast to brace for impact; he smashed into the ground face first. His nose crunched underneath the weight, the sound something like what an ice machine would make, as blood gushed out from his now narrower nostrils.

The old woman didn't let up, though. She took the knife out from his thigh and then stabbed him in the back again, just a few inches above the slash on his lower back.

"Look what you made me do! Look! Look!" She said, pulling the knife out and then stabbing it into his back again. "*You* made me do this!

She took the knife out and stabbed Larry again. And again. And again, and again.

Blood sprinkled up into the air with each pull of the blade, getting all over the front of her sweater and face and hair.

Larry tried to crawl away with the last inch of his life, but after the eighth stab, he went limp. His body nothing more than a carcass now, but the old woman continued to stab him until her arms grew tired.

In the distance, he thought he heard screaming, but in his half-asleep state, it was easy to ignore the sounds. The part of him that was awake felt himself slumping forward in the chair and kicked his legs out to keep from faceplanting into the dirt.

As he did, his eyelids fluttered open, and he saw a pair of lights coming toward him. Coming toward the camp. He blinked, thinking the deliriousness of needing to sleep was making him see shit.

But no. There were definitely lights heading his way. And they were coming fast.

He shot up out of the chair, any semblance of relaxation gone, dropping the can of PBR. It hit the ground and splashed some of the liquid on his shoe and the bottom of his pantleg, but Ray paid it no mind.

His eyes were glued on the lights. And now that they were closer, he saw they belonged to the front of a vehicle. A large vehicle, too, judging by the size of its grill. The vehicle began to slow as it came closer to the campsite, but whoever was behind the wheel seemed to barely have any control of the truck as it was weaving left and right.

Like a deer caught in headlights, Ray was too shocked to move a muscle. All he could do was watch as the vehicle got nearer and nearer, threatening to run over him and the rest of the campsite. It was an old truck, one of those that was essentially a heavy box of steel on wheels; it would flatten him into human roadkill and tear through their entire campsite with ease even at low speeds.

Before that could happen, though, the truck came to a sudden full stop on the other side of the campfire, only a few feet from running over it.

"What the fuck!" Ray screamed, feeling his mind and body finally reconnect. He shielded his eyes from the brightness of the headlights pointed directly into his eyes.

Ray stepped to the side, moving out of the headlights. At the same time, the old truck's driver side door opened. A giant man came rolling out of the vehicle and plopped down to the ground, stomach down.

The driver was enormous, maybe one of the biggest guy's Ray had ever seen, with a wild mangle of hair.

But the guy's stature and crazy hair wasn't the most disturbing part. It was the blood. He was covered in it. Bathed in it, really.

"Yo… Are, are you okay?" Ray said, not knowing if he should step forward or backward. Not knowing if the man was dead or alive or if he needed help or was danger himself.

The man didn't respond, just started squiggling toward him, forcing Ray to take a step back. And then, because the situation was growing ever more dangerous, he reached into his jacket pocket and pulled out his lighter. He held it out, as if trying to warn the man that he would burn him if he got any closer.

"Hey, man! Tell me who the fuck you are!" Ray barked, forcing his voice to sound deeper.

Before the man could respond, he heard screams from the woods behind their campsite. One of those screams belonged to his girlfriend, no doubt.

Ray's stomach turned sour, and his balls shriveled up close to his body. not knowing in that moment that this was only the beginning.

CHAPTER 4

KELLY AND DEBBIE came out of the trees and into a scene that was as confusing—and just as fucked up—as the one they'd just left back at the witch's campsite.

Ray was standing over a large man on the ground who was covered in dark red blood. One of Ray's arms was stretched out, holding a lighter toward the man. The small flame would be an insignificant threat given the enormity of this stranger.

The man on the ground was crawling toward him and seemed to be attempting to push himself up onto his feet at the same time but lacked the strength to do so.

Kelly and Debbie came to a halt, stopping between the tents. Their hearts fluttering in their chests, their minds rattled. They'd left one scene of chaos for another one.

"Ray! Ray! What the hell is going on!" Debbie shrieked.

Ray turned to them, his eyes bugged out, the color on his face drained white. He looked like he was on the verge of vomiting and passing out.

"I don't know—but run, Deb. RUN!" Ray screamed at them, then turned back to the man who was halfway up to his feet now.

Too much noise. Too much. Too much…Danger. And now there were three of them.

Varias Caras closed his good eye for a few seconds, trying to find the inner strength in his damaged body to pick himself up. The man kept shouting at him. Threatening him.

He wants to hurt me? It was Ignacio who thought this.

"Yes." Varias Caras uttered back, under his breath. "Ignacio… I need you… I need you to go away. I need you to go asleep."

You need me… to go to sleep…?

"Yes."

Ignacio has to go away? The voice in his head was high-pitched, almost soothing, but Varias Caras needed that side of his personality to be buried away right now. He was holding him back.

"Only… for a little while…" Varias Caras whispered back.

Ignacio listened. He gave Varias Caras more control of the body. Some strength returning to him now that the stronger personality was taking the reins, he planted his hands on the ground and pushed himself up to his feet.

"Hey, man! Stop!" the man shouted, then stomped down on his back, trying to force him back to the ground.

Varias Caras brushed the attack off, even in his weakened state he was much stronger than the man. This was going to be an easy kill.

He rose to his full stature, feeling all the wounds he'd sustained tonight flash with pain, but ignoring them for now. He knew if he could just get one kill, the two women watching in the distance would start to run.

Then he could eat this man and start to regain more of his strength. He just needed one quick kill…

Ray stared into the man's face, realizing for the first time that he was wearing a mask. Underneath the splatters and sprinkles of dried blood, he could see the brown, tattered leather stretched over the man's actual face.

The man's only good eye moved and met Ray's gaze, and it seemed like the man grew by another foot.

Ray gulped and felt his bladder relieving itself as a hot warmth spread over the front of his pants.

He sunk his weight down into his legs, meaning to turn on his heels and run, but he was too slow. The man grabbed his arm, the one that was holding the lighter, and pulled him forward.

"Get off me, you fuck!" Ray screamed and then swung his arm, meaning to clock the man on the side of the head.

Varias Caras turned the wrist he had a hold of, turning the joint inward, snapping the bone like a twig and tearing the ligaments apart with the torque.

Ray fell to his knees from the pain, letting out a loud whimpering scream. The lighter slipping out of his grip.

Varias Caras snatched it out of the air before it hit the ground with his freehand, still holding onto Ray with the other.

"Come on, man. Please, stop! Don't do this—"

Varias Caras shoved the lighter into his mouth and then, before Ray could react, let go of his wrist and punched him in the mouth.

The impact shattered the lighter while it was still inside of Ray's mouth. Plexiglas went shooting through the inside of his mouth. One piece got lodged into his tongue, a few others pierced through his tongue and cheeks. But it was the two pieces he swallowed that did the most damage. Their jagged edges shredded up the inside of his throat as they went down before getting stuck.

Ray grabbed at his throat, feeling the pieces of lighter poking through his throat, blocking it. He felt like if he could just pull on it and rip it through the skin, he'd be able to breathe.

He fell to his side, clawing at his throat, gasping for air. Unable to even scream. All he could do was lay there, tasting lighter fluid and blood in his mouth as he waited for death to end his suffering.

CHAPTER 5

To Varias Caras's surprise, one of the girls wasn't running away from him but was coming toward him. She'd grabbed a hatchet from somewhere and was charging him, the small ax held above her head with both hands, ready to bring it down on him.

Nearing striking distance, Debbie swung the hatchet down… Varias Caras sidestepped it, the head missing him by mere inches. So close he felt the wind from the attack against the side of his face.

Debbie had thrown all her weight into the attack, meaning to hack the hatchet through him as deeply as possible but now lost her balance as a result of missing. She gasped, realizing how vulnerable she was now.

Varias Caras seized the moment. He grabbed her by the waist and lifted her up about three feet, then threw her in the air toward the campfire.

Debbie landed inside the flames headfirst. A sharp part of the kindling found its way into one of her cheeks, while the fire seared at the skin on her face. She screamed as she pulled her head out of the campfire, her hair ablaze. The fire quickly burning her scalp and spreading down onto the collar of her jacket.

Varias Caras found the hatchet lying on the ground, which had slipped out of Debbie's grip as she'd been flying through the air. He picked it up and then turned to the girl, who was running around the campsite, flapping her arms through the air as the fire on her head continued to rage.

Varias Caras held the ax up, and lined it up with her, following her as she ran in desperate circles. This was going to be tricky, but it was needed. He didn't want to spend the energy chasing her.

Locking in his aim on the girl, he brought the hatchet over his head with both hands and threw it. The hatchet spun through the air, its edge shining silver when it pointed up at the night's full moon.

Four, five, six, revolutions and then it hit its target. The hatchet went into the side of Debbie's neck, hacking halfway through it. Blood spurted out of the wound like a sprinkler where a major artery had been sliced open.

Debbie fell to the side, nothing more than a corpse even before her body hit the ground.

Varias Caras watched his victim collapse, and made to move, but the night was catching up to him. His legs felt like Jell-O. He took three steps before he fell to one knee. Breathing heavily. His chest heaved in and out, his heart pulsing rapidly.

Somewhere in the short distance, through the trees, behind the campsite, he heard shouting. Two voices.

There were more of them. He wasn't sure he was going to be able to make it out of this night alive. He picked his head up and looked in the direction of the shouting, his vision blurring. So blurry the two tents looked like nothing more than oblongs against the dark.

More shouting. Feet moving. Moving fast. Someone running. And someone running after them, but they weren't coming in his direction.

They were running elsewhere. Somewhere deeper into the woods.

Maybe he had enough time to rest after all… Just a quick nap.

His head started to feel heavy, like it was filled with bricks, swaying left and right because his neck muscles were too weak to stabilize it.

"Just…a quick… nap…" Varias Caras said, letting himself fall forward.

He landed flat on his stomach on a patch of dry grass. His body weakening by the second, his limbs going numb. He closed his eye, and in a matter of seconds, Ignacio and el Monstro fell fast asleep.

CHAPTER 6

THE OLD WOMAN from the campsite was chasing after her. Kelly was running with no direction, no idea where she was going, unknowingly going deeper into the woods.

They entered an area where the trees started to thin out, and the full moon's light slivered through the trees like swords made of light. Kelly craned her neck over her shoulder to see where the old woman was, but she was still on her tail, bloody knife held up above her head. Her eyes were open so wide they looked like they were about to pop out of her skull.

"Get away from me!" Kelly screamed at her. "Leave me alone!"

"You get away from me!" The old woman screamed, then launched herself through the air, hand holding the knife stretched out.

Kelly shrieked and tried to kick her sprint into the next gear, but it wasn't enough. The old woman stabbed the knife into her shoulder, then used it as leverage to pull her back.

Kelly let out another scream, this one a mixture of shock and pain, as she was yanked off her feet. She crashed onto the ground, hitting it harder than she was bracing herself for, and felt the impact push all the air in her lungs out of her.

Still conscious of what was going on, she reached to grab the knife from her shoulder, but the old woman's hands beat her to it. Kelly's fingers curled around the air, then involuntarily her hand went to the wound, palm flat as she tried to plug it.

Kelly opened her eyes and saw the old woman standing over her. Her silver, frizzy hair a mess on her head, her icy blue eyes piercing through her. The old woman's hands came into view, holding the knife that was dripping with Kelly's fresh blood.

"Why… why are you doing this…" Kelly said in a weak voice, unsure if she was audible even in the stillness of these isolated woods. "Why…"

"I told you to stay away from my home!" The old woman screamed as she raised the knife above her head. "Stay away! Stay away!"

Kelly moved her hand from her shoulder down to where the old woman was aiming the knife. She felt the knife go through her hand and come out through the other side. She screamed as she kicked her legs to squirm away.

The old woman wasn't giving up though. She pulled the knife out of Kelly's hand and then stabbed her again. This time, Kelly was too slow to prevent the old woman from hitting her target. She felt the knife go into her chest, felt it stab through one of her lungs. And then, all at once, it felt like her body was beginning to fill with air. She only felt this for a second before the blood started pouring into the lung through the punctured hole, filling it. Hot blood gushed out of Kelly's mouth as she fruitlessly gasped for air.

Edith stared down into the young woman's face. Her eyes were open, but her body had gone still a few seconds ago, after a few more stabs in the chest.

Blood was still pumping out of her, but Edith knew enough about murder to know the girl was dead. The blood oozing out was just the last of it circulating through the severed veins.

Edith stared down at the front of her knitted lavender sweater. It was smeared with blood from stabbing both this girl and her boyfriend.

"Look what you made me do!" Edith screamed and stabbed the knife into the dead girl's body, right into one of her shoulders. "Look at this! You caused this!"

She pulled the knife out and then brought it down onto the dead body. Edith felt the knife pierced through one of her organs, her bladder or part of her stomach, maybe; it was hard to tell.

"You did this!" She shrieked, turning the knife.

More blood pumped out of the gash as Edith continued to twist the knife. She made the wound so large there was no resistance to her turning the knife anymore. Satisfied, she pulled the blade out and wiped it clean on the side of her pants.

"You made me do this…" she whispered to the dead body.

Edith shifted her focus, knowing there were more people out there. There was at least one more girl who'd been with these two she'd just killed. And she'd also heard some commotion coming from somewhere else in the woods. Shouting and an argument of some kind.

But the woods were silent now.

It could be a trap though. She had to be careful.

Edith tightened her grip on the knife and started making her way back to her campsite.

Edith could just see the light of a campfire through the trees. From this distance, it was a small, orange glow that was seemingly floating in the dark abyss. Easy to miss if you didn't know what to look for.

She retrieved her lantern from the spot where she'd dropped it after clocking that guy with it and re-lit it with a match from her tent. With the knife in hand and the lantern in the other, she started her way through the woods.

The dead leaves crunched underneath her feet. Dry grass brushed against the side of her legs. These sounds that would've been subtle just a few seconds ago were loud as if amplified by microphones in the dead-silent woods.

As she neared the other campsite, she stepped through some small shrubs. The small thorns on its bare branches clung onto her wool socks and made small perforations in them as she walked through the bushes.

Edith blew the lantern out and stopped behind a tree. She poked her head out to inspect the campsite. Three bodies were lying around the campfire. The body closest to her, a woman judging by the curves, had its face charred black; smoke was still rising from it in wisps against the cold air. The hair on the person's face had been completely burned off, nothing but ashes scattered in the wind. There was also a hatchet jutting out of the neck. The wound had been gushing blood, judging by the smattering of blood surrounding it.

The second body was facing away from Edith, so she couldn't see many details, but by the positioning of the arms, the person had died trying to grab at either their throat or their face. And the person was dead; there was no doubt in her mind about that. The body looked as stiff as the kindling inside the campfire.

The third body belonged to an enormous person. He was face down, covered in what looked to be bloodstains from head to toe. His hair was a tangle of greasy, black hair. She wondered if maybe the rodents wouldn't use it as a nest if he laid out there long enough.

Something in Edith's gut told her this man didn't belong to the group of campers who'd been snooping around her home.

A truck was parked on another side of the campfire, away from where the bodies lay. Its headlights were left on, the driver side door wide-open. Someone had been in a hurry to get out of the vehicle.

The scene was confusing. But one thing she did know, she'd taken care of those punk kids for trespassing. And now, it was time for her to take her spoils. With the knife still clutched in her hand, Edith started into the campsite, heading toward the tents.

The thing she enjoyed about living out here in these isolated woods was that rarely anyone bothered her, but the other side of that was being so far away from civilization sometimes made it difficult for her to get commonly needed items. Items that campers usually had on them, so whenever any wandered out this far, raiding their campsites was ideal.

And the easiest to raid, by far and for obvious reasons, were dead campers.

Edith came within a few feet of the enormous man's body before she realized he was still breathing. His chest heaved up and down. Despite how large he was, the movement was subtle enough that she couldn't see it until now. Until now that she was too close for comfort.

She saw his shoulders twitch, and one of his arms shot straight out. The meaty paw at the end of it digging into the earth, the dead half-frozen grass crunched in his squeeze.

Edith stopped, her heart fluttering in her chest like the wings of a hummingbird. The giant man's head snapped upward, and Edith found herself staring into a face that evoked so many feelings out of her at once, she took a step back and gasped.

She did a doubletake and realized the tattered thing she was staring into wasn't a face at all. It was a mask. A mask crusted with streaks of dried blood all over it. The thing she could tell about the man's actual face, though, was that one of his eyes was missing. One of the streaks on the mask was a mixture of ichor and blood, dried into a dark stain running down the mask from the socket where the eyeball was missing. The socket was crusted with a mixture made of the same grotesque ichor and blood. Parts of the optic nerve hung out from the hole like small little tentacles, like a small squid or octopus was trying to climb out of the man's head.

The image was enough to make Edith's stomach lurch. She forced herself to shift her focus to his other eye and met the gaze from his good eye. The pupil was black—black as a sky with no stars, black as infinite. Yet, it had a shine to it, like a piece of jewelry made from volcanic rock.

There was something beautiful about it. It had a certain innocence about it. Like the man had ended up here, hurt and covered in blood, but it wasn't his fault. Or at least, not *all* of his fault.

Edith took another step back as the man used his outstretched arm to claw into the earth and pull himself closer to her.

"You're not like them, are you?" Edith said, still staring in that beautiful dark eye. Caught somewhere between afraid and comforted by it.

The man didn't say anything, he just groaned. But a lot was said in that groan.

"They were trying to... trying to hurt you, weren't they?" Edith said, and as if to not confuse him, she cocked her head back, gesturing to where the two other bodies lay.

He nodded and then winced. His other arm shot out, planted against the ground, and he forced himself up into a sitting position. He brought his hands over his chest and crossed his legs. Gravity slumped him forward, but he seemed to have enough energy to keep himself up. Albeit, with a subtle sway as he was using whatever little energy he had to fight against falling.

Before Edith could ask him another question, he reached one hand underneath his long hair. There was a loud plastic snap, then he was pulling the mask off his face with both hands. The leather rasped against the blood that had dried between his face and the mask. In the silence of the night, it sounded like sandpaper grinding against sandpaper.

Edith stared into a face that reflected an even greater innocence than just the sole eye. Despite the man's size and the five-o-clock shadow on his face, the wounds on the man's face made her feel sorry for him. The eye that had been gouged out. The chunk of flesh that had been bitten off the side of his cheek.

"It wasn't just them, was it?" Edith almost gasped the question as the realization dawned on her. These injuries looked old. Like he'd sustained them at least a few hours ago. "There were others who tried to hurt you?"

He nodded again.

"Because they're afraid of you." Edith said, rolling up the sleeve of her sweater, revealing burn marks running up along her arms that had turned the skin into bumpy grooves.

"I think you've had enough action for one night." Edith said, daring to step closer to him. She bent down to be eye level with him and put a hand on his shoulder. "I live not too far from here. If you can make it there, I will help you. Fix up your bandages. Give you something hot to drink."

He grunted. It seemed the man didn't speak much or perhaps didn't know how to speak. Either way, the grunt was enough for Edith to know he was saying he understood what she was saying.

"But you have to be able to walk there on your own, you understand me?"

Another grunt, followed by an effort to get up. He swayed back and forth, looking like a giant baby trying to learn how to balance itself on its two legs. The giant man pressed himself against the tree at his back and used it as support to get himself up to his feet.

Now, at the extent of his height, Edith realized just how large the man was. He stood at least a foot over her; some loose strands of hair obscured his face. He smelled of body odor mixed with the coppery smell of the blood he was covered in.

Edith felt her courage waver, and a pang of panic went through her that suggested maybe this hadn't been such a good idea. That maybe she should have run away or killed this man.

She gulped.

Then saw him lose his balance and crash onto the tree, shoulders first. Another grunt came out of him, but this one was full of pain. She could see his eye through one of the curls in his face and saw them full of hurt. Not just physical, but mental and emotional pain.

The fear in Edith subsided, and a certain maternal instinct took over. Feelings she'd never had for anyone—not a pet or any of her nieces or nephews—except for her late son, Mason. She reached out and touched the man on the shoulder before she even realized she was doing it.

"I'm going to start walking. Do you think you'll be able to follow, boy?"

Keeping his eye concentrated on her, he bobbed his head up and down, then pushed off the tree. He swayed a bit before finding his center of gravity and stabilizing himself.

"Okay, then. Follow me." Edith said.

Side-by-side, the two of them started walking through the trees.

CHAPTER 7

She brought him back into her tent and laid him down on a rollout mattress Ignacio barely fit on. His sides spilled out over it, and he could feel a few small rocks and rough parts of the earth digging into his body through the tent's floor.

The old woman had been treating him for the last hour or so. Her touch was soft, but not in the same way as Judy's or Mamá's. No, her skin was soft in a way that made Ignacio think it might tear at any moment and start leaking blood all over him. Her hands were also cold—colder than the air outside, even—and clammy. They reminded him of the frogs and lizards he used to catch as a kid.

The old woman finished stitching the wound on his face where Judy's bruja friend had bitten a chunk of his cheek off. She lifted the excess stitching up into the air and snipped it off with a small pair of scissors.

She set the scissors down on the ground next to her and leaned back, inspecting her handiwork. Satisfied, she uncrossed her legs and stood up. The oversized sweater she wore unraveled and fell to her knees.

"It's going to take you a while to heal, but all-in-all, it doesn't look *too* bad." She said. "How's your head feel?"

Ignacio shrugged one shoulder. The old woman nodded.

"Get comfortable. I'm going to go make us some tea." She said.

Ignacio watched her grab some stuff from underneath a wooden table. He couldn't see what anything in that part of the tent was because the lantern by his bedside only lit his portion of the space. But he could track the old woman's movements through the shadows and watched her leave the tent.

This was all so confusing to Ignacio. The old woman reminded him of the witches his mother always warned him about. The witches who were supposed to be bad people. They were supposed to put curses on people and sacrifice animals to the Devil, not help people.

I'm scared. Ignacio said to Varias Caras.

"Shut up!" Varias Caras whisper-screamed, taking over Ignacio's body. "Do what I say. We need her right now."

We need her... right now... Varias Caras heard his weaker personality babble this in a childlike manner in his head.

"We have to play nice until we're better. Do you understand? We've taken a lot of damage, and even I can only take so much."

I understand. Ignacio understands.

"Good. Now, I'm going to give you back control so we don't scare the old woman off. But you have to do everything as I say if you want to see Mamá and Judy again, do you understand me?"

Okay. Ignacio understands. I will do what you say.

Ignacio felt Varias Caras slip into the back of his mind. With el Monstro hiding, he felt the wounds in his body flash hot with pain. All the wounds seemed to pulse in time with his heartbeat, almost as a reminder that he was lucky his heart was still ticking.

El Monstro was right. He needed to rest. Ignacio turned to his side.

Through the tent walls, he could see the glow of the campfire outside. The old woman's shadow was hunkered over it, moving things about that made metallic noises.

Ignacio closed his eye, trying to let his mind slip into the calmness of sleep. But he couldn't. An owl was hooting in the distance, the kindling in the campfire was crackling. It was too much stimulation. He couldn't relax.

A few seconds later, he heard the tent flap being pushed open. He lifted his head off the pillow and saw the old woman standing at the entrance, holding two porcelain mugs in one hand. A string dangled over their edges like dead serpents' tongues hanging out of their mouths.

He watched her cross the tent; steam rose from the mugs in thick plumes. The aroma of cinnamon and other spices and herbs filled the inside of the tent.

"You're still awake. Good." She said, stopping at Ignacio's side. She extended a mug out toward him. "Go on; drink it up. It'll help you sleep."

Ignacio grabbed the mug and blew into it the way Mamá had shown him to do so before sipping on a hot drink ever since he was a little boy. On the surface of the brownish liquid, he saw his own reflection staring back at him with his good eye.

"Can you talk, child?" The old woman asked him, still standing at his side.

Even though Ignacio was much bigger than her, he felt small in the current situation.

Don't say anything. Just shake your head. Varias Caras ordered him before he could even open his mouth to start talking.

Ignacio did as he was told and shook his head lightly. Mamá always told him not to lie to people, especially if they were older, but if he wanted to survive, he had to listen to what Varias Caras. El Monstro always knew how to get him out of trouble.

"That's okay." The old woman said, sitting down on the ground, cross-legged. She balanced the mug on her top leg, holding onto it with one hand. "The look in your eye tells me everything."

The old woman paused and swallowed hard. The loose skin on her wrinkly neck wobbled with the motion.

"I had a son who had that same look in his eyes." She said, taking a sip of her tea. "The other kids used to bully him. They would beat him up at recess, throw things at him, spit on him. You want to know why?"

Ignacio nodded. Then took a sip of tea. The cinnamon in it was overbearing, and there was a certain aftertaste that Ignacio didn't enjoy.

"It's an acquired taste." The old woman said, seeing the slight scowl on his face. "Think of it like medicine and just force it down."

Ignacio opened his mouth to repeat the instructions but then remembered what Varias Caras told him to do and turned it into a small grunt instead.

"I used to make this for my son when he was sick." The old woman's eyes turned watery all of a sudden. "You see, just like you, my boy was born different. He was born with a disease no doctor could figure out, but they thought it was some form of gigantism."

Ignacio blinked. He didn't know what she was saying, but he could feel the sadness in her heart.

"It affected his head and feet, mostly. By the time he was nine, he was already wearing size twelves—anyway, it made him a target to this cruel world. My son would come home crying from school almost every day. Sometimes he would try to hide it from me, locking himself up in his room and crying into his pillow to muffle the sounds—but a mother knows. A mother always knows."

She paused again. Took a few more sips of her tea and shifted her weight around before continuing.

"One day, he came home with patches of his hair missing. After a few minutes of begging him to tell me what happened, he finally told me a group of boys held him down during recess and took scissors to his hair. It broke my heart."

Pause. Ignacio stared at her, wanting to reach out to comfort her, but Varias Caras was telling him not to. That it would be a big mistake if he did.

"I saw some of my boy in you when I ran into you out in the woods, hurt and covered in blood." She jutted her head toward the front of the tent. "So, if you were wondering why I helped you instead of killing you, that's the reason."

She cupped the mug tight with both hands and then brought it up to her lips. Her slurping was the loudest sound in the tent for a few seconds.

"Don't think this is entirely altruistic—nothing ever really is…" She gulped to keep herself from crying, then let out a short cough to clear her throat. "I suppose I wanted you to come back here so I can be motherly to someone, at least until you recover. After that, you're of course free to go do whatever it is you're here in these woods for."

Without warning, the old woman got up, getting a view of the tea Ignacio had gulped down while she'd been talking. Her face lit up.

"Ah, very good, child." She said, smiling, showing teeth that were perfectly straight and pearly white.

She grabbed the empty mug from Ignacio and went over to a wooden table in a corner on the opposite side of the tent. Here, she rinsed the mugs out with water from a small plastic pitcher.

While she was doing that, Ignacio lay back in the bed, folding the pillow underneath him so it felt fluffier and got comfortable. He closed his eye, and almost instantly, his body started relaxing. He wasn't sure if it was the tea, the damage he'd taken tonight, or a combination, but his mind began slipping into the comfort of sleep.

Half-awake still, he could hear the old woman walking to the front of the tent. He heard her push through the flap, then stop.

"Pardon me, it seems I have forgotten my manners." She said, startling him awake.

He opened his eye and turned to her.

"My name is Edith."

"Ignacio." He muttered to her, feeling himself falling back asleep.

Her eyes got big, as if he'd just done a magic trick before her eyes. "So, you do talk?"

"Sometimes."

The old woman grinned. "And that's your name? Ignacio?"

"One of them," he muttered, then was fast asleep.

CHAPTER 8

It was light out when Ignacio woke up. A bird in a nearby tree was twittering at the top of its lungs, either in declaring its territory or trying to attract a potential mate. Either way, it signified to Ignacio that it was time for him to get up.

He focused his hearing as he slowly picked himself up off the mattress, listening for the old woman. He heard footsteps in the not-too-far distance, small feet attached to brittle legs shuffling through the woods, the soles of her boots grinding against the dirt and crunching leaves.

It was her. No doubt.

Ignacio made his way out of the tent.

Squinting against the golden morning sun, Ignacio watched the old woman returning to the campsite. She had a net full of fish slung over her shoulder that was leaving a trail of water in her wake. Some of the fish inside were still wiggling around, flicking water off their tails and fins through the mesh.

"I brought breakfast." The old woman said, stopping by a tree stump near the campfire where she set the net down with a wet thud. "I hope you like fish."

Ignacio nodded, wanting to tell her he ate all sorts of meat. Even human, but he knew Varias Caras would be mad if he did that.

"You look less haggard than you did last night. Did you sleep well?" Edith asked him, looking him up and down.

"Yes."

"And how are you feeling?"

"Better." Ignacio said, then pointed to his abdomen.

"That's very good news." Edith said. Then she moved over to the net and started undoing the knot at the top of it.

She reached underneath her sweater and unsheathed the same large knife she'd used to kill those people last night. She grabbed a fish from the top of the pile, set it on the stump, and beheaded it with one chop.

Ignacio watched her descale the fish, fascinated and admiring her handling of the knife. It was clear she had practice with this.

"I went to your truck this morning." Edith said, not looking up at him. She grabbed another fish from the net. "Found some interesting stuff in there."

Ignacio felt Varias Caras come awake. He shifted his weight from one leg to the other.

"The two severed heads stood out to me the most." She chopped the head off the fish and looked up at Ignacio.

He could see her cloudy, blue eyes through the strings of gray hair falling over her face. They seemed to be piercing through him, the same look Mamá would give him when she expected him to explain a mess he made in the kitchen or why he hadn't cleaned his room yet.

"A normal person would be afraid. Would probably have called the cops already."

Ignacio glanced at the knife in her hand, trying to gauge how many seconds he would have to take it from her. It would be easy, even in his injured state there was no way the old woman was stronger than him. The problem would be if she cut him open somewhere dangerous first before he could get a good grip on it. A slice to the throat or a stab in his eye was all she would need to take him out.

Wait. Not yet. Varias Caras said to him, reining him in.

"Relax, child." Edith said, noticing his hands had balled into fists. "I have no intentions of causing you harm or calling the police—not like they would come all the way out here, anyway."

She waved the knife through the air and then continued descaling the fish, her eyes trained on Ignacio the whole time.

"It seems we're more alike than I originally thought."

"More alike…" Ignacio muttered.

"Those people I killed last night weren't the first people I murdered."

Edith reached down for a bag leaning on the ground against the tree stump. She grabbed it and set it next to the fishnet. Then pulled out two wooden skewers and two glass shakers. One of the shakers was filled with salt, the other with black pepper.

"Those heads in your truck, do they belong to people you killed?" She asked him as she sprinkled salt and pepper all over the prepared fish.

Ignacio shook his head because that wasn't quite the truth. "They were people… women… that I loved."

"And someone took them from you?" Edith asked. She realized one fish wasn't going to be enough for her massive companion and grabbed two more fish to prepare for him.

"Yes." Ignacio said but didn't tell her that Judy had died by his own hand.

It was too painful.

"I'm sorry to hear that." Edith said, descaling the fish. She grabbed the shakers and started pouring the salt and pepper onto them. "But that's how this cruel, cruel world works. It gives you things you love and then takes them away without warning. And when you try to fight back, when you try to not let the world push you around, they call you a monster."

Edith pierced three fish into one of the skewers and one onto the other skewer. She held them up. "Want to cook your own?"

Ignacio nodded.

They moved over to the campfire.

Edith sat in the chair she had set up, while Ignacio sat on the ground. Both of them held the wooden skewers over the fire. Oil dripped off the fishes' skin as they cooked over the fire, sizzling as it came into contact with the flames. Every once in a while, parts of the skin would expand out into a little bubble and pop.

They hadn't talked since sitting down. They'd just been watching their fish cook, letting the sounds of the morning fill the silence between them. Songbirds singing in the distant treetops, an occasional autumnal wind blowing through the trees and surrounding foliage.

The bone chimes clattered in a macabre rhythm, something like a hymn of teeth chattering together. The sound was meant to keep unwanted visitors away, but of course, last night it'd had the opposite effect and had attracted the morbidly curious troop of campers.

"Those people we killed last night are still out in the woods." Edith said, breaking the silence, twirling the wooden stake to cook the other side of her fish. "All except the one I killed here. I buried him in the trees already while you were sleeping."

Ignacio went to move, thinking this was an order to go take care of them. The sudden movement caused the stab wound in his abdomen to flare up in pain, making him wince and rethink moving so fast.

"Easy now." Edith said, turning to look at him. "There's no rush, but we do have to get to them sooner rather than later. Before we get some unwanted critters crawling around our camp."

"Sooner rather than... later." Ignacio repeated, turning his focus back to the fish. They weren't getting crispy fast enough, so he held them closer to the flame. Close enough that the top of the flame licked at their skin.

"Last night wasn't the first time I killed someone, like I mentioned." Edith stated this like Ignacio had asked, "The first person I ever killed was my husband. Stabbed him with the same knife I carry with me."

She patted the sheathed knife hidden by her sweater, as if to remind Ignacio.

"Ironically, the knife belonged to him." She said, throwing her head back and letting out a high-pitched cackle that reverberated through the trees.

The laughter was shrieking, reminding Ignacio more of the sound a cat made when it was angry than the sound of a human finding something funny. He looked into the old woman's face, and saw her eyes were empty, void of anything.

Then, in a second, she snapped back. Her expression returning to normal as she sobered up from the fit of cackles.

"It was a long time coming." She said, her voice dropping down to a whisper.

She took the fish off the fire and started blowing onto it as she spun the wooden skewer around.

"About thirty years ago, he killed my son. We were staying at a camp not too far from here, and my husband took the boat and Mason Jr. to a nearby lake to go fishing.

I stayed back at the cabin to prepare dinner. Mason Jr. had been insisting on having pizza, and luckily, I had brought some French bread, tomatoes, and plenty of cheese for sandwiches and I was able to whip up something resembling my boy's request."

Edith paused and turned to look Ignacio directly in the eye. "I would have done anything for my boy. *Anything.* You understand me?"

Ignacio didn't reply. He just stared back at her, waiting for her to continue.

"Anyway, while they were out on the lake, my boy fell out of the boat. My husband dove into the water to try to get him, said Mason Jr. was thrashing like a loon, almost drowned himself trying to rescue him."

Edith stopped, using her free hand, she wiped the tears coming down her eyes with her knobby index finger. She took in a deep breath, then went on.

"I don't buy it for a second, though. He always resented Mason Jr. because of his birth defects. Always called him all sorts of nasty names; stupid, ugly, deformed. And worse, my husband was dry as the Sahara when he returned—said he toweled himself off and the sun dried him out, but it was all bunk. Bunk, I tell you!"

Edith shook her head. More tears were coming down her eyes, but she found her composure to press on. "I loved that boy more than anything. And I know my husband hated him. I know he threw him into the water and let him drown. I know it! I know it!"

Her icy blue eyes filled with rage, forcing Ignacio to look away. Instead, he watched the skin on his fish continue to blacken over the flames.

"I'd been fantasizing about killing him all this time, and about two months ago, I finally summoned up the courage. I took his knife from his side of the dresser where he always left it, and I stabbed him in the back in the middle of the night. Over and over. There was so much blood… so much blood…

I think he was dead after the seventh stab, but I gave him several more. Maybe ten or twenty or thirty more, I'm not sure. But when I stepped back and looked at the mess, it was the most beautiful thing I'd ever seen.

Bright, red blood was coming out of all the stab wounds, soaking the sheets and the mattress underneath them. My husband's body was still as I literally watched the fluids that had been his life essence drip out of him. Knowing that it was all due to my hand made me feel like a *god*, my boy."

Edith took a bite from the fish, pausing to let the statement hang in the air. The food was hot, but she powered through and quickly chewed it down.

"That's why I'm here." She continued. "The lake my son drowned in isn't too far from here. It's where I got this fish from."

She took another bite of the fish and then said, "For some reason, visiting the place where he was last alive and eating the fish from there makes me feel inexplicably connected to Mason Jr. Almost like his essence was left in the lake when his body and soul separated from each other."

Ignacio leaned forward and blew onto his fish.

Edith was halfway to biting her fish but paused to look over at Ignacio. It sounded like he was blowing raspberries at the trout rather than trying to cool them off.

"You have no idea what I'm talking about, do you, boy?"

"Yes." Ignacio said. "Lake. Nearby. Ignacio knows."

"You've been in these woods before?"

"Yes."

Edith was surprised by this answer. "For what reason?"

"To be close to her." Ignacio said, chomping on a fish, eating half of its body in almost one bite. He chewed fast, realizing how ravenous he was now that he had his first taste of food, and swallowed just as quickly. "To be close to Mamá."

"I'm not understanding."

Ignacio giggled. "It… is you who does not know what Ignacio… is talking about."

"No. I don't. Start making a lick of sense, please."

"Fantasmas." Ignacio said, taking another bite of his fish.

"I don't know that word, boy."

"Ghosts." Ignacio said, nodding as the bite went down into his tummy. "They are everywhere."

"What are you talking about?"

"There are ghosts in these woods. Ignacio can see them." He said. "Ignacio can… help you…"

"Help me how?"

Ignacio took a bite of his second fish. "I can help you... see your son again..."

Edith stirred. She tightened her grip around the wooden skewer and balled her other hand into a fist, wondering if this man wasn't trying to yank her chain. She'd had plenty of experience with so-called mediums who preyed on her grief and conned her out of money to "talk to her son." They'd all been full of it and gotten even the most miniscule details wrong—like the one who told her Mason Jr. told her he wished he could have grown up to be a star football player. It was a ridiculous statement because her boy was into collecting bugs, reading nature books, and had never once in the eight years he'd been alive had an affinity toward anything physical.

It was unlikely Ignacio was one of these, but this conversation was getting stranger by the second. She was wondering if maybe he hadn't been badly concussed last night while he'd been attacked.

"It is why...you feel that connection when you eat the fish." Ignacio explained to her, sensing she was disbelieving him. "Your son's ghost... Ignacio can show it to you... when I feel better..."

"Show it to me? His ghost? Is that what you're trying to say?"

"Yes... Ignacio has candles... in his truck." He said, bringing the fish close to his mouth and taking a big bite of it.

Edith leaned in slightly closer to him and saw the sincerity in his face. He believed what he was saying. There was no con happening here, at least, none she could sniff out. Whether she believed this man had actual connections to the spirit world, she wasn't sure.

She pondered this while Ignacio sat eating his fish. A period of silence stretched between them.

"You know, I wish I would've thought about keeping my son's head." Edith said, breaking the silence. "That's quite the ingenious memoriam."

CHAPTER 9

IGNACIO AWOKE FROM his third nap the same day. She'd been giving him that tea that made him sleep all through the day. Even when he woke up, he was still sleepy.

Except now, it was different. It was nighttime.

Ignacio sat up. The only light was coming from the campfire outside the tent. He could hear a pot of liquid boiling. The smell came in through the unzipped flap, the aroma of garlic and onions and meat wafted into the tent.

Ignacio's stomach grumbled. He knew whatever it was she was cooking wouldn't be enough, though. She'd given him another meal earlier: a mix of some leafy greens, mushrooms, and chunks of some wild bird. But it hadn't been enough to satiate el Monstro.

Varias Caras was still hungry. Ravenous, even.

I will be okay. He heard Varias Caras say, el Monstro surfacing to his mind. *We can't let her know about me. Not yet.*

"Why… not?" Ignacio said, scratching his head. "Because she will… be afraid of me…?"

Yes. Just like Judy was. Just like everyone always is.

"But she says she understands." Ignacio said, shaking his head.

She doesn't. No one understands. No one except me. And Mamá and Papá, but they are—

"They are gone." Ignacio muttered this, feeling a pang of sadness ring through him.

He leaned back onto the mattress, looking up at the tent ceiling. Or at least, what he could see of it in the darkness.

At the other side of the tent, the tent flaps were pushed open. Ignacio turned his head to see Edith coming in, a lantern in her right hand. She strode into the tent toward the wooden table where she kept all her medical supplies, tools, and cooking utensils. From it, she gathered some material and then came to Ignacio's side.

"Were you calling for me?" she asked, kneeling next to him, setting the medical supply and the lantern next to her.

Varias Caras shook his head.

"Ah, thought I heard you talking."

Tell her you were praying. Ignacio heard Varias Caras order in his head.

"Ignacio was… praying."

"I see," Edith said, nodding in approval. "I was never a church woman myself. Maybe I should've been. Maybe I wouldn't have married a damn devil."

Ignacio nodded.

"Here, pick your head up. I'm going to clean your wounds and change your bandages, then I have something to show you."

Edith undid the bandages, being careful not to rip the wounds open again. Then she poured in a green powder, a holistic medicine made from local herbs. It felt refreshing in Varias Caras's wounds, kind of reminded Ignacio of when Mamá would rub VapoRub on his chest when he was sick and coughing to try to relieve his lungs.

A few minutes later, Edith was done cleaning him up and replacing his wounds. She leaned her posture back, making sure all the bandages looked perfectly wound.

"Any of them too tight?" she asked him, grabbing his sweater from where she'd placed it on the ground next to her.

Ignacio shook his head.

"Perfect." Edith said, then reached into the neck of her sweater and pulled the leather string hanging around her neck, revealing the eight teeth dangling from them. "These belonged to my Mason. I pulled them out of his mouth after my husband brought back his body from the lake."

She paused, swiped a finger underneath her eyes to clear them of the wetness.

Ignacio stared at the teeth. They looked like they came from different mouths given the variety in size. The tops of some of them were jagged, while others had an unusual flatness to them. Perhaps they were a snapshot of the defects the old woman's son had.

He started to reach out with a finger to touch them, but the old woman smacked his hand away. She did it without thinking, like a cat batting at a ball rolling past it.

"Don't touch." She said, her eyes peeled. "Did you not hear me? They belonged to my boy!"

Ignacio snatched his hand away and nodded.

"They were just to show you." Edith said, coming out of her defensive state. "I just wanted to show you…"

Ignacio nodded again. "You miss… your son. Don't you?"

"More than anything."

"I miss Mamá." Ignacio said, his eye dropping down to look at his legs at the end of the mattress. "Miss Judy, too."

"Is that the girl's name? The blond one whose head you have in the truck?"

"Yes."

"We seem to be more alike than I originally thought." Edith smiled, a weak smile, but it was a real smile. Ignacio could tell. "It's strange that it took me moving into these isolated woods to run into someone like me."

"Strange…" Ignacio said, just understanding what she was saying.

"Perhaps it was destiny, or something like that, that brought us together." Edith let out a small laugh, then got up off the floor, grabbing the lantern and medical supplies in the process. "Anyway, I'm making soup for dinner. I'll be back once it's done. Rest up, child."

Ignacio nodded.

He watched her put the supplies back on the wooden table then leave the tent. When the flap was closed behind her, he laid down flat on the mattress.

There was a warm feeling inside of him. Not the same kind of warm feelings Judy made him feel like this back at the hospital—no, that had been a different kind of warmness, one Ignacio had never felt before. This warmness coming from the old woman was familiar. The kind of warmness he'd only felt from Mamá.

It won't last long. Varias Caras growled in his head. *Don't get attached, tonto.*

Ignacio went rigid. He hadn't been expecting Varias Caras to start talking to him in the moment.

She is only keeping you alive because she wants to use you. She saw what you did to those people. She wants you around to protect her.

"Only wants me alive… to protect her…" Ignacio muttered, letting the words jog around in his head. Something dawned on him, and in the lowest whisper he could muster, he said to Varias Caras, "Are you—are you going to kill her?"

Let me handle things. Don't worry about it. Just listen to what I say.

"No, no," Ignacio sat up, squeezing the sides of his head, using all his willpower to talk in a low voice so the old woman wouldn't hear him. "No, no, no. Please don't kill her, please."

Stop this. STOP! If you want to see Mamá and Judy again, stop!

"Mamá…?" Ignacio let his hands drop to the side, feeling the headache subsiding, feeling himself become one with el Monstro again.

Varias Caras was right. If he wanted to see Mamá and Judy, he had to listen to him. Varias Caras knew what to do. Always did.

I'm what's keeping you alive.

"Keeping me alive…" Ignacio repeated.

He glanced over to the wooden table crammed with the ointments, bandages, and creams the old woman was using to heal him. A small part of him wondered if maybe it wasn't her keeping him alive and not el Monstro.

The thought disappeared as he felt Varias Caras take some more control of his mind.

We will help her. Don't worry.

"We will?"

Yes. You and I. Working together. Like always.

"Working together… like always…"

She is sad and lonely.

Ignacio nodded. He understood those two words perfectly.

But we will help her once we've healed up.

"How?"

By bringing her back to her child.

CHAPTER 10

Varias Caras reached into the lake, grabbing the net by the corners, and with a quick yank, pulled it out of the water. The fish flailed about as they broke through the water's surface. Ignacio closed the top of the net, making a tight knot and slung it over his shoulders.

"Good, good." Edith said, watching him from a few steps away.

Ignacio walked over to her, the net dripping water behind him. He still felt sluggish, but he was doing much, much better than before. Food, resting, and the old woman's care had done wonders for him these past two days.

"You're very good at following instructions, you know that?" Edith asked, looking him up and down.

Ignacio knew that look. It was the way people sized up horses at the racetracks Papá used to take him to. It was the look of someone judging him. Trying to figure out how he could be useful to them. The same way all his bosses had ever looked at him.

She's just using you. Remember that, Ignacio. Varias Caras said to him.

Ignacio knew he wasn't supposed to talk to el Monstro while the old woman was around, so all he did was furrow his brow subtly to let Varias Caras know he was on the same page.

"Are you okay?" Edith asked, confusing it with a wince.

"Ignacio is okay." he responded, coming up to her side.

Edith turned around and waved to him to follow her.

They started walking back to the campsite, Ignacio a few paces behind Edith. Water still dripped from the bottom of the fishnet, leaving a trail behind them. It was a crisp, cold November morning. A thin layer of frost had built up on the dying grass that melted as the droplets from the fishnet fell on the blades.

"The lake and the nearby rivers will be freezing soon." Edith said, following a few steps behind Ignacio. "It'll make fishing more difficult."

Ignacio grunted in response.

They continued walking through the woods in silence. Ignacio listening to everything surrounding them, now that he was about eighty percent recovered, his senses were all firing at a level they hadn't since Halloween. Since he'd had to get rid of all those people in the way of him getting to Judy.

He homed in on the sounds of the woods. The birds chirping in the treetops in the distance, leaves and branches slapping together from a gust that had just blown, animals—both small and large—crunching on the leaves and twigs on the ground as they scurried and stamped around. It felt like home.

But soon, when he would go back to the point where he could always feel Mamá's ghost the most, it would feel even more like a homecoming.

A mile and a half later, they were back at Edith's campsite. The bone windchimes struck together, their macabre cacophony seemingly welcoming them back.

Ignacio slung the net over his shoulder and plopped it down onto the tree stump by the firepit. It made a wet, meaty thump. The motion riled up some of the more resilient fish that were still alive, and they started to thrash, sprinkling water through the air. The whole net jiggled with the motion. Ignacio watched, pitying them.

"Come," Edith said, taking his attention off the fish.

She took him behind the tent where a large wooden barrel was sitting.

"Do you think you have the strength to lift—"

Before she could finish her sentence, Ignacio moved and swooped it up like it was a tin can. He put it on one of his shoulders, holding it in place with only a single arm.

"Very good." Edith said, then led them back around to the middle of the campground. "Right there."

Ignacio placed the barrel next to the tree stump.

"As we get deeper into the winter, fishing won't be as easily accessible. We'll have to rely on hunting mammals." She said, as she headed into the tent.

She came back out of the tent with a large container of salt and put it next to the fishnet.

"But it's also smart of us to have some extra food kept in here." Edith said, tapping the lid of the barrel.

"I can cut." Varias Caras said, gesturing toward the fish.

"I know you can. I looked through your stuff and saw your machete." Edith laughed to herself.

Varias Caras nodded, then made his point clearer, "I can cut the fish."

"I know what you meant, Ignacio. Sometimes I just like to amuse myself." She said, reaching underneath her sweater to unsheathe the knife.

She handed it over to Ignacio, then sat down on the ground cross-legged. Using one of her bony hands, she stretched her black skirt over her legs and took out the wrinkles.

Meanwhile, Ignacio grabbed the fishnet and started undoing the knot at the top.

"I have gloves in the tent—" Edith started, then saw him snatch one of the fish from the net.

Ignacio's massive hands seemed to glide through the air as he beheaded the fish, descaled it, chopped it into pieces, then set the chunks to the side.

Edith watched this in fascinated silence, her mouth almost agape. For a few minutes, the loudest sounds in the vicinity were the knife clinking against the tree stump and the windchimes humming from a slight breeze.

"The dead bodies…Ignacio should take care of them soon?" Without taking his eye off the task of cutting through the fish in front of him, he gestured his head in the direction where the corpses of the campers had been left.

"Yes." Edith said.

Ignacio nodded, then held a fish up in the air, right at chin-level. His eye slid up past the fish's open mouth and locked with Edith's eyes.

A chill went up her spine. It was inexplicable to her, she hadn't felt any much around him despite his size, but now there was a look in that eye that hadn't been there before. Like the innocent part of him was beginning to hide now that he was recovering, now that he was regaining his strength and speed.

"Ignacio helps and helps and helps everyone."

"Y—yes." Edith said, involuntarily gulping. "You're a good helper."

"Ignacio will take care of those bodies." He said, setting the fish down on the stump and taking its head off with one chop of the knife. "Then, when nighttime comes, I will take you to see your son. Nighttime is when the fantasmas come out."

"Is that why you're here?" Edith said, feeling herself relaxing now that his focus was back on the fish. "Because you can see your mother's ghost here?"

"Not see. Feel." Ignacio explained to her. "Mamá did not die here. I can only see the ghosts of people who died here. Some Ignacio killed. Others, I did not."

"I see…" Edith said, pondering this.

"The candles in Ignacio's truck will help." he said, nodding.

He used the blade to put the pieces of fish in front of him to the side. At the same time, with his other hand, he grabbed a fish from the net, which drew Edith's attention.

She saw there were only two fish left in the net. It was incredible. He'd gone through fifteen fish like it was nothing while they'd been conversing. This man was quite the physical specimen. And if he indeed did have this ESP—then he was a being like no other.

"You don't believe Ignacio." he asked, snapping Edith out of her thoughts.

"I was never one to believe in things like ghosts or spirits, no." Edith said. "And the only psychics or mediums I've ever ran into were full of shit."

"Full of…" Ignacio couldn't bring himself to say the bad word. Instead, he shook his head. "Ignacio will show you."

Edith didn't respond. She just stared into his face. Into a face that was somehow both innocent and stern at the same time. Maybe it was his natural features, she wasn't sure. But there was something about this man that exuded a calmness, but now he was becoming terrifying to be around. It was more than his stature, something that Edith couldn't quite pinpoint.

The scariest part, though, was that she believed him when he said he could see ghosts.

Edith gulped, feeling the taste of anxiety coating her mouth and throat.

Ignacio set the knife down next to the pile of fish. "I am done… I can take care of the bodies now, yes?"

"Yes," Edith said, then cleared her throat because her voice came out smaller than she intended and tried again. "Yes, you go do that. There's a shovel inside the tent. I'll take care of the fish."

Ignacio nodded to her, then headed into the tent.

CHAPTER 11

IGNACIO RETURNED TO the camper's site, and even though it wasn't very far from the old woman's campsite, it felt like a completely different location. It served as a reminder of just how isolated and how dense these woods in Northern Pennsylvania were.

Everything in the campsite remained the same: the campers' tents, the chairs they'd been using, the beer cans littering the ground, and even the game of Monopoly they'd been playing on a foldout table by the tents was untouched. The campers had paused the game, at the time thinking they still had their whole lives ahead of them. Never once had it occurred to them that a few hours later, they'd all be dead.

The guy Ignacio had killed was lying on his back, a few feet away from the campfire. He'd died on his back, letting Ignacio see his face from where he stood. The corpse's face purple and bloated from when he'd choked on the shards of glass and his own blood. A maroon crust of dried blood that had gushed from his mouth covered his chin. One of the shards of glass lodged in his throat was poking the skin from the inside, stretching it upward into a fine point, threatening to break through at any moment.

The girl lay a couple feet away from him. Her face a crisp, black burned mess. All the hair had burnt away, and the wind had scattered its ashes, leaving nothing on her blackened scalp. The hatchet stuck out the side of her neck. The way the blood dried around the wound and the head of the hatchet made it look like the girl and the tool were melding together.

Ignacio leaned the shovel against one of the trees he was standing next to, then crossed the campsite. Dead leaves crunched underneath his heavy boots as he made his way to the Bronco on the other side of the campfire.

As he came near the vehicle, he looked through the windshield and could see the red marking on the door locks indicating they were unlocked. Ignacio threw open the driver side door. The key was still in the ignition, shining silver from the spire of sunlight coming in through the windshield.

Ignacio grabbed the key, then circled around to the back of the Bronco. Using the key, he unlocked the trunk door and opened it. The door hinges let out a squeak that sounded like a whine, as if the vehicle was protesting that Ignacio had left it abandoned these last few days.

From the middle of the pile of his belongings, Ignacio grabbed the gym bag. He unzipped the main pocket, and all his masks—pieces of his victims, really—stared up at him. The smell of leather with a hint of death escaped from the opening. Ignacio breathed in deeply, letting the scent fill his nostrils as the cold crisp air rushed through his nasal passage and into his lungs. A rush of blood spiked up into his brain, his strength returning to him even more now.

He reached into the bag and pulled out a mask the color of an eggshell with black studs protruding out of it. The eyeholes in the mask were wide so it wouldn't be tight against his wounded eye socket with the missing eyeball. It was perfect for the task ahead.

Ignacio unzipped one of the gym bag's side pockets and took out his hunting knife from it. He clipped it to a loop on his jeans, then closed the trunk.

There was only one thing left to do.

It's time to let me take control. Varias Caras said.

"Let you… take control…" Ignacio muttered, slipping the mask over his face.

Half an hour later, Varias Caras was done burying the corpses in the shallow graves he dug behind the tents. He stuck the shovel into one of them, then rubbed his hands together to clear them of dirt.

Ignacio had given el Monstro a lot of control, but handling the cold, stiff bodies had roused Varias Caras. He could feel him taking over even more.

His stomach grumbled. Louder and longer than ever.

I need more control, Ignacio!

Ignacio put a hand up to his forehead, feeling el Monstro slipping into the forefront of his mind. It felt good.

He flexed his muscles as he let el Monstro take over, as he felt himself cross that zenith where Ignacio Calderon took the backseat, and he became Varias Caras.

The third body wasn't very difficult to find. The girl had only gotten a few yards away from the campsites before the old woman had caught up to her and the stabbing had commenced. Varias Caras walked over to her, admiring the old woman's work like the corpse was a piece of modern art.

The old woman had stabbed the girl multiple times. He couldn't see how many knife wounds were in the body underneath all the blood, but the old woman had probably stabbed her well past the point of necessity. Way after the girl had already been dead. That was the part that impressed Varias Caras the most.

He stopped in front of the body, laying the shovel down next to him as he crouched to get a better look. The low temperatures of the last few nights had turned the blood covering her torso into a dark red crust. At a quick glance, it looked like the corpse was encased in some sort of rusted-out metal.

He looked at her face. It was pretty despite being twisted up with the pain and panic of being murdered. Varias Caras touched her pale face—which had been pale in life but had turned even whiter after death. Her skin was cold and hard to the touch. Not quite frozen.

Refrigerated. Varias Caras thought, his finger still pressed to the girl's cheek.

A thought dawned on him. The meat might still be good to eat, despite that the body had been sitting out here for days. It'd been cold enough that it probably hadn't started to spoil just yet.

Varias Caras dug the knife out from his back pocket. Then, despite rigor mortis, used his index and thumb to pry the girl's mouth open. He stuck the edge of the knife against the side of her mouth and started sawing the blade through her cheek a few centimeters, then sliced on an upward angle to the cheekbone. Once at the cheekbone, he circled the knife down until he got to the jawline. From this point, he swiped the blade across and up until the blade was back at the point he'd started cutting. With the tip of the blade, Varias Caras peeled the cheek from the skull. The sound of the meat separating from the bone underneath was wet and meaty.

He did the same thing to the other side of her face. He set the two floppy pieces of meat down on her chest for the moment. Then he reached into her mouth with two fingers and pulled on her tongue until it was several inches out of what was left of her mouth. Using the knife in his other hand, he cut through her tongue. Varias Caras set it next to the cheeks.

There was one more thing to do before he would get started on digging the grave. He went down to one of her pantlegs and cut a square out of it, then grabbed the tongue and cheeks and folded them up in the denim.

Done with this, he put the knife in his pocket and grabbed the shovel as he stood up. He surveyed the area for a good spot to bury the corpse. Luckily, in woods these expansive, anywhere with a sizeable clearing of foliage made a perfect spot for this.

Varias Caras picked a spot between two large bushes and started digging.

CHAPTER 12

By the time he returned, the sun was going down. Edith was by the campfire, stirring a pot hanging over the flames. The wind pushed the smell of what she was cooking into Varias Caras's face just as he was coming through the trees. It smelled like garlic and onions and some sort of meat.

His stomach grumbled. So loud, Edith heard it as he came up next to her.

"You took care of them?" she asked without turning to look at him, just feeling his shadow eclipsing her.

"Yes." He said, reaching into his back pocket for the piece of denim with the meat.

As he unwrapped it, he knelt down beside Edith. The skewers they'd used for the fish this morning were still leaning against the firepit. Ignacio grabbed one and stuck the cheeks and tongue on it. He held the skewer out near the flame, a few inches below the pot.

The movement broke Edith's focus, drawing her eyes. First thing she noticed was the skewer. The chunks of flesh were indiscriminate enough that she didn't know what they belonged to. But the long, pink chunk was a whole other story. She was close enough that she could see the tastebuds on one side of it, making it obvious that it was a tongue.

She stirred but couldn't bring herself to ask him about it. Or move a muscle, really.

"Ignacio is hungry…" he said, his voice sounding different. Like it had a slight growl to it that hadn't been there before.

Edith looked past the skewer and up to his face and noticed the strange mask on his face for the first time. It was the color of eggshell and had several black studs protruding out of it. The studs were about half an inch long, and she couldn't quite tell what they were, except that they looked like tiny pins.

The temperature of the air seemed to drop as a wave of fear went through Edith, the skin on her arms and back turning into gooseflesh. For some inexplicable reason, Ignacio wearing this mask was more frightening than finding his severed heads.

Maybe it was because, on some level, she could understand the murdering. But this mask seemed to be coming out of nowhere.

"They make Ignacio feel better." He said, answering the question she was too stunned to ask.

Edith saw the reflection of the flames dancing in his good eye for a split second before he turned to look at her. They eye met her eyes. With the mask on, it felt like this was an entirely different person than the one she'd been caring for the last few days.

"They hide Ignacio from the world…and make him… not afraid…" He nodded, then broke eye contact and went back to watching the meat cook on the end of the skewer.

Edith didn't respond. She just turned away from him and stared at the boiling pot of soup, uncertain of anything.

By the time they were done eating, the sun was down. Varias Caras had scarfed down the human parts and then two bowls of Edith's soup. Edith had just one helping. The confusion and fear (though, it was lessening) had curbed some of her appetite.

They'd eaten in silence. One of those silences that became more and more uncomfortable the longer it stretched out. Neither of them looked at the other.

Edith got out of her seat and went over to the tree stump, going around it so that she and Ignacio were facing one another. She set her bowl down, and without making eye contact said, "That meat you ate. It belonged to one of the dead bodies, didn't it?"

Before he could answer, she shook her head vigorously, her thin gray hair flinging through the air, and said, "Never mind. Maybe I shouldn't ask questions I wouldn't like the answer to."

She turned and went inside the tent. When she came out, she was holding a gallon bottle of water. She walked over to Ignacio with her hand out.

"Your bowl and spoon, please." She said, reaching for it but still not looking him in the face.

Ignacio obliged. Then, as she was turning, he stood up, making Edith pause midmotion.

"The ghosts," he started, staring at her with his single dark eye as he towered over her. "They are awake now."

Edith couldn't bring herself to even make a noise, much less respond with anything resembling a coherent sentence.

"I will get the candles… in my truck… Then we will go…" Ignacio said, and without waiting for her to respond, he turned away and headed for the Bronco.

CHAPTER 13

EDITH FELT LIKE she'd given her free will away to some unseen force. If someone asked her why she was following this gargantuan man—who was little more than a stranger despite having taken care of him these last few days—and why she was letting him keep their only source of light out here in these dark, dark woods, she wouldn't have an answer for them.

She'd done some crazy things in her life, but following Ignacio had to be up there with stabbing her husband to death.

They hadn't talked at all since leaving the campsite. They'd been communicating solely with body language and movement to coordinate this excursion out in the dark. The silence seemed to envelope them, somehow more present than even the shadowed trees surrounding them.

Leaves crunched underneath their feet. The wild, dry grass rustled against their pantlegs. Occasionally, the toe of their footwear would kick loose a rock stuck in the earth and send it tumbling through the grass, bumping into other rocks or the base of a tree. Ignacio was carrying a plastic bag in his hand that crinkled with every other step he took.

They came through the trees and into what could be considered the bank of Willow Lake. Fireflies hovered above the grass, their lights turning off and on in erratic patterns. The full moon reflected off the surface of the water, a slight breeze made the water ripple, distorting its image. At the same time, the willow trees on the perimeter of the lake swayed through the air.

This all made the night eerier to Edith. But she had no way of imagining just how much worse it was about to get.

They stopped near the edge of the bank, maybe two feet away from where the water and the dirt met. Edith stood next to him, almost touching. Meanwhile, Ignacio just stared straight ahead, as if something had caught his attention across the lake. But they couldn't see anything from here except the vague outline of the trees on the other side.

Without warning, he dropped down to one knee, setting the lantern and bag down. Then he got to untying the knot at the top of the bag and pulled out several candles from it. He cradled them in one arm and stood back up.

"Ignacio used to watch… the witches in Mexico… do this… It is how Ignacio knows." He said to Edith, keeping his eyes focused on the ground as he decided where to place the first candle.

Edith felt the temperature in the air drop, making her shiver, unsure if the night truly got colder or if it was the strangeness of what was happening that gave her the sensation.

Yet, at the same time, she realized she had an answer for why she was here. The truth was, if there was even a slim chance she could communicate with her dead son, she would take it. Even if it meant following a strange man deeper into the woods. She realized, then and there, that she would do anything just to hear her sweet boy's voice one more time and to tell him she loved him.

Ignacio had been walking around in a circle around Edith, placing the candles about a foot or so apart from each other. He placed one in front of her, completing the ring.

Ignacio went back to the plastic bag. From it, he pulled out a box of matches. He took one out and struck it against the side of the box.

The orange flame at the tip of the match looked different to Edith. It was brighter somehow. Once again, she wasn't sure if it was just in her head or if the flame actually was burning differently.

Ignacio started lighting the candles one by one. The flames on the wicks weren't particularly big, but each one that was lit changed the ambiance in the night. A mood that hadn't been there before began to take form around them. A certain somberness that had been absent before.

Edith felt something stir in her. Something she'd only felt twice in her life—once when she saw her mother's ghost at the house she grew up in, when she'd gone to clean it out after her mother died, and a second time in the laundry room years after Mason had died. She'd been folding clothes when she thought she felt someone walking down the steps into the basement. When she looked, there hadn't been anyone (or anything, for that matter) there, but the feeling that an apparition of some sort been lurking around had felt too real to ignore.

This moment now, in these Pennsylvanian woods, far away from her home, validated those feelings. Made her sure that she hadn't "just been imagining" things the way her husband had dismissed it when she'd brought up these events to him.

Ignacio lit the last candle, blew out the match, and flicked it into the grass somewhere. He stood up, grabbing the lantern as he did so.

"You can feel them… can't you…?" Ignacio said, turning to face her. He brought the lantern up near his lips and blew it out with a puff of his breath.

Smoke billowed out from the openings. Ignacio's face was obscured by the darkness, as now the only lighting they had was the circle of candles.

Edith wasn't sure what he was asking her, so she had no idea how to answer him. All she could do was stare at him and gulp.

He walked over to her side, turning around to face the same direction as her. "You were right... me... and you... we are not like other people."

Out the corner of her eye, she saw him swaying. Frontward and backward, so he wasn't in danger of falling on top of her, but just the same, it was strange. Discomforting.

Edith felt her whole body tensing up.

Ignacio reached out with a meaty hand. She turned to look at him. And now, given the situation, given what was happening, given the eeriness of the night, she realized how large he was. How truly dangerous he was by just his sheer size.

The person who'd reminded her of her son, who she'd felt this need to nurse when she first saw him down on the ground and bloodied, seemed to have disappeared. Instead, all she saw was an enormous man wearing a mask who'd been traveling with severed heads in his car.

His hand reached her shoulder, and she felt something transcendental happening, like her soul was being lifted from her body.

"The necklace." He said and reached for her neck with his other hand.

Edith was so flabbergasted and overwhelmed by everything happening that, for a second, she thought he was reaching out to choke her, but then she felt him pinch the leather string around her neck with two fingers. This time, though, she didn't smack his hand away; all she could do was continue to stare at him as he pulled it up over her head.

Ignacio clutched the top of the leather string, letting Mason's jagged teeth dangle in the air. He turned to look out across the lake, into the shadowed trees on the other side.

Edith started looking that way, too, but for some reason the details on one of the candles nearest her caught her eye. The candle was tall, with a blue label on it that she'd been mistaking for just a department store logo or something like that, but she saw the angels on it clearly now. They were floating up into the sky, their eyes looking onward. Looking up to their father, their creator, into clouds parting and partially revealing a celestial palace beyond the ray of light shining out from them.

She looked around and realized all the other candles had religious iconography on them. Most of them had similar angels and bright skies on them. But there were two taller ones with images of Jesus. One was of him on the crucifix, with a backdrop of clouds and rays of sunshine. The other one, though, was a profile shot of him wearing the crown of thorns. He was looking up into the sky, blood dripping down onto his face, perhaps asking his father for the strength to survive the punishment—Edith wasn't sure, she'd never even thumbed through a Bible in her lifetime.

"Now watch," Ignacio said, breaking her concentration.

She looked out into the darkness across the water, but she didn't see anything. She felt Ignacio tighten his grip on her shoulders, and suddenly, the night got more bitter. The flames on the candles moved in one direction, as if a breeze was blowing, but there was no such thing happening. Edith's large sweater and hair remained in place.

This was something else.

In the distance, somewhere in the trees, orbs of light began to appear. They had a certain blue hue to them, making them impossible to confuse for any sort of ordinary lights. They were suspended in mid-air, too low to be the stars, but too high up to be headlights from any vehicle.

The lights began to blink on all around them like fireflies—but much too big to be bugs. The closest orbs to them were about the size of a decent orange. In a matter of seconds, they were surrounded by these floating orbs, encompassed by them.

Edith felt every hair on her body stand up. The image of herself as a shrieking cat, back arched, flashed through her mind. In any other circumstance, perhaps this image would've been comical, but there was nothing humorous about this situation.

"Think about him…" Ignacio said to her. "You will be able to feel him… if you think about him…"

His voice sounded almost alien given how much had changed in such a short amount of time, she'd almost forgotten Ignacio was here with her. But now that she was aware of his presence again, she felt him clamping onto her shoulder. Edith dared a glance at him and saw him staring straight ahead.

There was a certain glow to him. Nothing dramatic, nothing like Hollywood special effects, but there was an incandescent layer outlining him that hadn't been there before.

An orb came floating out from the lake. But it didn't exactly break through the surface, no, the orb seemed to be coming from another plane of existence than the lake existed on.

We're somewhere between the living and the dead. Edith thought, watching the blue light coming closer to them.

The orb began to shapeshift as if an invisible hand was giving it form. It stretched, contracted, and bent until it had the shape and size of a human child. Details began to surface from the light. The outline of fingers and toes, then the rest of the hands and feet. The effect continued, revealing more and more of the person whose spirit this belonged to.

But Edith knew who it was before the face was revealed to her. She'd known who it was as soon as the light had shaped itself a big head.

There was no mistaking it. It was her sweet boy, Mason. Ignacio had really done it. He'd really let her see into some in-between world. A Limbo, if you will.

"M—Mason…" Edith muttered, as his face appeared from the light. Barely having any control of her lips and having no control of her emotions whatsoever, she fell to her knees.

"Mami!" Mason said, eyes big. His face broke out into a big smile, revealing his mouthful of crooked teeth.

"It's you… it's really you…" Edith said, feeling her whole body trembling, but she'd managed to find some of her composure.

She reached up and wiped the tears from under her eyes, but it was fruitless. The tears were flowing, boiling hot in contrast with the night of the dark. But it didn't matter. Nothing did.

She was back with Mason. Reunited with her sweet, sweet boy.

Varias Caras hadn't been sure if it was going to work. He was just as surprised as the old lady was that it had.

Tapping into this world was something he knew he and Ignacio could do, but up until now, he didn't know he could bring other people here. It must've had something to do with the fact that the old woman's son had died in the lake, so the energy from his spirit was tied here. Bound here by some supernatural force, perhaps. That combined with the boy's teeth must've enhanced the effect.

He watched the woman and the spirit of the boy with the big head, towering over them. It made Ignacio think of Mamá—made him miss her hugs and her warmth.

"No!" Varias Caras growled, putting his hand up to his forehead. He felt a splitting headache as Ignacio tried to wrestle control from him. "No, no!"

This hadn't been a part of the plan. He hadn't meant to reunite the old woman with her son. He thought his abilities would help her hear him or feel his spirit at best, but this… this was making him weak.

Don't kill her, don't kill her, don't kill her! Ignacio shouted in his head, still fighting to control his body.

"Go away! You're not… you're not…" Varias Caras tensed his muscles. He moved one arm behind him and took out the knife. "You're not needed anymore, Ignacio."

No! No! No!

Varias Caras stared at the knife, the moonlight reflecting off the blade silver, making it like a mirror. He could only see his good eye on the reflection, but he could feel the bandage over the missing one. The wounded socket that had been a result of Diana Santos stabbing his eyeball out with a windshield wiper pulsed with pain. She'd gotten the best of him out in the junkyard because he hadn't been in full control—Ignacio had still been somewhere in his mind—but not anymore. He wasn't going to let that personality slow him down or weaken him any further.

El Monstro was in control now.

He tightened his grip on the knife handle and flipped it in his hand, positioning to use it. With his other hand, Varias Caras clamped down on Edith's shoulder.

Edith felt a shift in the air before she felt anything else. The candlelight surrounding them went out. The orbs in the distance began to disintegrate. Not dim out, no, it was more like the particles of light were splitting up into a million little grains.

It was happening to Mason, too. Right before her very eyes, her sweet boy was disappearing. She was losing him again, and somehow the second time felt much worse. She tightened her arms, but there wasn't anything to hold onto; his torso was gone.

All that was left was his big pumpkin head and his smiling face.

"Buh-bye, Mamá." Mason said, and the next second he was gone.

With the spirits gone, and the candlelight extinguished, the darkness enveloped her.

But the most terrifying part was yet to come. Edith suddenly felt like another presence was out here with them. Some sort of entity that hadn't been here before. The hairs on the back of her neck rose, then she felt Ignacio clamp down on her shoulder.

She turned her neck to see him, seeing that his enormous body was now blocking out the moonlight that had been slanting through the trees. He was staring down at her, his single eye focused on her. Transfixed.

"I—Ignacio… what's going on? What happened? Where's Mason?" Edith asked, standing up to her feet.

She felt her heart thumping in her chest and her thoughts racing. Her mouth was dry, as if she'd just eaten a burnt piece of toast. And she realized, in this moment, she was more afraid than she'd ever been in her life.

Ignacio swayed back and forth, putting one hand up to his forehead, like something was trying to force itself out from his skull and he was pushing it back in.

"Ignacio… Ignacio is not here anymore…" he muttered, barely audible, but just intelligible enough for her to receive the message.

Before she realized she was doing it, Edith was reaching underneath her sweater for the knife at her waist.

He saw the old woman lift her large sweater and reach for the knife. He saw her slide it out of the sheath clipped to her waistline and start bringing it toward his stomach in an upward arc. He saw this all happening in slow motion and shot his arm out.

Varias Caras caught the old woman's wrist, stopping her inches away from when she would've stabbed him and squeezed the joint as hard as he could. There was a series of snaps and pops as her old bones shattered into several pieces. The knife fell out of her hand by the wayside as she screamed in pain.

The scream reminded Varias Caras of the sound coyotes in Mexico would make late at night. He didn't like those sounds or the sounds the old woman was making.

But that was okay. Because he was going to stop it soon.

Varias Caras stabbed the knife into the middle of her throat. He drove it all the way through. The blade pierced through the back of her neck, sending a thick spray of blood through the air as it punctured through the skin.

The old woman kicked and flailed as the life seeped out of her, but Varias kept her from falling to the ground by continuing to hold onto her arm.

He looked into her face, watching as best as he could in the darkness as the life drained out of her. He felt her arm going limp in his hold and her struggling got weaker and weaker as more blood pumped out of the wound.

A few more seconds passed and then her body went still. He felt the shift in heaviness as she went from a living person to deadweight. He took the knife out of her throat and let the corpse drop to the ground.

The body hit the ground with a loud thud. Her thin, gray hair spread out over the ground like the wings of a dead bird. The blood coming out of the wound at the back of her neck almost immediately began to form a pool on the leaves she landed on top of.

Varias Caras stared down at her, wiping the blade of his knife clean on the side of his pants as he did so.

She'd taken care of him. Nurtured him back to health. Killed some of the people who might've gotten the best of him the first night he'd returned to the woods. Was the reason he was standing here, alive, really.

But he didn't feel anything as he stared down at the old woman's still body. Maybe Ignacio would've felt something, but Ignacio was nowhere to be found.

There was only Varias Caras now.

CHAPTER 14

Varias Caras returned to the old woman's campsite. He took everything out of her tent before taking it apart and rolling it up. It was strapped to the top of his Bronco now.

He was finishing up loading all the useful things he found inside the tent into the truck. The old woman's herbs, medical supplies, some knives, kitchen utensils, plates, a few bags, fishing nets, and a variety of spices.

He closed the trunk door, then slid into the driver seat. He stuck the key into the ignition and cranked it. The engine sounded like an explosion in the quiet of the isolated woods, even scaring away some birds perched on a nearby tree and sending a few chipmunks scurrying for cover under some bushes.

Varias Caras put the Bronco in drive and navigated it through the woods, heading to his destination.

II.

CHAPTER 15

Noelle had re-read the article on the "Halloween Massacre" that morning over a bowl of oatmeal and a cup of coffee to refresh herself of the details. She'd spent the last few months after the events at Camp Slaughter combing through all the Pennsylvania smalltown news sites she could find, trying to see if there were any reports of the cannibal being caught by the police in the surrounding towns.

At a certain point, she gave up on this idea and thought maybe they'd killed him. Maybe the ax to his chest and Gavin bashing him with the rock had been enough to leave him dead. Maybe by now his corpse was lying in the secluded woods, picked apart by rodents.

But something in her gut told her it was just wishful thinking, and she continued to check news articles every night and morning. She was obsessed because she needed to know if he was still out there killing people or not; it was the only way the nightmares would end.

The cops and the journalists she'd reached out to hadn't been helpful. The police just told her they were "looking into it" and the journalists all treated it like it was just another run-of-the-mill backwoods murder.

After a few weeks of getting the runaround from the police and ignored as some crazed crockpot by the media, she was feeling discourage. She was about to give up on all of this and try to deal with the trauma in another matter (perhaps a healthier way), when on the first of November, she opened up the article about the slaughter near a small town about four hours from where she lived.

Everything described in the article matched up with the description of the cannibal from the campgrounds: his size, his hair, and the fact that he'd been wearing a mask. The details of the killings were sparse, but the journalist had described it as a "graphic and brutal scene"—which matched up with what Noelle had seen him do at Lakewood Cabin.

The smoking gun, so to speak, was the picture of the man. It was terrible quality because it was a photograph of the photograph on his driver's license. It'd been provided to the press by the police after they'd gone through the records at the junkyard the cannibal had been working at the last few months.

Despite how pixelated the photo was, there were enough details that Noelle had a face behind the mask now. And that, in some way, made things much more terrifying.

In other ways, it made things easier because now she knew he was just a human. Sure, he was massive and strong and tough. But he was still just a man. And all men could be killed.

She just needed to be prepared.

Noelle had been thinking about these things the entire time as she drove up the highway, as the hours passed, and towns were replaced with farmland and stretches of wilderness.

Noelle thought about Diana Santos, who had nearly been one of the cannibal's victims, and wondered what she must've been thinking. In the same article that talked about the killings on Halloween, there was a brief but detailed account of the girl's experience. She'd broken down on the side of the road and been kidnapped by the cannibal after she witnessed him kill two brother who themselves were trying to kidnap her.

The cannibal had kept her in the attic of the home he was renting near the junkyard where he worked, feeding her mystery meat (that very well could've come from a human) and calling her his "Barbie."

The article had also detailed her heroic escape from the cannibal. She'd had a physical confrontation with him at one point in the night where she managed to jam a windshield wiper into his eye and then choke him unconscious with a chain. She'd thought she'd managed to kill him, but the cannibal had killed two police officers only minutes after.

Diana Santos had been driving for her first big job interview after college, but it seemed life had a cruel twist of fate for her. The thought of this enraged Noelle and made her thirst for revenge worse.

She clenched her jaw, clutched the steering wheel tighter, and stepped on the gas.

Up ahead, just barely legible from this distance, she saw a sign that read:

EMERGENCY STOP
HILLTOWN HOSPITAL
3 MILES

CHAPTER 16

MAYBE IT WAS all just in her head because she'd known what happened in the town, but there seemed to be a blanket of gloom hovering over Hilltown. Pedestrians, mostly retirees at this hour of the day, walked down the sidewalks in winter clothing and accessories. They seemed to be dragging their feet, and their shoulders seemed to be slumped.

Noelle looked through the windows of the shops and cafes and restaurants and saw a similar type of gloom in all of them. The patrons and shop owners moved slow and rigid, like they were just going through the motions and would rather have been at home mourning the deaths of the cannibal's victims.

It was like the whole town was still shellshocked from the massacre that had occurred on Halloween, and the Santa Clauses, hollies, bells, and snowflake stickers decorating the buildings and their windows did nothing to offset this feeling.

Noelle kept her Jeep at a low speed as she made her way through the heart of the town. The main purpose of coming here was to speak to Sheriff Olmos, but she also wanted to see the town. She wanted to see where the cannibal had been living these past few months.

She could almost sense him being here. Like his presence still loomed in the darkest corners of the town. She wished there'd been some way she could've known he was here before. It would've made things easier.

She could've gunned him down right here in the middle of town. Maybe in front of the hardware store as he was coming out with lumber and metal bars to build the cage he held Diana captive in. Noelle could've taken her pistol out and emptied a clip into his chest, ending everything right there and sparing these poor, unsuspecting residents of Hilltown the sadness he would bring to them.

"Would've," "could've," "should've" never did anything for anyone, though. Noelle thought with a pang of sadness.

The sadness was quickly replaced with excitement as she saw Gregorio Olmos sitting in a booth inside the Hilltown Diner. She hadn't been too sure she'd be able to find the man at all, so it felt a bit like finding Waldo on the very first glance of a page. He was at a booth near the window, across from him sat a broad-shouldered gentleman in a brown police uniform.

Mr. Olmos's hair was longer, he had a beard, and he was wearing a black and red flannel, but Noelle was positive it was him. She parked in a parking spot along the curb across from the diner and shut the Jeep's engine off.

The diner had large windows, and she was almost directly across from it, so she had a clear view of Mr. Olmos and his companion. She watched them for a few seconds. From the looks of it, they were finishing up an early lunch. The policeman was handing the waitress a pen and a receipt holder as Mr. Olmos checked the lid of his to-go coffee cup to make sure it was on tight.

Noelle watched them chat for a few more seconds, then they slid out of the booth and started making their way out of the diner. They waved at some of the patrons and even stopped for some small talk with two couples along the way. At the front of the diner, they grabbed their jackets and pushed through the front door, both waving to the hostess behind the podium.

Once outside, the gentleman in the police uniform put on a sheriff's hat. Noelle wasn't entirely sure what was going on, but maybe the Halloween slaughter had become bigger than Hilltown and this was a sheriff from another town.

Either way, it didn't concern Noelle too much. She was here to talk to one man only.

The enemy of my enemy is a friend. Noelle thought, feeling these words and this sentiment coming from a dark part of her mind.

The dark part she didn't know she had until surviving Camp Slaughter. It was a part of her mind she didn't like sitting in too long, so she brushed the thoughts away and refocused on Greg Olmos.

He talked to the sheriff for a few more seconds outside the diner, then they shook hands and headed their separate ways.

This was Noelle's cue.

She slipped out of her vehicle, her eyes tracking Greg Olmos walking up the sidewalk the entire time.

The bitterness of the cold surprised her, forcing her to put the hood of her rainslicker up. Noelle stuck her hands in her pockets and proceeded to follow Gregorio Olmos from across the street.

The moment she watched him go into the flower shop, she knew where the man's final destination would be. Noelle watched him sort through the bouquets of flowers, but much like the rest of the town, she could practically see the dark cloud hanging over his head. She could practically see his sadness, as if a gray aura were seeping out from Gregorio Olmos's body.

Noelle was sitting on a bench underneath a bare tree that likely provided better shade when it had leaves, pretending like she was answering important emails on her phone, glancing up every once in a while to see how far along Mr. Olmos was on his shopping.

As far as she could tell, no one had noticed her shadowing Mr. Olmos. She'd been properly discrete the last six blocks she'd followed him. Even still, this was a tricky operation, so she was being careful to not be suspicious. And now that she knew the man was buying flowers for his dead daughter's grave, a bit of guilt was working its way through her.

These were the moments where she would have to let the dark part of her mind take over. She did so, and the guilt was wiped away. Or maybe it was just suppressed; she wasn't sure.

Either way, she continued to watch Mr. Olmos. He'd taken the flowers to the register and was reaching into his wallet while chatting with the girl behind the register. He threw a few smiles at her and then a real big one as the cashier handed him his change and he grabbed the flowers off the counter. Noelle only had a profile shot of the man, but she didn't need to see his full face to know those smiles were merely a façade.

The pain on the man's face returned as soon as the transaction ended, and he was turning away from the cashier. Noelle watched him shuffle out of the flower shop and walk down the stoop before continuing up the sidewalk in the same direction he'd been heading.

She waited a few beats, then put the phone in her rainslicker and proceeded in that direction as well.

Noelle was standing two rows away from him. Luckily, there wasn't anyone else around. The old woman—a widow coming to visit her husband's gravesite, perhaps—was leaving just as she'd been entering the Hilltown Cemetery a few paces behind Greg Olmos.

Noelle waited a few moments, giving him a chance to get the grievances out of his system before she would approach him. It was the least she could do since she was stalking the poor man.

A small drizzle had started falling, but Greg Olmos was none the wiser. Something told Noelle he wouldn't have noticed even if a bomb went off in the middle of the cemetery. His focus was entirely on his daughter's grave. He bent down to touch the plot of dirt, which gave Noelle a clear view of what was engraved on the headstone:

JUDY OLMOS
LOVED BY ALL
1999-2022

The pile of flowers sitting atop the grave was evidence of the words being true. It was like the whole town had come together to honor the girl's death. Watching the light rainfall drizzle over the colorful petals gave Noelle a melancholy feeling. It felt a bit like the blanket of sadness hanging over the rest of the town was concentrated here, as if where Judy Olmos was buried was where it began and spread.

Greg Olmos rose from his crouch. Something about his body language suggested to Noelle that he was done grieving for the moment. It was time.

Noelle took a few steps closer to him and cleared her throat. Then said, "Are you the sheriff of Hilltown?"

"Not anymore." He responded, back still to her. He pointed his thumb in the direction of town. "The man you're looking for is likely at the police station."

"You're Greg Olmos, though, right?"

"Yeah, who's asking?" he asked, turning around, his movements suddenly not so cumbersome as before.

"If you're Greg Olmos, then you're who I'm looking for."

He knit his eyebrows together and said, "What are you? A journalist or something?"

"Not quite." Noelle said, shifting her weight from one foot to the other.

"Then?"

"I'm someone who might be able to help you avenge your daughter's death." She said, jutting her chin toward Judy's headstone.

"Lady, I don't know what you're talking about." He said, his expression changing from confusion to anger.

"You guys never caught the guy who killed all those people on Halloween," Noelle said. "Am I right?"

He didn't respond. He just stared back at her, shooting daggers at her with his eyes. Noelle remained steadfast, though and pressed on.

"My name is Noelle." She said, pulling the hood of her rainslicker down. The fading droplets of drizzle tickled the top of her hair, but other than that, the hood wasn't necessary. All it seemed to be doing was putting Greg Olmos on edge, anyway. "A few months ago, that same cannibal attacked me and my friends out in the woods. He killed most of us. I'm one of the few survivors."

"Well," he said, stirring. There was a flicker in his eye that told Noelle she was making some headway here. At the very least, his interest seemed piqued. "I'm certainly glad to hear you survived. I still think you want to tell this to the sheriff. Don't know what you think this has to do with me."

"I want you to help me kill him." Noelle stated, her tone flat. Vocalizing her intentions boosted her confidence, and she took a step toward him. "I think I might know where to find him. Mr. Olmos, have you ever heard of a place called Camp Slaughter?"

"Camp what now?" he said, shaking his head. Then, it was like a lightbulb came on inside his head. His eyes widened and were flooded with realization. "You mean that story about the campgrounds in the woods? Where people disappear from?"

Hilltown was geographically four hours or so eastward from the location of Camp Slaughter, but it seemed the legend had traveled even this far.

"That's it." Noelle said. "But it's not just a story, Mr. Olmos."

Greg Olmos shook his head. "I'm not following—what do these campgrounds have anything to do with the Ignacio and my daughter's death?"

"The cannibal attacked me and my friends a few months ago. The campgrounds were where he lived before he showed up in your town."

"How do you know that—how can you be sure it's the same guy, I mean?"

"I read the article on the Halloween massacre—"

"Slaughter." Mr. Olmos corrected her.

"What?"

"Halloween Slaughter. That's what they're calling it." He shrugged.

"Quite a coincidence."

"Indeed." He nodded.

"The description of the cannibal matches up perfectly with the guy who attacked us at the campgrounds." Noelle said, bringing the conversation back on track. "Everything from the masks to the size of the man. This, I truly believe isn't a coincidence."

Mr. Olmos shook his head. "Let's say you're right, okay? I'm still uncertain what you want me to do with this information. Like I said, this is better information for the police. And like I also said, I'm retired, young lady."

"You probably know this better than anyone: the police won't do anything about it. I've reported it to all the counties within the area, as well as the state police, and nothing has come of it."

"Smalltown police forces are small. We don't exactly have the manpower and resources to investigate every single murder." He stopped himself and took in a breath before correcting himself. "They don't, I mean."

"Yeah, because you're retired." Noelle said. "I know. Which, I wasn't aware of until now, but honestly, I think that works in my favor."

"Because what you're proposing is vigilantism."

"What I'm proposing is a chance at revenge against the guy who took your daughter's life." Noelle said. "I know you had a confrontation with him at the junkyard, and he escaped from you. I'm offering you a second chance here."

"How can we even be sure he's still in those woods?" Greg Olmos said.

"We can't. But it's a good place to start the hunt." Noelle said. "I sat around waiting for someone to do something about the cannibal. But I'm done with that. I'm going to find him and kill him—whether you join me or not."

There was no reply from Mr. Olmos. He just dropped his eyes down to the ground and let out a big sigh.

"Look, Mr. Olmos, I know I caught you at a bad time, at a bad place," Noelle took a second to gander around. As if placed there like props to illustrate her point, she could see a murder of crows perched on the cemetery gates over Mr. Olmos's shoulder. "So, I don't expect you to give me an answer now, but I'd like to leave you with my contact info."

He looked up at her, then with a slight hesitance, reached into the pocket of his bomber jacket for his cellphone. "I'm only entertaining this because I can see the determination in your eyes, you understand?"

"Yeah, I understand." Noelle said, grinning.

He unlocked the phone and handed it over to her. Noelle punched in her contact info—including her email address—and handed him the phone back. "Contact me if you're ever ready, and I'll send you the details of what happened to me and my friends at Camp Slaughter."

"Okay," he nodded. "But if I were you, I wouldn't hold my breath. I'm more interested in fixing things around my home than doing any sort of heroism nowadays."

"You were sheriff of this town for most of your life, correct?" She didn't wait for him to answer before adding, "Something makes me think you're still interested in heroism."

A smile spread over his lips—one that seemed more authentic than any of the ones he'd given the cashier back at the flower shop. "You have a good day now, young lady."

"You too, Mr. Olmos." Noelle said.

She watched him put the cellphone in his pocket, turn away from her, and head toward a side exit in the cemetery. Noelle watched him for a few seconds, noticing his feet weren't dragging the way they had been when he'd been walking through town.

There was an extra pep in his step. And if she could actually see auras, something told her that his aura wasn't just gray anymore but flickering red now.

CHAPTER 17

Greg Olmos sat down on his porch. Sharon wasn't home yet, and since it was the middle of the afternoon, none of the neighbors were around. They were all at work and their children were all in school. The street was quiet, leaving him by his lonesome with his thoughts and the freshly brewed coffee in his mug.

He felt an indescribable way after the strange encounter. It wasn't a *bad* feeling per se, but it certainly wasn't a good feeling, either. Even stranger, the phone sitting in the pocket of his bomber jacket somehow felt heavier now that he had that girl's contact info.

Greg took the cellphone out and unlocked it. He paused to gaze at the wallpaper picture of him and Judy on the boardwalk. The picture was from their trip to Cony Island two years ago. Sharon had snapped the picture, and it was his favorite one of them.

Judy had a broad smile on her face, as she always did, because she was naturally photogenic and loved being in pictures. Greg was the total opposite, always uncomfortable and not sure what to do with his expression or his hands. But in this picture, he had a big smile on his face.

He remembered Sharon commenting on that, asking him why he never smiled like that in pictures of her and him like that. It'd been a joke, of course. There were plenty of pictures with him and his wife where he was smiling like that, but there was something special about this picture.

The wind had blown just as the picture was being taken. The breeze had moved some of Judy's hair into her face and ruffled parts of his button-up shirt. The effect made the photo look animated. And any time he looked at it, for a fleeting second, he felt like he was there that day again. Standing underneath the afternoon sun, feeling the stickiness of the ocean breeze.

Most importantly, though, it made him feel like he was standing next to Judy, feeling her warmth.

And now that she was gone, he tried his very best to hold onto that feeling for as long as he could. But unfortunately, the magic only lasted so long before reality brought him back to his sadness.

Only this time, it wasn't sadness that replaced that impossible feeling. It was something akin to anger.

Because that girl was right. He hadn't realized it until she spoke the word out into the open, but somewhere deep down inside of him—in the darkest part of his mind, perhaps—he had an itch for revenge.

He clicked his contacts list and scrolled down until he got to the letter "N" and stopped at the newest addition:

Noelle.

The name stared back at him, as if daring him to contact her. But he didn't.

Instead, he locked the phone, watching the screen go black as he clicked the button. He put the coffee up to his lips and drank some. It was piping hot—almost scalding—but he would do anything to ignore the blooming urge to accept the girl's offer.

But he knew he would only be able to ignore this feeling for so long. Because Gregorio Olmos always wanted to make things square.

And there was a certain cannibal whom he owed a few bullet holes.

CHAPTER 18

Gavin Briggs was sitting down, watching the sunset from the balcony of his apartment, his cellphone in one hand and a glass of sparkling water in the other. Gavin Briggs' drinking days were (what felt like) long gone. He'd been trying to reform since the events at Camp Slaughter.

It'd been a difficult road, but he was on month number three now of no weed, cocaine, alcohol, or cigarettes. He didn't even drink caffeine nowadays unless he really needed a pick-me-up after the gym or a long study session.

Behind him, he heard the balcony door slide open. He turned and saw Connie, the girl he'd started dating two months ago, come out holding two mugs. Steam rose from the top of them, and Gavin could see the little marshmallows floating atop the hot cocoa.

"Thought I'd make you something to warm you up." Connie said, walking across the balcony. The rubber at the bottom of her fuzzy slippers made funny noises as they pattered against the concrete.

Gavin had been studying for a midterm the whole night and told her he needed a break and was going to get some fresh air. Connie, meanwhile, had stayed in his room watching something on Netflix—some sort of cooking show or something.

Connie settled on the seat next to him and handed him one of the mugs. The other one she nursed in her hands.

"Thanks," Gav said, taking a sip of the hot cocoa. It was piping hot, but delicious. Much better than any mug of cocoa he'd ever made for himself.

They stared out into the city skyline in silence for a few moments. The darkness was beginning to consume the last rays of sunshine as twilight dwindled away to nighttime. A telephone wire happened to be in the perfect spot, and the sun was shining on it in just a way that its surface was shiny and black, reflecting the light up into something like a silver lining on it.

The moment was interrupted by Gavin's cellphone chiming in the pocket of his joggers.

"Shit." Gavin said, fumbling to get it out. "I thought I had it on silent."

He looked at the notifications on his screen and saw an incoming message from a number he didn't have saved in his contacts. The message read:

I know you still think about what happened this summer.

"What the fuck?" Gavin said, rereading the text message and checking the number to see if he didn't recognize it.

"Gav, you okay?" Connie asked.

Out of his peripherals, he could see her straining to look at his phone screen, and for the first time in their short relationship, he had the instinct to hide his phone from her.

Before he could do such a thing, another message from the same number came through:

We need to talk. Call me.

Gavin shifted in his chair and gulped. His throat was dry. *Okay, this is getting weird as shit.* He thought.

"Gav? Hey, Gav, you okay?" Connie was standing in front of him, grabbing onto his shoulder.

He looked up at her and clicked the lock button on his phone. Embarrassed, but he had to do what he had to do. They hadn't been dating long enough for him to show her he could be vulnerable.

"Uh, yeah. I just, uh, need a moment to myself. Is that cool?"

Connie's eyes were big and round and full of worry. It was in this moment that he knew this girl truly cared about him, and he felt emotions pulling at his heartstrings. For Gavin Briggs, this was a new sensation, a sensation he hadn't even been sure he could've experienced until right now.

Connie bent down and kissed him on the forehead.

"Yeah, of course," she said, stepping back from him. "I'll be inside, okay?"

"Alright. Thank you." Gavin said. "I'll join you shortly."

Connie gave him a weak smile before grabbing her hot cocoa off the metal table she'd set it on and headed inside.

Gavin watched her disappear behind the blinds. He waited for them to settle, for the clatter of the plastic blinds bumping into each other to die off, then turned back to his phone.

He opened the text message thread from the unknown number. There were previous messages in there, which meant it belonged to someone he'd previously been in contact with. It only took him reading two older messages to realize who the unknown number belonged to: Noelle Remington.

He'd deleted her contact info two months ago after deciding to try to move on from the events at Camp Slaughter. He hadn't spoken to her since and had been trying his best to not think about her or the events at Camp Slaughter.

He started typing back a message, then rethought it. A phone call would be more effective for what he had in mind, so he dialed her. Noelle picked up on the third ring.

"Hey, Gav."

"Yo. What's that text message about?" He said, putting the mug of hot cocoa on the table next to him and standing up to walk across the balcony. He leaned against the railing.

"You know what it's about." Noelle stated in a flat tone.

Gavin puffed out some breath in frustration. "Unfortunately, I do."

His apartment was on the third floor of the building, and below, he could hear the cars on the busy streets. Horns blared, tires grinded against the blacktop as brakes were slammed on, people were shouting. It was just another night in Philadelphia.

But Gavin felt disconnected from all of that because his mind was elsewhere. His mind was transporting him back to the seclusion of Northern Pennsylvania. Back to Camp Slaughter.

"He killed more people, Gav." She said, and he swore he heard a crack at the end of her voice. "After his encounter with us, he went into a town and killed a group of kids around our age on Halloween night."

"Noelle, I don't care—"

"I'm going to try to stop him." Noelle said. "I think the only way I'll stop having these nightmares is when I know he's dead for good."

"Look, Noelle, I'm trying to move on and get over this." Gavin said, clutching his phone harder. "I suggest you try to, too. Now, goodbye. Stop contacting me."

He took the phone off his ear and ended the call. Then, before she could call back, he blocked Noelle's number.

There. That takes care of that. He thought. He was really putting in a concerted effort to be a nicer person since the events at Camp Slaughter, but sometimes he had to let his old self come out and do shit like this for him.

The last thing he needed—or wanted—was to be out here in the cold talking about the maniac cannibal that had killed his little brother.

Gavin turned around and saw Connie through the glass door. She was sitting on the couch, wrapped in a throw blanket with a bowl of popcorn on her lap. The colors of the television glowed on her face. He watched her smile at whatever she was watching—probably some corny romcom—and as much as Gavin hated those movies, sitting on the couch with her was where he wanted to be.

He grabbed his hot cocoa and headed inside the apartment to relax.

In the back of his head, a little voice told him that whatever relaxation he would find tonight was only temporary. Because all his thoughts—all the roads if you will—would eventually lead back to the camp.

Noelle stared down at her phone. After trying him three more time, it was obvious Gavin had either blocked her phone number or turned his cellphone off. Either way, that was another person down.

This "recruitment" wasn't going very well.

Noelle was sitting on her couch, every light off in the apartment, the only thing illuminating was the backlight from her phone screen. She'd been spending more and more time alone in the dark. There was a certain comfort to it that made her feel invisible. Made her feel like she wasn't in this world while hidden by the darkness.

The events at Camp Slaughter truly had changed her. Maybe for the best. Maybe for the worst. That, she decided, would be something she would determine after everything was said and done. For now, though, she had to be focused.

Focused and prepared if she was going to kill that damn cannibal.

Noelle set the phone down on the couch and got up. She crossed the living room until she got to the desk that was pushed up against the wall leading into the kitchen. Noelle found the little chain on the tiny desk lamp despite the darkness of the room and yanked it.

The light shined over the clutter scattered across the desk. It was mostly pieces of notebook paper with Noelle's handwriting from her research into Camp Slaughter and Ignacio Calderon. There were articles printed out from various websites, too. The most recent was from the killings the cannibal had done at Hilltown.

But there was one paper in particular she was interested in. It had the neatest handwriting on it, and the other sheets cluttered around it seemed to be encircling it like it was the belle of the ball.

Indeed, though, it was one of the most important papers on Noelle's desk. At the top of it, in large capital letters she'd written: **SURVIVORS.**

Underneath it, she'd written down the names of the people she meant to reach out to and in the order she was going to do it:

~~Sheriff Greg Olmos~~

Gavin Briggs

Diana Santos

Brooke Florentine

She grabbed a pen from a plastic pencil at the corner of the desk, and just as she'd done to Gregorio Olmos's name, she crossed out Gavin Briggs's name.

This one stung a little because she thought they'd bonded over surviving the cannibal together. She thought he'd at the very least hear her out, but things didn't always go as planned.

Noelle sighed. There were only two people left. If they weren't in, this would have to be a solo mission.

So be it. She thought, grabbing the little chain on the desk lamp. She pulled on it until it clicked. The bulb went off, leaving her in the dark apartment once again.

CHAPTER 19

Gavin shot up in bed. Sweat poured down his face. His back was sticky and slimy, and he knew he'd have to wash his sheets in the morning from how gross they'd gotten since he'd gone to sleep.

Another nightmare. The same fucking one, too.

Gavin looked over at the empty side of the bed. The sheets were wrinkled, vaguely in the shape of where his girlfriend had been lying. They'd only been together for two months—three, really, if one counts the elusive in between stage of not knowing what 'you are' with the other person—and she'd only stayed over a handful of times.

Tonight was not one of those nights. Gavin wasn't sure if he was glad about that or not. On one hand, it saved him the embarrassment of waking up in the middle of the night frightened over a nightmare like a child. On the other hand, he'd feel better if she was lying next to him right now.

Something in him stirred, and he realized he missed her. Gavin had never in his life missed any girl—it had driven Fred Meyers crazy, and probably made his best friend respect him less. But that was the truth of it.

Guess this is growing up. Gavin thought, then shook his head. Another possibility popped into his head. *Or maybe it's just the nightmare fucking with my head.*

He pushed the sheets off him and swung out of bed. He was thirsty. His lips were dry and borderline cracked, even though the rest of him felt slimy and sticky.

As he walked through the darkened apartment at this hour of the night, he could hear every creak in the wood underneath the carpet.

In the kitchen, he flipped the light switch on, retrieved a glass from the cupboard, and filled it up with water from the Arrowhead jug.

He leaned against the kitchen counter and drank the water in one gulp, then headed back to the bedroom.

In his haste (and because he didn't really need them to see) he'd left the bedroom lights off. But now, at the doorframe, something made him stop. Something was different about it.

He thought about flicking the lights on, even reached for the switch on the wall, but stopped himself. A feeling in his gut told him that turning the lights on would just make this worse. It was as if the danger would be able to find him before he found it.

Whatever "it" was….

Gavin scanned the darkened room. He looked over at the curtains—the ones Connie had forced him to put up so his place would actually start to feel like a home, as she'd said. There was nothing behind them.

He looked over at the bed. He could see the shadow of his pillow pushed up against the headboard, bent in half, just as he'd left it. The comforter he'd thrown off was bunched up at the foot of the bed, but there was nothing ominous about it.

Underneath the bed, maybe? But it was too dark to see anything.

Oh, fuck this. You're way too old to be afraid of Boogiemen BS. He thought and slapped on the light switch.

He went over to the side of the bed where the nightstand was and grabbed his cellphone, then turned on its flashlight. Gavin got down on all fours and shined the light underneath the bed. He swept the cellphone left and right to inspect underneath it.

Just as he was going to determine there was nothing, a small spot on the carpet caught his eye.

His heart began racing again, thumping against the front of his chest.

There, directly in the center underneath the mattress was a dark stain. A purplish color against the dark beige carpeting that still looked wet. For a second, he thought about reaching out to touch it. Then thought better of it. Instead, he angled the phone to shine the light up toward the bottom of the mattress and the wooden slats.

Another stain. And the source of the smaller one—kind of anyway.

Blood was leaking from the mattress. No, not from. *Through* the mattress. It collected in the spot he was looking at until the mattress and fabric couldn't hold it anymore, at which point it would drip down to the carpet.

"What the fuck." Gavin said, vocalizing it because it felt like the only appropriate response.

He jumped up to his feet, a bad feeling forming in his gut. He looked at the bed and saw Connie was laying there. She hadn't gone home after all. In fact, she'd been laying there this whole time, and he'd somehow missed her.

She was dead. Lying on her back with three massive gashes across her stomach. Her pink bathrobe was open, letting him get a clear view of the wounds, a clear view of all the blood coming out of her abdomen. Blood and entrails were spilling out the side of her body, drenching the sheets.

Connie turned her head toward Gavin, her eyes lifeless—yet, somehow pleading him for help.

Gavin reached out to touch her, as if he could take her skin and close it up and she would be okay, but before his hand got anywhere near her, everything went black—

—He woke up in bed again. Chest heaving. Hair stuck to his forehead with sweat.

Fuck. Not again. He thought, glancing at the empty spot in the bed next to him where his disemboweled girlfriend definitely wasn't lying.

No blood or entrails, either, for that matter.

He leaned over the bed and turned on the lamp on the nightstand. The yellow light flooded the room. Gavin grabbed the glass of water sitting by the lamp, turning it until the NASA logo was facing him. He reached into the nightstand drawer and pulled out the piece of paper with his handwriting that said:

If you see the NASA logo, you are awake.

It was batshit crazy, but every night before bed, he would write this note to himself, that way he would know with absolute certainty if he was awake or not. Even crazier, though, he would change out the cup in case the nightmares somehow caught on to what he was doing and would try to replicate his "code."

It made him feel like a total loon, and it wasn't foolproof, of course, but it hadn't failed him yet.

Gavin grabbed the glass of water and gulped it down. The water was chilled, which meant he hadn't been sleeping that long before he'd woken up. Gavin unlocked his phone. It was only five minutes past midnight. Connie had left about two hours ago, and Gavin had only just gone to bed around an hour ago.

He set the glass back onto the nightstand, turned the lamp off, and lay flat on his back.

He closed his eyes, but he knew it was fruitless. It was going to be a long night. Tonight, he wouldn't be getting any sleep. He would lie there in the dark, tossing and turning, trying to find a comfortable position to fall asleep in.

And somewhere, amidst this struggle and constant failing, he would realize that Noelle was right. The only thing that would stop these nightmares, and these endless nights, would be knowing the cannibal was dead.

CHAPTER 20

Someone had once said old habits die hard, and Greg Olmos knew that more than ever now. Even though he was retired, he still woke up at 5:00 a.m. and couldn't fall back asleep no matter how much he tried. He lay in bed listening to his wife moving about in the kitchen. A spoon scraped against the bottom of a skillet as something sizzled inside of it (bacon, it seemed, by the smell wafting into the bedroom).

Despite the obvious onset of depression setting in on her, Greg knew his wife was trying to keep herself busy. Trying her damnedest to hold onto the miniscule amount of normalcy in their lives after the cannibal had ruthlessly murdered their daughter.

He'd had been trying to downplay her death since it happened, that Judy's death could have happened to anyone. That his daughter just happened to be at the wrong place at the wrong time, that she hadn't been the cannibal's target. It'd been making it easier to accept she was gone by doing this, but this morning was different.

The meeting with Noelle had changed something in him. It was like the girl had given him that extra little push he needed to feel something other than an infinite sadness.

The first thing he'd felt was motivation. He'd researched Ignacio Calderon last night after Sharon had gone into the bedroom to sleep. There wasn't much on the man; the name was somewhat common, so he had to click around until he found something interesting.

There was an article about a nurse in Pennsylvania who'd been killed in a home invasion. The picture of her and her son was all the evidence Greg needed to see to know this was the same Ignacio. The article claimed the boy was eight at the time the picture was taken, but the kid on her lap looked about double the size of an average child that age.

His hair was cropped short and combed upward into tiny spikes near the front instead of the long curly hair he had now, but everything else looked like a young version of the guy he'd interviewed at Harvey's. The thick eyebrows, the broad-shoulders, and bearpaws for hands that he would eventually grow into.

Reading the article made him sick to his stomach. There was something discomforting about the connection between the cannibal's mother and his own daughter being nurses. Something that made this whole thing much more disturbing to him—because he realized that his daughter hadn't just been killed randomly.

Worse yet was the part of the article that stated Ignacio's mother had been beheaded. Just like Judy.

As a lifelong policeman, Greg knew home invaders weren't likely to take the time to behead someone. That type of criminal never really even intended to kill; the weapons were there "just in case."

Ignacio *had* beheaded Judy, though. That he knew for a fact.

Knowing all of this, his sadness had turned into anger. Somehow, though, he'd managed to shut his laptop off and go to sleep last night. This morning, however, the anger was fully blossomed.

His wounded heart was seeping out nothing but hatred, yearning for revenge. Noelle Remington had been right all along. He couldn't simply just "move on" from his daughter's death. He needed to avenge it.

But first, he had to do what would perhaps be the most difficult part of this whole ordeal. He would have to lie to the woman he loved.

Greg pushed the covers off himself and rose out of bed.

Retirement for them was supposed to bring peace for them. It was a thing Greg had always talked about with Sharon—especially lately, as he'd been getting closer and closer to retiring from the department.

Judy's death had forced him into an early retirement since he no longer had the motivation or wherewithal to be the sheriff of town. He couldn't even protect his own kin, how in the hell was he supposed to protect the whole town?

Ignacio Calderon—Varias Caras, as Diana Santos had told him he'd called himself—had thrown a wrench into Greg Olmos's retirement plans.

Shit, if I decide to go through with this crazy plan, this will be more dangerous than anything I ever did in my entire police career. This thought invaded his mind as he entered the kitchen.

Sharon turned away from the counter to face him as he was coming in. She held a plate with fluffy scrambled eggs, two pieces of toast, and three crisp pieces of bacon. It was a picture-perfect breakfast. Sharon already had a natural ability to cook and plate food, but the need to distract herself from the depression had her working on her skills even more and the breakfast looked phenomenal.

It made him want to postpone the conversation—the *lie* he was about to tell her—but he thought better of it. The sooner he did this, the sooner he would be able to get over the guilt.

Greg sat down at the kitchen table as she put the plate down in front of him. "Morning, honey."

"Morning," she said, bending down to kiss him on the cheek.

It didn't matter how old they'd gotten and how long they'd been together, she did this every morning they spent together.

But this time, there was something different. She stepped away from him after kissing him and stood up straight, one eyebrow cocked up, like she was trying to figure out one of those funky paintings at a post-modern museum that may or may not be the shape of something recognizable.

She knows. Greg thought, swallowing. *She knows me too well.*

Then, she relaxed, and half turned toward the fridge. "Juice or coffee?"

She's giving me a chance to come clean. He thought. Out loud, he said, "Juice."

"I think we have apple juice and a little bit of orange juice..." her voice trailed off as she fully turned away from him and started rummaging through the fridge.

"I was talking to some old friends last night." Greg said, letting the first lie drop.

"Oh?" Sharon asked, turning around with a carton that had a big orange on the front of it. She walked over to the cupboard. "From high school? Who was it?"

"Elementary school." The lie came out before he could really think it through.

Greg Olmos's family had been one of the rare families that had actually moved *into* Hilltown back when he was ten years old. It was the only part of his life that had any sort of mystery to Sharon. The lies were coming out naturally, which made him feel guiltier about this whole thing.

Having grabbed a glass, Sharon came back to the kitchen table. "I thought you said you didn't talk to anyone from elementary school?"

Greg shifted in his seat and then attempted to correct her with a lie. "No, I said most of my friends from then were dead."

"Right." Sharon said, unscrewing the cap on the orange juice. "Okay, so what did you talk to them about?"

"We're going on a fishing trip. It's going to be about a weeklong or so." He said, watching her fill the glass. Anything so he wouldn't have to look at the love of his life in the eyes as he told a boldfaced lie to her.

"Oh, like a reunion? That should be fun! When?"

"I—I'm not sure." He said, because the truth was, he wasn't even sure if Noelle would want him to go hunting for the cannibal anymore. Maybe she might've changed her mind after he'd tucked his tail and ran away from the offer yesterday.

Sharon walked around the table and hugged him from behind and leaned her head against his.

"You need this to stop thinking about her, don't you?" she whispered to him and then kissed him on the head.

"I think it would be good for me, yeah." Greg said, swallowing. He felt himself tense, and with that, he felt like he'd given himself away. There was no way she was buying the lie. She knew.

Somehow, she knew. A wife's intuition if you will.

"Promise me you'll be careful on this fishing trip?" she said. "I already lost half of my world, I don't want to lose you, too."

"I'll try my best." He said, fighting back tears.

He reached up and put one of his hands on top of hers. For a moment, they just stayed there, holding one another. The loudest sounds in the kitchen were the hum of the coffeemaker's hotplate and the bird clock on the wall ticking away. This was similar to the moments before he'd gone out to the junkyard on Halloween where he'd had his first confrontation with Varias Caras.

And now, here they were, recreating this moment before what he would plan to be the next confrontation with the man.

No, not just the next one. The final confrontation. One way or another, he or the cannibal would be dying out in those woods.

"But," he said, breaking the silence.

"But what?" Sharon said.

"No promises on how safe I'll be. A big fish might bite my line and pull me over the boat—and you know how bad of a swimmer I am."

He grinned as he said this, and Sharon laughed. But this was the most honest thing he'd said to her all morning. Because promising his safety to her was too big of a lie to commit.

CHAPTER 21

The timer on her phone sounded, signaling the end of the meditation session. Noelle opened her eyes. As per usual, the sun coming in through the windows into her apartment appeared brighter. She let out one big, final exhale.

Noelle stood up, slowly, feeling the weightlessness and relaxation that came with a thirty-minute meditation session after a three-mile jog. This was how she started her morning nowadays. Preparing. Because she knew the showdown with Varias Caras would require her to run at some point, but more than that, she would need to keep calm, too.

She wasn't sure she would find him in the woods, specifically, but she knew they would have another confrontation eventually. She wasn't sure how she knew this, but she was as sure of it as the sun rising tomorrow.

And when it happened, their fight would test her mettle. Of this, Noelle had no doubt.

Noelle went over to the coffee table where her phone was ringing. There was a new text message from Gavin in her notifications. It read:

> You win. I'm in.

Noelle smiled, feeling a bit victorious. She just hoped these small wins would lead her to winning the big one.

She locked the phone and put it back on the coffee table. For now, responding to Gavin would have to wait. She had elsewhere to be.

Noelle walked to a café near her apartment, laptop bag strapped to her shoulder. She'd ordered a latte with oat milk, even though she didn't much feel like having a drink, but she needed to blend in here. There was something about what she was about to do that always felt illegal. She wasn't sure if it was, but as her father once told her: if it feels wrong and works in your favor, it's probably against the law.

Noelle sat down at a booth in the corner of the café, her back to the wall so there was no chance anyone could sneak up behind her. She put her latte down on the table, and then slipped the laptop out of its case and opened it.

As she typed in her login password, she glanced around the café. There were only four other patrons here besides her.

A beefy kid with sandy blond hair was staring at a laptop screen. He wore flipflops despite the fact that it was sub-forty degrees out and had a pencil in his mouth that was covered in bitemarks. There was also a notebook open in front of him with some of the worst handwriting Noelle had ever seen.

Sitting a few tables behind him was an old man whose getup was the polar opposite of the college student. He was bundled up like they were living in the Arctic. He wore a shiny, puffy jacket and a thick scarf that looked like it belonged to an era long ago. One of his gloved hands was wrapped around a large coffee he'd taken the lid off of. Steam rose from it as he took a small sip from it. The whole time he drank from the cup his eyes were glued to a thick paperback novel with a broken spine that had pieces of tape holding it together.

The only other people here in the café were a couple. The man was wearing a baggy, dark blue sweater and the woman was in a flowing cardigan. Judging by how the man seemed to gaze into the woman's eyes, they were either in the honeymoon phase of their relationship or on a first date. Noelle wasn't sure, but either way, it was good. It meant they were distracted.

She glanced over at the counter where the young kid with the afro who'd made her latte was cleaning the countertop, going over the same spot over and over with lackadaisical movements. He stopped midmotion, tilted his head back, and let out an enormous yawn.

Sure that no one was curious as to what she was up to, Noelle brought her focus back to the laptop. She connected to the café's Wi-Fi, opened up the web browser, and went onto Gmail.com. She navigated the cursor over to the text field asking for an email address and entered one belonging to a dead man. Then, in the password field, she typed in the one she'd invented and hit LOGIN.

The password was accepted, and she was in Emeril Dantes's account now.

Getting into the man's email hadn't been easy. She'd had to do a lot of shady stuff she wasn't proud of. First, she had to do extensive research on both Emeril Dantes and Molly Sanger—who she learned about from Gavin while they'd been recovering in the hospital.

She'd paid for those creepy services that reveal people's private information like addresses, possible relatives, all forms of contact, and so on. The kind of sites that were generally used by private investigators or spouses suspecting their significant other of cheating, but they also worked to help break into a deceased man's accounts, as Noelle found out.

The first thing she tried to find out was if Emeril Dantes or Molly Sanger had any children—turned out neither one had. In fact, neither of them had ever even been married for the duration of their lives, according to multiple of the spy sites Noelle had used.

The next thing she did was look up their relatives. Molly's family was a total dead-end. All their stuff was set to the maximum privacy; all she found out was her parents name and that she was an only child.

Emeril Dantes, however, was another story. She found his half-sister. According to what Noelle could piece together, his mother had remarried after being widowed for several years. The thing that caught Noelle's eyes was that his half-sister had a daughter named Marie Parton who was around Noelle's age.

It was perfect. Marie was close enough in blood to Emeril that people would believe she would be trying to access her deceased half-uncle's accounts to tie-up loose ends and reach out to friends who only he had contact with. At the same time, it was possible that Emeril and Marie didn't have any relationship, and the real Marie wouldn't be trying to access his account, which would work in Noelle's favor.

As it turned out, the latter was the truth. Posing as Marie Parton, Noelle had contacted Google from a throwaway account. After going back and forth with them for a few days, and using info she gained from these shady sites, she managed to convince them she was his surviving half-niece.

They'd reset the password on his account and emailed her instructions on how to take it over. Within minutes, she had access to all his Google accounts—but the two most important ones were his email address and the Google Drive account.

The Drive account was the one he shared with Molly Sanger and had tons of footage of their unfinished Camp Slaughter documentary. As shady as she'd felt breaking into the man's account, something about opening those files felt like a step too far. Something about watching videos of the dead man and his dead business partner when they'd still been alive, still been hopeful about their project, made her deeply uncomfortable.

She stuck to just reading his emails (which, in and of itself was highly intrusive, but there was a mission she needed to accomplish).

Emeril's inbox was filled with emails from fans of his YouTube channel; most of the new ones were people asking when the Camp Slaughter video was coming out. Amidst these were emails from Bigfoot aficionados calling him an "idiot" or "moron" or "asshole" for his video on the exploration in the Pacific Northwest, where he'd claimed the ape crypto was nothing but an elaborate hoax.

Noelle hadn't done anything with the account besides read through his emails. Not up until two days, ago, though. Two days ago, she'd finally summoned up the courage to send off an email to the man who'd been Emeril and Molly's informant when they'd been researching Camp Slaughter.

This man's reply sat at the top of the inbox. Noelle opened his email and read it:

From: TheLivingtribunal86@gmail.com
Subject: RE: Need to meet

Hey there, old chum! Thought I'd never hear from ya again!

Sure, I'm available to meet. When were ya thinking? How's the doc coming along? I guess maybe we could talk about that in person, though, right? Hehe

Tell Molly I say hello!

Anyway, let me know when and where you wanna meet.

P.S. If this is to ask me to be in another movie, the answer is yes. But give me a heads up so I can clean up a bit, you know? Ha! Anyway, see ya soon.

Noelle fired back an email, telling him that wherever he wanted to meet was OK with her. Harold Buckley had sent the email am hour and a half ago, while she'd been at the gun range practicing with her new pistol.

Noelle didn't have Emeril Dantes's accounts tied to her phone, so she'd missed it. The only time she accessed the dead man's account was when she could connect to a public Wi-Fi network. It was her attempt to cover up her tracks in case someone tried to figure out who was using Emeril Dantes's email address.

Noelle wasn't technologically sound enough to know if doing this was enough to cover her digital footprints, but it felt like the right thing to do, so she stuck to this rule.

If Fred Meyers were alive, she would've asked him… but of course he wasn't… because Varias Caras had murdered him back at the campgrounds.

Pain, anger, and sadness flashed through her. Noelle pushed these thoughts away and refocused herself. She looked at the inbox. Harold Buckley hadn't emailed back yet, so she took another look around the café.

The old man continued reading his paperback. The couple continued staring into each other's eyes over their coffees. The college student was the only doing something different. He was hunched over, typing away at the keys, chewed pencil balancing on the top of his curled-up lip.

Noelle took a big sip of her latte and brought her gaze back to the laptop screen. She stared at the inbox, trying to will Harold Buckley to reply. She didn't have all day to sit here in the café.

Just as she was about to give up and logout of Emeril Dantes's email, a new message came through:

From: TheLivingTribunal86@gmail.com
Subject: RE: Need to meet

Hey there,

How about we meet at the Green Lizard Tavern again?

P.S. Looking forward to it.

P.P.S. I'm assuming by your lack of an answer to the question, this is not about another doc?

> Noelle wrote back, hoping he was still in front of his computer:

The Green Lizard Tavern sounds good. What time works for you?

And no. It is not for another doc. Need more info on Camp Slaughter.

> Harold Buckley wrote back almost immediately:

From: TheLivingTribunal86@gmail.com
Subject: RE: Need to meet

How's tomorrow at 8:00 p.m. sound? Camp Slaughter still, eh? Well, you know I'm your guy. Sort of, ha!

> Noelle sent off another email, telling him that the time worked. She didn't bother to wait for a follow-up email. She logged out of Emeril's account, cleared the browsing history, and exited out of Chrome. She had no idea if doing this was helping her cover her tracks or not, but better safe than sorry.

Noelle closed the laptop and put it back in its bag. She stood up, swooping the coffee up from the table as she did so. The motion was a bit dramatic, but she was feeling good. She was feeling accomplished.

Things seemed to be coming together.

As she marched out of the café with her shoulders a little squarer than when she entered the place, she wondered if maybe she wasn't feeling a little *too* good about all this.

The time for her to find out would soon come.

CHAPTER 22

GREG OLMOS SHUFFLED into the diner and sat down in his usual spot: in a high-top chair on the far right-side of the counter, where he could get a view of the restaurant and the front door at the same time. The waitress working this section was a heavyset girl with curly hair and the prettiest blue eyes anyone had ever seen. She was one of the owner's daughters, the youngest one who didn't work here that often and whose name was escaping Greg at the moment.

The girl looked up from the notepad she'd been scribbling in and walked over to him, flipping to a new page.

"Morning, Sheriff."

"Not sheriff anymore." Greg said, looking over at her and trying to give her his best smile.

"Ah, well, you'll always be the sheriff to me." She smiled, showing a set of teeth that were almost too white. "Childhood memories and all."

"Mr. Olmos is fine nowadays." He said, nodding.

"Sure thing. What can I get you this morning, Sheriff?"

Greg opened his mouth to correct her, but he stopped when he saw her knit her brows.

"You say you're not the sheriff anymore, but yet you're wearing that." A shadow cast over her eyes as she said this.

The lighting in the diner got dimmer. Greg couldn't remember if there were people in here when he'd come in through the front doors, but if there were, they were gone now.

He looked down and saw he was wearing a brown uniform with a sheriff's badge pinned to it. He was wearing his boots, too. The laces untied on one of them, the two ends hanging to the side in mid-air like small serpents.

Greg looked up and saw the girl smiling at him again. This time it was different, though. This time the smile so big it seemed to take up her whole face—stretch it out, even.

"Orders up, Sheriff!" The woman said, reaching for something underneath the counter.

Whatever it was, it was heavy because she had to use both arms to grab it. Her arms came back up into his view, and he saw she was holding onto a glass cake holder. The walls of the carrier were specked with blood but not so much that he couldn't make out the details of what was inside—no, it was clear it was a severed head inside.

More than that, though, he knew whose head he was staring at.

The blue eyes. The blond hair. The pink lips turned into an O.

"Judy—!" Greg screamed and reached out for the cake carrier, reached out for his daughter's head.

The girl stepped back, snatching it away from him, causing his fingers to swipe at nothing but air. She reached up with one hand and grabbed at the top of her face, right where her hairline was, and ripped the skin off her own face.

Instead of muscles and blood and veins, there was a mask underneath. A brown, tattered mask.

The rest of the woman shapeshifted, and now he was staring at the cannibal.

Greg jumped off the stool, knocking it over in the process. Its metal frame clattered against the hardwood floor. The metallic clang rang through the empty diner like a church bell.

"No!" he screamed, but unlike the metal echoes, his voice was swallowed up. Made to sound smaller than it felt.

The cannibal stared at him through the eye hole of his mask. He had only one good eye. The other eyehole had a stream of blood pouring out of it, running down the length of the mask.

"No!" Greg screamed again, then reached for his gun without taking his eyes off the cannibal.

He felt the butt of his pistol, unholstered it, and aimed at the monster that killed his daughter. Though his hands were shaking, he managed to find the trigger with his index finger.

"I'm... dreaming... this isn't real..." he muttered, his lips quivering.

"But even here... You are powerless." Varias Caras said and then threw his head back and laughed. His laughter bouncing off the walls, reverberating through the diner, seeming to come from every direction at once.

Greg felt himself squeeze the trigger—

And woke up on his Lazy Boy, reclined all the way back. Sharon was at work, and besides an episode of *Deal or No Deal* on the television, the house was quiet.

Sweat poured down Greg's forehead. His skin felt slimy, the way he imagined a frog's would feel after it came out of the water and the sun hadn't yet dried it off. In his left hand he was clutching the TV remote instead of the pistol, but his index finger was curled as if on an invisible trigger.

The nightmares had been getting more and more intense these days. No one told you when your loved ones died, that they would die and die again in your nightmares.

This thought, though fleeting, sent a shiver up his spine. Greg stirred, then put the remote on the Lazy Boy's armrest and moved to get up. On the television, the contestant won the next briefcase. The crowd cheered.

Happiness. Clapping.

The sound was faint, the volume low. But the emotions they were expressing were even further away for Greg.

Judy was dead. Not just in his wicked, vivid dreams. In real life, his daughter was dead.

He turned to look toward the mantel hanging over the fireplace, where a picture of him and Sharon and Judy gathered at a family friend's wedding were. It'd been from two years ago, but it felt like a lifetime ago. Shit. Halloween felt like a lifetime ago.

Halloween had been the last time he saw her alive. She'd come to pick up the neighbor girl to go to the party where her fate would ultimately be sealed (and the neighbor girl's as well, for that matter). She'd dropped off peanut butter cookies for them. In a rare night, he'd been home at the time and sent her off along with Sharon. It'd been almost like the universe knew his daughter would be gone soon and the universe was allowing him one last chance to get a look at her alive.

A knock at the door brought him out of these awful thoughts, and he realized he was standing in the middle of the living room staring at the picture. If someone had been peeking in through one of the windows, they would've thought he was a loon or high on drugs.

The irony, of course, was that he'd never felt lower in his life.

"Greg, it's James." The person behind the door said, giving the door another rap with their knuckles. This one more of a love tap than a full out knock.

"Coming." Greg said, shuffling toward the door.

He could see the outline of the sheriff's hat through the opaqued glass windows on the front door. It made him feel a certain way. He couldn't pinpoint the feeling because it was a strange mix of both good and bad. Nostalgia with a hint of envy. No. A *bite* of envy was more accurate.

He opened the door. The first thing that caught his eye was how shiny the sheriff's badge on James's shirt looked. The morning's sunrays bounced off it like it was a polished mirror.

"Morning, Greg." Sheriff Rooney said. "I got your text message and came over as soon as I could."

It took Greg a few seconds to remember he'd texted James an hour ago—and had promptly fallen asleep afterward. A part of him wondered if this wasn't another dream, and the sheriff wouldn't suddenly pull out a hacksaw and start cutting his own head off or something like that.

"You alright, Greg?" The sheriff said, looking him up and down with a puzzled look on his face.

"Yeah, yeah. Sorry. Just got up from a nap and a bit groggy." Greg said, making room for him to come in.

Sheriff Rooney took his hat off as he stepped into the house. Greg led him into the living room.

"Make yourself at home," Greg said, motioning toward the seats. "Can I get you something to drink?"

"I think I'm okay." Sheriff Rooney said, settling into the Lazy Boy. "What did you want to talk about?"

"Cutting right to the chase, huh?" Greg said, sitting down on the couch, diagonal from the sheriff.

"It's not every day you text me, Greg." Sheriff Rooney said, giving him a weak smile. "You said you had a lot on your mind. I'm guessing it has to do with—"

"More specific, that night." Greg said, cutting him off before he could even start to make the 'j' sound in his daughter's name. He would try his hardest to talk about this while avoiding talking about her death. Lord knew he thought about that enough as it was.

"What about it?"

"Do you remember what you said about the babysitter he killed?"

"Yeah," Sheriff Rooney nodded. "That it seemed like the guy had killed before."

"I had a visit from a girl a few days ago." Greg said, shifting in his seat.

Sheriff Rooney nodded. This was a different nod than the previous one. It was the universal police gesture that said *I don't know where you're going with this, but I'm all ears so proceed*. Greg had given it to many people during interrogations and questionings.

"This girl had an encounter with our cannibal—Ignacio Calderon." He let the words hang in the air and let the sheriff digest them.

"She was there at the party or something?" The sheriff asked.

"No, no. Before coming to our town, Ignacio was out in the woods. Living at an abandoned campsite." Greg rubbed at his face.

"Go on."

"County isn't out looking for this man, are they?"

The sheriff shook his head. "They've got bigger fish to fry than some nut who attacked our small town. You know how it is better than anyone, Greg."

Unfortunately. He thought.

"The girl—Noelle Remington is her name—thinks he went back into the woods." Greg said, a scowl forming on his face. "Which would make him pretty much a free man."

"Certainly, yeah." The sheriff concurred.

"What if…" Greg stopped himself, trying to find the best way to word it. The best way to not make what he was about to say come off as crazy or as silly as it seemed. But of course, as soon as the idea would come out of him, he would realize there was no other way. "What if we could find him?"

He felt the shift in the room. Something akin to tension, but not quite. More like the sheriff was waiting for the other shoe to drop, waiting for the punchline to the joke or for the second half of the suggestion that would make it make more sense.

Sheriff Rooney coughed, then shifted his feet, the heels of his boots making small scraping sounds against the floor.

"Greg, you're… uh, you're not a cop anymore." He said.

"I know." Greg said, smiling. "I'm retired, not senile, James."

To his relief, the sheriff smiled at this crack.

"What exactly are you suggesting? That we go on a vigilante manhunt through northern Pennsylvania for this guy?" The sheriff grabbed a tissue from the box Sharon kept in the center table and wiped his forehead with it before tucking it into his shirt pocket.

"You don't have to come." Greg said. "I know how much work being sheriff is."

Sheriff Rooney nodded. "Then why exactly are you telling me this?"

"Because you're my friend, James."

"Right." He responded. "Of course."

Greg saw him relax into the Lazy Boy.

"I mostly want your opinion on this."

"I think the idea is—pardon my French, Greg—fucking insane."

"So do I. But he's still out there, James. And he's going to kill again. You saw the pictures of the people in his fridge. Butchered up and packed like beef chuck."

"And what's the plan exactly? To just camp out in the woods and hope he finds you?"

"I guess." Greg said, breaking eye contact because when he put it that way, the plan didn't just seem insane; it seemed flat-out silly. "The girl—Noelle—seemed pretty convinced he would return to those campgrounds."

"What does she know?" James said, shaking his head. "She just managed to avoid being one of his victims. Why would she know anything more than anyone?"

"I don't know. Good question." Greg said, pondering on it himself. "But I have to try, James… I have to try…*something*. It's… been hard to live since he killed Judy. And Officer Roos and DiLossi and everyone else…"

"I understand." Sheriff Rooney said, swallowing.

"I consider it the biggest failure of my career, by a longshot." To his surprise, he let out a chuckle, a chuckle that was void of any humor and was more a defensive mechanism. "Talk about retiring on a low point."

"I understand your feelings and where you're coming from." James let out a small sigh and fidgeted in his seat. "And I know you're going to do whatever you want, but I really hope what's driving you is justice—"

"I've been retired from the police department for weeks." Greg said, bringing his eyes back to him, and in particular to the badge on James's shirt. "When I wore that badge, it *was* justice I was seeking."

A pause.

"But that seems like a lifetime ago. What I'm seeking is revenge."

"Hey, Greg, I think I need some fresh air." James said, standing up.

Greg understood what he was trying to say. He wasn't going to argue with him or try to talk him out of this, so it was time for him to go.

Greg stood up with him and they went out onto the porch. Greg settled on the porch swing, while Sheriff Rooney remained standing by the railing, staring out across the street.

By now, the Halloween decorations had been stored away for weeks, but several of the houses in the neighborhood still had pumpkins and gourds in their windows and on their porch railings. The town was in that transitionary period between Halloween and Christmas, where fall was celebrated for about a week until the candy canes and Christmas lights started to make their annual appearances.

"Like I said, Greg, I know you're going to do what you're going to do." Sheriff Rooney turned away from the railing, the muscles around his eyes unflexing now that he wasn't staring out into the morning sun but was looking into the shade underneath the awning. "I just hope you make it out alive—for Sharon's sake."

James had said something to this effect on Halloween night.

But the truth was, ever since Judy died, he had a hard time facing Sharon in the mornings. He thought that the feeling of letting the whole of Hilltown down that night would eventually pass. That time would help to heal the wound of his failure and of his daughter's death, but no such thing happened. If anything, it seemed to get worse.

Nowadays, he wondered if it was even worthwhile to continue to live.

This was all too much to tell anyone. Even James, who'd been his righthand man basically his entire career as Hilltown sheriff.

Instead, what he said to the sheriff was, "I'll keep that in mind, James. Thank you."

Sheriff Rooney looked down at the watch on his wrist. "I have some stuff to take care of. Couple of rednecks broke into a house the other night—gonna drive by and make sure the residents on the street know I'm patrolling the area."

Another tremor of envy went through Greg, feeling like another person was doing the duty he'd once held so dear to his heart. And apparently, given the reaction, still did.

"Have a good rest of your day, Greg." James said, going down the porch steps. At the bottom of them, he stopped and turned to look at him. "And in case you wanted to know, yes, you have my blessings on whatever you do. Good luck, friend."

"Thanks, Sheriff." Greg smiled. "You have a good day as well."

James put his sheriff hat on, then saluted him and made his way to the curb where his cruiser was parked.

Greg waited until the sheriff's cruiser was driving away, then pulled his cellphone out. He tapped the screen, opening the contacts list, then scrolled down to the newest name on the list.

CHAPTER 23

Gavin had driven over to Noelle's apartment after a brief conversation. They hadn't seen each other in months. The first thing Noelle had noticed when he took his jacket off was that his chest and shoulders looked smaller. He was still muscular, there was no doubt about that. She could see his bulging biceps underneath the loose Champion sweater, but he wasn't as bulky as he'd been in the summer.

"I've gotten soft." Gavin said, sitting down with a Coke he'd retrieved from Noelle's fridge. He cracked it open, looking at it like he wished it was something stronger. "I tried to change after the stuff that happened at Camp Slaughter… but…"

"You can't move on." Noelle finished for him.

"Yeah," Gavin put the can up to his lips and drank some, almost emptying it out in one go.

"There's a liquor store down the street if you'd rather have some alcohol—"

Gavin was waving his hand through the air when Noelle's phone started going off. It was sitting on the coffee table;. Its screen lit up and the vibrations made it buzz against the surface, vying for their attention. They both saw it was an unsaved number calling.

"I have to pick this up." Noelle said, thinking she knew who it was. "One moment, please."

Gavin waved again, this time more of a dismal type of wave. It wasn't like Noelle needed permission, though, she'd already been swooping the phone off the table and walking toward the kitchen.

"Hello?" she said, turning the light on in the kitchen and crossing the room. She leaned against one of the counters.

"Noelle. It's Greg Olmos."

Hearing the name made Noelle smile. Partly because her hunch had been correct, but mostly because she knew what him calling her meant: he'd changed his mind.

"Thought I'd never hear from you." She said.

"Yeah, well, I had a lot to think about since we last talked."

"And what did all this thinking make you conclude?"

"That you're right." He said, breathing into the receiver. "I think in my heart of hearts, what I want the most is revenge for what he did to my daughter."

"We'll get him, Mr. Olmos." Noelle said, her voice booming with confidence.

"So, what's the plan, then?" he asked. "We waltz into the woods and hope he's there?"

"Basically, yeah." Noelle said. "If he's not there, we'll keep trying to find reports of a cannibal that matches his description."

"Yeah, not much of a plan."

"One thing at a time." Noelle told him, feeling like she was the adult in this dynamic.

She would think back to this conversation a little later and realize that this was the moment she knew she was the leader of this excursion—that everyone going along with this revenge plan was counting on her.

"Right." Mr. Olmos said.

"Mr. Olmos, I have a guest over—a friend of sorts—we'll have to pick this conversation up some other time. I can call maybe later tonight."

"Okay, that's fine. If I don't pick up, it's because I'm spending quality time with my wife." A pause, and Noelle could practically hear his thoughts rolling around in his head. "Maybe one of the last chances I get to do so."

"Try to take it easy," she said to him, knowing damn well she couldn't take that advice herself.

It made him laugh, and to her that was almost as good. "I'll give that a shot, young lady. But no promises."

"Fair enough."

"If we don't talk later, have a good night, Noelle."

"You too, Mr. Olmos."

They hung up.

Noelle looked at the phone with some morose. She could hear the man's inner turmoil through his voice—a man who both wanted to move on from the nightmare his life had become but also knew he had to put himself in grave danger in order to do so.

She understood his feelings well. Maybe even too well.

Noelle put the phone in her pocket and went back out into the living room, surprised to find it was empty.

A few minutes later, a knock at the door made Noelle spring up from the couch. She'd been sitting down on the desk, going over the notes she had on Varias Caras in a composition notebook.

She opened her apartment door, and Gavin stood there with a six-pack of Yuengling.

"I caved." He said it like a boy telling his sins in the confession box. "In my defense, desperate times call for desperate measures."

"Relax." Noelle said, making space to let him into the apartment. "I'm not judging. I don't care."

"Good." Gavin said, moving past her. He slumped down onto the couch and put the pack of beers on the floor between his shoes. He regarded them for a few seconds, like they were an old friend he'd neglected. "Because I don't think I could do this shit sober."

"I hope you'll still be able to function. We'll need all our wits about us if we're going to kill Varias Caras."

Noelle was about to ask him if he wanted a bottle opener, but then he used the corner of the coffee table to pop the cap off his Yuengling.

"Don't worry," he said, taking a long pull on the beer. "I'm an expert at this."

"Can I ask you a deeply personal question?"

Gavin's response was to shrug, then drink the rest of his beer. He grabbed another from the case and popped its top off the same way he'd done to the first one.

"What are your nightmares like? Like, what are they about?"

"Mostly I see the cannibal killing my little brother." Gavin said, his voice as small as Noelle had ever heard it.

"Yeah, I have a younger sister that died, too. All I had for about a year was nightmares of the car crash that killed her."

"Fredster told me about your sister. I didn't know it happened in a car crash."

Noelle nodded. "I was driving, and we got t-boned. The car tumbled and tumbled down a hill on the side of the road. Rachel smacked her head so hard her brain started to bleed. She died within minutes of impact, way before the first responders ever showed up."

"Damn."

"For the longest time, I felt like it was my fault—still feel that way, sometimes, to be honest. I keep thinking… if we would've left the mall earlier that driver would've never hit us. Or if I didn't insist on her going with me because I 'wanted company', she'd still be alive…"

Gavin drank some of his beer. "Do you feel like you'll get some retribution if you kill the cannibal?"

"I don't know." Noelle said. "I do know that I was doing better about not blaming myself for Rachel's death, up until I ran away and left Dalton and Wayne to die in the cabin."

"Wait, who?"

"Dalton. Brooke's cousin."

"Oh." Gavin said, nodding. "You could've given me a million guesses and I would have never remembered his name."

Noelle grinned. "Fred told me you always managed to lift his spirits up even in the worst times."

"It's my gift to the world." Gavin said, drinking more of his beer. "And how I justify being an asshole most of the time."

A laugh escaped Noelle, then she brought the conversation back. "In some ways, I feel like I'm responsible for your brother and Dalton's death."

"How come? Because you ran?"

"Yeah, when they needed me most."

"Hm," Gavin put a thumb up to his lips and sat there pensive for a few seconds. "More than likely, he would've killed you, too."

Noelle couldn't help but scowl. "You don't know that."

"The old man—Emeril—he had a gun and couldn't do shit to him."

"A fair point, but maybe if it'd been three of us—"

"We outnumbered him at the camp, too." Gavin cut her off, shaking his head. "None of us had a chance that day. He was on a rampage."

"We... we don't know that."

"We know he killed all of us but three with ease."

"Not quite. You and I almost had him on the ropes. With a little more energy and us being less scared... we could've killed him. There was also a girl at Hilltown that almost killed him—he *can* be killed."

"I'm not saying he's invincible, Noelle."

"Then what are you saying?"

"I'm saying that maybe things went exactly how they were supposed to."

"This sounds like some hokey shit people repeat to deal with their trauma."

It was Gavin's turn to laugh.

"Maybe so. But still. If you hadn't bailed when you did, we wouldn't be here right now. I would've probably caved and started drinking again eventually, anyway. Except, instead of doing anything to try to avenge my little brother, I probably would've just drunk myself stupid every night and cried."

Noelle could tell by his body language that he wasn't a man used to being this open and vulnerable around people. It made her want to go over there and embrace him. But she also could tell Gavin Briggs wasn't the kind of guy that liked being hugged.

"So, I have to ask, who was it that called?" Gavin said when she didn't respond.

"The sheriff—or rather, former sheriff—of the town where the cannibal last killed."

"Is he helping you research him or something?"

"More than that," Noelle said, grinning. "He's coming along with us."

"Oh… well, damn." Gavin said, bringing the beer bottle up to his lips. He frowned a little when he realized it was empty, then grabbed a new one and opened it.

"There's a lot I have to catch you up on." Noelle looked at the clock hanging on the wall past Gavin's shoulder. "How much time do you have?"

"As much as you need."

Noelle nodded in approval, then started by telling him about the Halloween Slaughter.

About half an hour later, Noelle had him caught up to speed. She told him everything she'd found in her research thus far: the name of the cannibal, terror he'd caused on Hilltown, the fact that Varias Caras was injured from a scuffle with Diana Santos, the motivation the sheriff had for coming with them, and so on. The only thing she'd left out was the reason she believed they would find him there.

Gavin sat back in the couch, taking the last drink of the last beer in the six-pack. After a few seconds of silence, he let out a deep sigh.

"Varias Caras?" he said, putting the beer in the case to join the other empty bottles. "Is that French?"

"Spanish." Noelle corrected him. "It means 'Various Faces' or 'Many Faces' depending on the translation."

"And that's a reference to his masks."

"Yeah, exactly."

"Okay, two big questions off the top of my head. First, what's of Diana Santos? Have you, uh, reached out to her or something?"

"I haven't." Noelle said. She got up and went over to the cluttered desk and grabbed the sheet in the middle of it. "I wrote this list down in order of who was most likely to go along with the plan. She was up next after you."

Noelle held the list out for Gavin to grab. He did so, scanned it, and looked back up her. If she didn't know any better, she would've thought he was a bit hurt by what he saw.

"You struck me out?"

"You were staunch in not going. Even hung up on me and blocked my number if I'm remembering correctly."

Gavin opened his mouth as if he was going to say something, then pressed his lips together into a tight line. Then said, "It's not an easy decision to make, you know."

"I know." Noelle said. "A part of me kind of wishes someone else was taking on this task."

"No kidding." Gavin said, then looked back down at the list. "Why's Brooke at the very bottom? I'm guessing you haven't talked to her recently?"

"I haven't. Not since we all met up for dinner."

Two weeks after the three of them survived the event at Camp Slaughter, they'd met at a Nifty Fifty's. Brooke had treated them to dinner—fancy fries and milkshakes included—and they discussed the horrific camping trip and the aftermath. Brooke apologized multiple times throughout the dinner for abandoning them and essentially leaving them to die.

Noelle accepted the apology, of course, because it seemed genuine. But to Noelle, that single action told her everything she needed to know about the girl: she couldn't be trusted or counted on. In fact, now that she'd shared the list with Gavin, she wasn't sure why she'd put her name on the sheet at all.

"She wouldn't come anyway." Noelle continued.

"Yeah, I know."

"Have you talked to her recently?"

"Like a month or so ago." Gavin said. "She's moving to Hollywood. Said she's going to try to get a book deal or something about this whole ordeal."

Noelle burst out laughing. "She'll likely need more luck than us for that to happen. No one around here seems to care except us. And she thinks they'll care on an entirely different coast?"

"*Camp Slaughter: The Truth Behind the Myth.*" Gavin laughed. "I can see it on the marquee in bright lights."

"What was the other big question? You said you had two off the top of your head."

"Yeah." Gavin said, leaning forward now. "What exactly make you so sure we're going to find this fuckin' guy in the woods?"

It was Noelle turn to be uncomfortable. She shifted in her seat. "If I tell you something, will you promise not to think I'm crazy."

"I'm going on a manhunt into the woods to find a murderer who chops people up and eats them. I don't think I have much room to judge."

"Fair." Noelle said, then cleared her throat to bide herself some more time. "Okay, so you know how the sheriff's daughter and Ignacio's mother are both nurses?"

"Yeah."

"And how both bodies were found decapitated."

"Uh-huh. I see that connection, what's that have to do with—"

"Let me finish." Noelle said.

"Yikes. *Excuse* me."

"Something… weird happened out in the woods to me. After we crashed into the car."

"Okay."

"Do you believe in ghosts?"

"Not at all."

Noelle couldn't help but smile. "Not surprised. But anyway…"

"You think you saw one?"

"I *know* I saw one." Noelle said. "I saw my sister's ghost."

"Noelle… are you sure you weren't just seeing shit? I mean, the accident was pretty bad, you probably knocked your head."

"No, no. Trust me, Gav. I know when I'm seeing stuff, and this was different."

She saw him gulp, and in that slight gesture, she saw a guy starting to question his beliefs.

"Different how, exactly?"

"She pulled me through the windshield. It was like, she was able to pull me into, uh, the ghost world for a brief second or something."

"Huh…"

"Believe me, Gav. I've always been agnostic when it came to stuff like this." She shook her head. "But there's something going on in those woods. I'm sure of it."

"Okay, let's say it happened. My question is, what's this gotta do with the cannibal?"

"Well, I experienced something supernatural there, which means other people must've too. What if the reason he was there in the first place is because he can see his mother's ghost while he's in the woods?"

"That'd make him the biggest momma's boy I've ever heard of."

Noelle let out a small laugh. "Seriously, Gav."

"Okay, okay." Gavin straightened up; his broad frame went square. "Okay, so if I'm understanding you correctly, you think he uses the heads as what? Some sort of like 'token' to manifest the ghosts?"

"Yeah, maybe." Noelle said, shaking her head again. It seemed she did a lot of this nowadays. "It makes more sense in my head."

"I'm following the logic, even though I don't necessarily believe in the ghost aspect of it all." Gavin reached over and rested his hand on her shoulder. "Either way, I'm going back into those woods with you. And if we find him there, we'll finish what we started months ago."

Noelle put her hand on his. It was large and rough, a bit like a piece of sandpaper, but there was some comfort in it. Not in a romantic sense. No, not at all. She and Gavin could never date each other for a myriad of reasons, but it was comforting to know she finally had someone on her side.

Since she thought of this plan, she'd been ready to venture into those woods by herself, thinking there was no way anyone would want to go through with such a wild idea. But here she was, sitting on the couch with someone who had as much skin in the game as she did.

"Thank you." Noelle said.

"You're welcome." Gavin said. Then, judging by the expression on his face, something dawned on him. "May I suggest something, though?"

"What's that?"

"Can we bring a vacuum in case we have to fight ghosts?"

Noelle slapped his hand and then moved it off her shoulder. "Get out of here, Gav!"

They were at the front door, Gav halfway out of the apartment with a bottle of Poland Spring in one of his hands. After Gavin mentioned that he might stop by the liquor store for some "road sodas," they got into a little argument in which Noelle convinced him to take a water bottle and get home as quickly as possible instead.

"Tomorrow." Noelle said. "Don't forget."

Gavin was going with Noelle to go meet Harold Buckley at the Green Lizard Tavern tomorrow. He'd gone from blocking her number to being in this as deep as she was rather quickly.

"I won't. I'll text you when I'm on the way." He said, stepping out into the hallway. "I'll see ya."

"See ya, Gav." Noelle closed the door behind him.

She heard his footsteps down the corridor for a few seconds, the floorboards underneath the carpet creaking, and then the apartment building went quiet. She could hear the murmur of the television in one of the neighboring units, but other than that, the place was still.

Noelle leaned against the door and then slid down to the floor, wondering how her life had gotten to this point.

Gavin sat inside his Honda Civic and pulled the door closed. He slid the key into the ignition, then wondered the same thing as Noelle.

How the hell did I end up here? An image of his little brother's decapitated head in the cabin flashed through his mind, along with all the blood that had been splattered in the room. *Oh right. That's how.*

He looked up at the Noelle's apartment. From this side of the building, he was looking at the living room windows. He saw someone's shadow moving through the room, the figure long and enigmatic, but it retained enough of its shape that he could tell it was feminine.

He watched the shadow roll along the off-white walls and over a bookshelf, then the lights in the living room went off.

He couldn't see anything now, so he cranked the key in the ignition. The Honda Civic's engine roared to life. Gavin took one last glance up at Noelle's darkened apartment. The shadow had clearly been Noelle shutting down the lights to get ready for bed, but for a few beats while he'd been watching that shadow, Gavin had begun to believe that maybe ghosts did exist.

CHAPTER 24

SHE'S INSIDE OF a car, driving down a windy road surrounded by trees. Someone is in the passenger seat, but she can't really tell who it is. Not right now, anyway. She'll know, eventually.

Everything about this moment feels familiar, like she's been here before a hundred times. No, a thousand times.

Yet, something seems off. Like when you run into someone from grade school years after graduation and their hair is different or their weight changed or they're applying their makeup differently or—

Her thought is interrupted because she sees a pair of headlights coming down the other side of the road. Bright and brilliant. Could easily be the lights that would spill out when the pearly gates are opened if it weren't for the grill of the pickup truck she's staring at.

The grill is silver and shiny. And as the vehicle nears, it seems to pick up speed.

The headlights begin swaying left and right, the truck threatening to go into their lane. The driver has lost all control of the vehicle.

Noelle clutches the steering wheel as tight as her grip will let her, so tight she can feel the plastic wheel against her bones. The car is continuing to swerve, getting closer to them, inching over to their lane more and more.

It's going to be a head-on collision if she doesn't act fast. Next to her, Noelle can hear Rachel screaming. She's screaming words, mostly expletives, but it's all nonsensical to Noelle. Though, the string of words has a certain cadence of warning and instructions on how to avoid the danger.

But Noelle knows what she has to do. She has to avoid those headlights.

She takes a split second to look out the window and sees the road they're on is on a cliff. The steel guardrail doesn't look as strong as it once did. And the shoulder is much narrower than it seemed seconds ago.

The truck is so close to them, she can see the silhouette of the driver. He's hunched over the steering wheel. His broad shoulders enormous.

There's no more time.

Noelle cuts the wheel to the right, effectively running her car off the road. She hears the sidemirror crash against the guardrail, a loud tink *that is somehow audible over all the other sounds.*

The truck driver blasts the horn as they pass, just missing hitting one another by mere centimeters.

Rachel's screams turn into shrieks, and then Noelle can hear the side of her car scraping along the guardrail, can hear the sparks shooting through the night air.

But still, Noelle manages to steal another look into the truck. She sees the driver. The driver turns to look at her, and through strands of long curly hair that are somewhat obscuring his face, she can see his mask. There're crude eye holes and an even cruder mouth hole cut into the tattered leather.

Then, Noelle feels her car start running off the road, off the side of the cliff. The guardrail has ended. The front passenger side tire is off the road, floating in mid-air, spinning, but there's nothing underneath it.

Noelle feels all of this, knows what's about to happen, but her gaze is locked on the truck driver. On the mask. On the single eye, because Diana Santos destroyed the other one, she knows this somehow. She's not sure how, but she's sure she knows it.

Never been surer of anything.

The thoughts are broken—no, completely demolished—as she feels the car sailing off the side of the cliff. She takes one last second, or maybe more—she's not really sure or able to tell given how strange time seems to be moving at the moment—and sees the truck driver still staring at her.

The truck has stopped. Somehow defying the laws of physics, it's come to a full stop and the driver is watching Noelle's car with fascination. Like it's a spectacle to behold.

And maybe it is, Noelle thinks, as the car goes airborne.

She turns to see Rachel in the passenger seat. Her face as white as snow, an expression of sheer panic plastered onto it. She thinks she can practically feel Rachel's heart, then realizes it's her own heart she's hearing.

The car hits something solid underneath it and then they're rolling down the side of the cliff.

Tumbling down. Each revolution causing a new inward dent to appear in the car, jutting into the interior like an invisible giant is punching at it. As they spin, and go upside down several times, Noelle can feel herself getting dizzy, her stomach souring.

The sound of glass breaking surrounds them. Rachel is screaming. They're hoarse screams because her sister's voice is starting to go.

Then, Noelle feels something hot against her skin. A spray of it. Like someone just opened a garden hose and stuck a finger into it.

Noelle opens her eyes, which she hadn't realized she had squeezed tight until she's opening them, and sees the blood going every which way. It's not her own; she knows this somehow.

She knows this because she's always protected in this moment in time. The harm isn't done to her. It's always done to—

"Rachel!" She screams, just as the car comes to a halt at the bottom of the cliff.

There's a shard of glass in Rachel's throat. Judging from the angle and where it came from, it's either from the broken windshield or the passenger side window.

Either way, Rachel's eyes are opened big. There is pain mixed with the panic now.

Rachel turns to her. Her head swiveling on her neck in an unusual way, like she's a mannequin made of wood and her head is turning on a screw.

"Do you remember?" She asks Noelle.

Noelle feels her heart skip a beat. Confusion and sadness coalescing into one ambiguous, nebulous emotion she can't—will never—shake off.

"Do you remember where we were going? Before this?" Rachel looks out the window.

By some impossibility, the car has turned up right now. The car had landed sideways at the end of their momentum, after tumbling down the side of the cliff. Noelle is sure of this, but it's changed. They're seated normally now.

Noelle looks past Rachel, past the broken window, and sees a cloud of smoke rolling over the car. Dark gray plumes block her view of their surroundings, but somewhere in the cloud, she can see the outlines of some trees.

Rachel's question comes back to her. Where were we going?

"You know, sister." Rachel says, smiling. Blood begins to ooze out between her curled lips. Flowing down to her chin. Dripping. Spilling onto the front of her chest.

Noelle takes a gander inside the interior of the car and sees the blood splattered everywhere. She looks down at her own chest. Her clothes, all sprinkled with blood, but none is hers.

She looks back up at Rachel, who's still staring at her.

Past her, outside the car, inside the smoke, she sees a figure approach. A long object in one of his hands. A machete.

Then, without warning, the shape of the object in the figures hands changes. It gets bigger at the top. Wider. But shorter, too. And then she sees the teeth on its edges.

"I know where we were going!" Rachel says, and grabs onto the piece of glass stuck in her throat. She pulls it out.

She doesn't even wince or flinch and the smile on her face doesn't even quaver. Though it has to be painful, Noelle knows it has to be.

From the wound where she just plucked the glass, blood shoots out like a broken fire hydrant, splashing onto the dashboard.

"I know where we were going, Noelle! I know! I know! Because—"

"Because all roads lead back to the camp." Noelle finishes the thought for her.

Outside the car a chainsaw revs.

Noelle woke up, drenched in sweat. Her room was dark, but through the gaps in the curtains, she could tell it was bright outside. Somewhere nearby, outside, she could hear one of the landscapers running a hedge trimmer.

That explained the chainsaw in her nightmares. At least, partly, anyway.

Noelle pushed the covers off herself and swung her legs out of bed. While she felt around with her feet for her slippers, she saw her cellphone was lit up on the nightstand.

In contrast with the darkened room, it looked like a runway signal. A text message had come in seconds before the hedge trimmer—the chainsaw revving in the nightmare—had wakened her.

Noelle swooped the phone off the nightstand and looked at the message. It was from Mr. Olmos:

Call me

It seemed urgent. But it would have to wait until after her morning run and meditation session. Preparation took precedence over everything.

CHAPTER 25

Varias Caras had been stalking the girls through the woods for the last half hour, keeping to the trees. They were walking around in circles, staring down at a map and a compass, unaware of his presence.

They'd been bickering back and forth out of frustration—and fear, too—about which direction they needed to walk to find their tent. Varias Caras was focused on their heartbeats, not what they were saying, though.

He could hear them thumping in their chests. The pace getting faster as their panic increased.

He watched one of the girls pull down on the bill of her baseball cap as she stared a hole through the map in her hands. And for some reason, this seemed like his signal that it was time.

Varias Caras reached to the back of the utility belt around his waist and pulled out a clawhammer.

It was killing time.

"We're on the west side of the map, so why would we go *east?*" Geena argued, snatching the map from Shelby's fingers.

"Because you're looking at the wrong side of the map." Shelby said, tapping her index finger onto a landmark labeled 'rough cliffs' on the map. "See? This is the cliff we walked past like fifteen minutes ago. If we head that way—"

The words got caught in her mouth as she saw a gargantuan man jump out of the trees. He was only a few feet away from them, holding onto a hammer. Shelby tried to scream, but nothing was coming out, so instead she just pointed.

Geena hadn't noticed him yet but saw the hand movement. Thinking Shelby was just showing her the direction she wanted to walk in, she looked away from the map to where her friend was pointing and saw the massive man who seemed to have appeared out of thin air.

Geena dropped the map. It fluttered through the air, long forgotten in a matter of seconds. Then, both girls screamed.

The massive man moved toward them, hammer ready to be swung.

Shelby and Geena started running through the woods, the direction moot now.

Shelby screamed as she felt the man's massive shoulder smash into her lower back. She went spilling forward, her momentum too fast for her to brace herself, so she crashed chin first into the ground. Her glasses went flying off her face, bouncing and shattering in the process.

Her survival instincts were telling her to push up off the ground, to get up and run, but then she felt the man's heavy boot stamp down on her back.

Once again, Shelby's screams filled the air.

Varias Caras kept her pinned down with his boot, then brought the clawhammer down onto the back of her head, full force. The flat of the hammer struck right where the base of the skull and the spine met. The bones and skull shattered and cracked, killing the girl instantly. He felt her stop squirming—and go silent—underneath him.

A quick glance told him everything. Her fingers were still twitching, but the rest of her was still. She was nothing but deadweight.

Varias Caras shifted his focus. The other one was running through the trees. He could hear leaves crunching underneath her boots and branches whipping against the sides of her coat as she sprinted through the woods.

She wasn't very far. And he knew how to cut her off. Varias Caras took off running to do just that.

As he raced through the woods, he could feel the wind blowing his hair back. Could feel the cool, crisp air seeping through the gaps of his mask and touching his flesh like chilly, delicate hands.

This was the kind of hunting he'd been missing while at the town. Chasing down prey through the elements of the wilderness, their ability to escape into such a vast hunting space gave the chase an extra thrill. Made him feel primal.

Made him feel alive.

He could hear the girl's breath getting shorter and shorter—at the same time, he could hear her heart beating faster and faster. The pace of it wasn't just from the exertion of running. No. That was just part of it.

The other part was fear. Fear as cold and as raw as the winter air.

He could almost hear the girl's thoughts as she ran, as her body began to slow. Could almost hear her wondering if this was the last day she'd be alive.

It most certainly was.

Varias Caras cut to his left. The path he'd taken was clear of any large shrubbery, meaning he'd been able to run as fast as he could without worrying about any impediments and was ahead of her.

He could see her through the trees now, struggling against the terrain changes of the path she was running on.

Varias Caras jumped out from behind the trees. The girl saw him and screamed. At the same time, she attempted to stop herself, but she had too much momentum. She all but ran right into him.

Varias Caras unsheathed the machete from his back. He saw the girl's feet shuffle as she tried to book it in the opposite direction.

But Varias Caras was too fast for her.

He grabbed the front of her coat, lifted her off her feet, and swung her into a nearby tree. The girl crashed into the trunk, back first, and let out a pained wheeze as she fell to the ground on her ass.

Varias Caras grabbed the machete with both hands and then brought it down onto her head, point first. The girl's eyes went wide as the blade pierced and broke through the top of her skull. Then they rolled to the back of her head as the machete punctured through her brain. The sudden damage sent the girl's central-nervous system into shock, causing her whole body to convulse.

Varias Caras let go of the machete and took a few steps back, watching the girl's body twitch uncontrollably. The blade had stopped about halfway through her head, and blood was pouring out of every one of her orifices, hot and sticky. It flowed out from the wound at the top of her head, too, and ran down her face like a crimson waterfall.

After a few seconds, the girl's body stopped convulsing. He watched the blood continue to seep out from her head for a few more breaths, but the show was over.

Varias Caras grabbed the handle of the machete and began dragging the girl's corpse behind him.

It was supposed to have been Geena and Shelby's get away from their daily life in rural Florida. But it ended up being their last day alive.

CHAPTER 26

From a bird's eye view, the campgrounds were a bald spot in the woods. The log cabins that had once made up what was known as Camp Lakewood—Camp Slaughter to others—were all nearly burned down to the ground by the fire Varias Caras had set to the place.

A few cabins managed to retain a bit of their architectural structure, but even these were scorched black and had walls that looked like they'd crumble and wash away during the next rainstorm.

All the grass, shrubbery, and trees on the campgrounds had been burned away, reduced to ashes and scattered throughout the woods by the wind. The only thing left on the ground was dirt and roots poking out from it like they were hands reaching for new life.

Maybe come next spring, their efforts would pay off and a new generation of foliage would crop up in these spots. But as of now, the temperatures of fall and early winter had caused them to decay and shrivel up.

Varias Caras came out of the trees, carrying the first girl on his shoulder. The second girl he pulled behind him by the handle of the machete.

He'd left a small trail of blood behind by dragging the corpse like this, but that was OK. There were hardly any campers around here this time of the year, so there was no danger that anyone would be around anytime soon.

Really, he'd been lucky that these girls had been out there at all. Lucky, but not because he didn't have food. No, that wasn't it at all. The four others he'd killed would be enough if he rationed their meat right. Lucky because hunting animals wasn't anywhere near as thrilling as hunting down humans.

Varias Caras stopped at his encampment, the spot where the camp's eatery hall had once stood. Now, however, it was more accurate to describe it as the epicenter of the fire's damage. He'd set up the tent he got from the old woman and made a firepit outside of it. His Bronco was parked off to the left, and behind the truck was the barrel with the salted fish in it.

He dropped the first girl's body onto the ground, then shifted his attention to the one with machete in her head. He pressed his boot to her throat, then pulled on the machete handle. It slid out with a wet, clinking sound as it passed through the girl's skull and freed itself from the muck of gore and blood that had coagulated around it.

Varias Caras took the machete inside the tent.

Pushed up against one of the tent's walls was a small wooden table he'd taken from the old woman. He walked over to it and crouched down to grab a gallon-sized plastic jug filled with water (another object that had belonged to the old woman) from underneath it. With one hand, he unscrewed the cap off the container, then rinsed the machete clean. Once done with this, he put the cap back on and tucked the jug back in its place, then stood up.

Varias Caras crossed the tent to the opposite wall. Here, his masks hung on rows of rusty nails he'd pierced into the canvas.

He took the mask off his face—a thick leather one with several stitches on it—and put it on one of the nails.

Varias Caras waited a few seconds, anticipating the second personality to begin trying to take over the body now that the mask was off. In the past, this was how it went. When the masks were off, the weak personality would be active. That personality would interact with people at work, at stores, and do all the mundane things needed to live among the civil world.

When the masks were put on, though, that was when Varias Caras would surface. When Ignacio would let him do what he wanted—but was actually what they both wanted, really.

Now, though, it didn't seem to make a difference. Varias Caras couldn't feel or hear Ignacio.

He's all but dead. Varias Caras thought, finding it strange that now there was only one singular voice in his head. *I've completely taken over this body.*

He felt better than ever. The monster was in the driver's seat with full control. And there was more to it than that, though. These woods seemed to have a power of their own, a power that enhanced Varias Caras's super abilities. He felt like he was moving faster, processing things faster, his hearing was sharper. It was like his brain and body were in perfect alignment with one another.

And it wasn't just because he'd recovered from his injuries, either. No. He hadn't felt this way while he'd been in the town at all, even when his health was back to normal. There was a reason he'd stayed in these woods, on this spot where the campgrounds had once been, for so long.

A reason he'd come back, too, for that matter.

Varias Caras entered one of the cabins that had been formidable enough to not burn down to the ground. Like the others, though, it wasn't exactly a building anymore. For starters, its ceiling had no ceiling anymore. Second, there were only two walls high enough to even be considered walls. The other two had been reduced to about four feet of height, more like wooden dividends than anything.

All four walls were damaged beyond repair, jagged at the top where the flames had been burning through them the harshest. The glass in the windows that remained had burst from the heat, and glass was scattered inside and outside the husk of the cabin. A few shards clung to the frames on the taller walls like shark's teeth.

The two tall walls touched one another, forming a dark corner. It was here that Varias Caras walked over to.

He stopped in front of the three severed heads stabbed onto wooden stakes. Mamá's head was in the middle. Judy's head was to her right.

The third head, on Mamá's left, belonged to the old woman. Ignacio had returned to where he'd killed her and severed her head off with the machete, then fixed it onto a wooden stake the same way he'd done to Judy and Mamá's head. It was the least he could do after she'd nursed him back to health.

Varias Caras took a matchbox from his back pocket, then knelt and started lighting the candles at the foot of the severed heads. The light revealed the flowers, candles, and the rosary he'd put here as a tribute to the three women.

Once all six candles were lit, he swiped the rosary off the floor, and then stood up. He put the matchbox back in his back pocket. Holding the rosary between his palms, and letting it dangle, he began to recite *Padre Nuestro*.

At the end of the prayer, he opened his eyes, expecting to feel Ignacio surfacing. But no such thing happened.

"Are you there?" he asked the empty cabin. "Come out, come out, wherever you are…"

But nothing. The other voice was gone.

"You better not come back to try to take my body away!" He screamed, then balled one of his fists and punched himself on the side of his head. "Don't come back! You hear me?"

He let the rosary drop from his hands, the beads clattering against the dirty wooden floor. Then he pressed his palms on his temples and squeezed tight, as if he were trying to make his brain shoot out from the top of his head.

"Don't come back! Don't come back!" He growled, thrashing about.

He did this until he felt the front of his boot knock over one of the candles. He opened his eyes and realized the day had gotten dark all of a sudden.

A series of thick, dark gray clouds had rolled over the woods while he'd been yelling at the air.

Varias Caras looked up to the sky. A few raindrops fell from the cloud, two of them hitting his exposed skin near the eyeholes of his mask. He blinked against their icy touch.

A few seconds later, the clouds unleashed a torrential downpour. Varias Caras was soaked in a matter of seconds. The flames on the candles were extinguished. Thunder cracked in the sky, and less than a mile away, a streak of lightning tore through the darkness. Varias Caras felt the ground rumble underneath his feet as everything in the vicinity flashed blue.

"You finally get it, mijo." Someone inside the shrine said.

Varias Caras took his attention away from the sky and looked where the voice was coming from. Papá's ghost was standing behind the severed heads. He was in that same ghastly, white form he'd been in back at the junkyard. And although he was wearing sunglasses, Varias Caras could tell he had his attention on Mamá's head.

"I knew one day you'd understand what I meant when I said that deep down there's a monster inside all of us." Papá said, taking his sunglasses off and staring right at Varias Caras. "Today is that day, Ignacio."

Varias Caras put a hand to his forehead, feeling a splitting headache coming on. He shook his head, as if that could've gotten rid of it, then through gritted teeth said, "Ignacio... is not here. Ignacio is dead."

Papá let out a small laugh. "No, mijo. You're just reborn."

CHAPTER 27

Noelle finished her meditation session, took a shower, and put her hair up in a towel to dry it. The meditation was supposed to take her mind off Camp Slaughter and the cannibal, but it was failing to do so. A team was forming, a plan was coming together, and something in her gut told her they would find the cannibal in the woods. Which meant the end was near…

Noelle grabbed her phone from the coffee table and settled back into her couch, then called Mr. Olmos. He picked up on the second ring.

"Hello?" his voice had a slight croak to it, like maybe the phone call had woken him up from a nap.

"Hi. Sorry I didn't get back to you sooner. Had a lot going on this morning."

"Um, yeah, that's okay." He said over the sound of bedsheets rustling. "I was just calling to finish up the conversation from last night."

"Yeah. I meant to call you, but I went to sleep early after my guest left."

"That's OK. I was busy making chicken alfredo with Sharon—my wife—last night, anyway."

"We have someone else joining us on the hunt." Noelle said.

"Oh? The more the merrier." A pause, then he said, "Or maybe 'strength in numbers' is more appropriate in this case."

"He's the one who fought the cannibal with me. The one whose little brother was killed."

"Great. So, he knows what we're up against."

"Right." Noelle said. "I have two more names on the list of people who will potentially join us, but I think the three of us should be enough."

"We're leaving Diana Santos out of this." Mr. Olmos said, his voice stern. "She's been through enough."

Noelle cut her eyes across the living room to her research desk, where the paper with the names, which did indeed include Diana Santos's, was sitting the middle of. "If I didn't know any better, I'd think you've seen my list."

Mr. Olmos laughed. It was a good laugh, like the kind a grandparent gives to their grandchild when they surprise them with a joke they hadn't heard before. "No, Noelle, I'm just starting to see what kind of a team is being put together."

A team thirsting for revenge. Noelle thought the words, but neither of them spoke them.

"I see." Noelle said. "Very astute, as I would assume a lifelong sheriff would be."

"What's the plan, then? When are we doing this?"

"Me and Gav are going up to meet Harold Buckley—the contact the YouTubers were using to gather information on Camp Slaughter."

"Yeah, I remember the name."

"I'm going to see what sort of information I can get from him. See what he knows about the cannibal and the campgrounds."

"Any reason for this?"

"Not really. I just don't want to leave any stone unturned. The more prepared and informed we are heading into the woods, the more likely our survival."

"I didn't think our survival was in question."

Noelle couldn't help but smile at this. "I like how you think, Mr. Olmos."

"Let me know what you find out."

"Would you like to come with us?"

"No, thanks. I'm going to try to find some normalcy in my retirement before our hunting expedition."

"That's fair." Noelle said, wondering if it would at all be possible all things considered. "After meeting with Harold Buckley, my next move was to book Lakewood Cabin. Once I get that done, I'll touch base with you, Mr. Olmos."

"Sounds like a plan." He said. "Can't exactly say I'm looking forward to any of this, but I'm ready to get things moving."

"Me too." Noelle said. "I'll talk to you soon."

"Yeah. Good luck with your meeting."

They hung up. Noelle looked at the time on her phone. She'd killed most of the day running, meditating, and preparing meals for the next few days. Gavin would be coming to meet her here in about two hours, which meant she had to hurry if she was going to make it to the gun range.

Noelle put her phone down and hurried into her room to get her pistol and all her equipment.

Hours later, she and Gavin were pulling up to the Green Lizard Tavern. Unknowingly, they parked in the same spot that Emeril and Molly had parked when coming to meet the same man they were here to find.

Gavin cut the lights off his Honda and stared at the bar. It was a typical one-story Podunk establishment with a brick façade and a rinky-dink wooden patio sitting in a lot in the middle of nowhere. There was a neon lizard in one of the doors, some sort of gecko or skink, perhaps. Next to the light the name of the place was printed in Old English letters that were beginning to peel and fade away.

"I'm almost afraid to cut my headlights off." Gavin said, taking a gander around the lot. "Feels like our cannibal might be lurking in the shadows around here. Jeez."

There were only three other cars besides his Honda. At least one had to belong to someone working the bar, which meant there wouldn't be very many patrons. That would be to their advantage in terms of privacy, of course, but the dark and isolated surroundings were giving him the creeps.

"This is nothing compared to where we'll be going." Noelle said, flashing him a grin.

"Yeah, yeah," Gavin said, shutting the headlights off. Despite his concerns, the two lampposts outside the bar provided decent lighting to the lot. "I'm embellishing."

"Come on," Noelle said, unbuckling her seatbelt and unlocking the door. "I'd like to get back home at a decent time."

Without another word, the two of them got out of the car and headed into the tavern.

CHAPTER 28

There were only three patrons inside the Green Lizard Tavern. A man with a giant red beard was seated at the bar staring through a big mug of beer in front of him. Judging by his posture, and the color of his eyes, this wasn't his first drink. Behind him, at one of the bar tops, was a woman with long black hair and pockmarked skin she was trying to hide behind copious amounts of makeup. She kept looking around the place with skittish eyes.

Noelle couldn't tell if she was waiting for a date or worried if someone was following her. Either way, it didn't matter much. The person sitting two tables behind her, underneath a wall lined with old rock n rock albums, was who she was here for.

There was no mistaking the guy with the shaggy hair, glasses, finger-less gloves, and oversized plaid jacket was Harold Buckley. He was sticking a piece of monkey bread into his mouth when he noticed them approaching him.

"You're Harold Buckley, right?" Noelle asked.

"I am," Harold said, chewing through the monkey bread he'd just plopped into his mouth. "Uh, may I ask who's asking?"

"I'm the person you've been emailing back and forth." Noelle said, watching his eyebrows knit together in confusion.

"Wait, huh? Where's Emeril?" He looked over at Gavin, confused. "Are you guys like… his assistants or something?"

"No," Noelle sat down on the stool on the other side of the table. Gavin followed suit and settled into the one next to hers. "Emeril Dantes is dead."

"What the heck…" Harold shook his head and ran his fingers through his hair. The leather gloves on his hands rasped against his scalp. "What? How? How did you get access to Emeril's email address? What do you mean he's dead?"

"The first part is a long story for another time." Noelle said, bluntly. "To answer your second question, he was killed at Camp Slaughter while trying to make his movie."

"Oh, holy crap!" Harold cupped a hand over his mouth, then quickly took it away. "No way! How do you know this?"

"We met him and Molly in the woods when they were filming for their documentary." Gavin cut in.

"Holy moly…" Harold said, picking up a piece of monkey bread and rolling it between his hands in a nervous tic. Something told them this man had a lot of those. "And Emeril was killed? How?"

"Both him and Molly were killed, actually." Noelle said. "There's a cannibal out in those woods that attacked all of us."

"Wait… cannibal? He's real?"

"Unfortunately." Gavin said.

"So, we were right… the cannibal people were right." Harold nodded, then shook his head. "And pardon my bluntness, but who exactly are you guys? I'm still a little lost on that."

"We're just people that were at the wrong place at the wrong time." Noelle said. "We had a run-in with the cannibal."

"And barely survived." Gavin added.

"So, what exactly do you guys want from me? Are you guys like… inspired to make a movie about these events? Writing a book or something?"

"Not quite." Noelle said. "But you were Emeril's go-to guy for info on Camp Slaughter."

Harold nodded.

"We want to know everything you know about that place." Gavin said.

"Sorry if I'm being intrusive, but for what if it's not to write an editorial piece on the place?"

Noelle leaned over the table. "We're going back into the woods to find him and kill the cannibal."

Harold's eyes got big behind his thick glasses, and he scanned Noelle's face for any trace that she was just pulling his leg. He found no such thing but was too flabbergasted to speak.

"So, we'd appreciate it, Harold, if you told us everything you know about Camp Slaughter." Noelle continued.

Harold shook his head. "Looks, all I really know is what I emailed Emeril. My interests in Camp Slaughter waned after they interviewed me…but…"

"But what?" Gavin said, his voice coming out baritone.

"If you read through my emails with Emeril, then you know he found me through these weirdo forums. Anyway, there are people on there that obsess over one topic—one of my buddies on there is all about Camp Slaughter."

Noelle and Gav exchanged a look, then Noelle took her cellphone out of her jacket. She set it in the middle of the table.

"Give me his contact info."

Harold regarded the phone for a second, as if waiting for it to transform into a serpent and bite him or something, then picked it up. He tapped in his buddy's contact info and his own, then handed the phone back to Noelle.

"He might ask for money in exchange." Harold said in a small voice. "We spend a lot of time researching this stuff with no real payoff unless people like you or Emeril come along."

"That's okay." Noelle said, glancing at the info Harold had punched into her phone. The area code was a local one. That was a good thing. "Okay, so now let me give you my phone number."

Harold looked at her like a deer-in-headlights. It was obvious he was hardly ever given people's number, much less from women. Or maybe never. It took him a second to realize what he had to do, but then he picked his phone up and handed it to Noelle.

"There," Noelle said, finishing putting in her phone number and giving him his phone back.

"Sorry I don't have much more info on Camp Slaughter." Harold shrugged, putting his phone in the pocket of his jacket. "Been researching other stuff, though. So, hey, if you ever have a run-in with any mole people and need info on them, I'm your guy."

"We'll keep that in mind." Noelle said, standing up.

"Wait, mole people?" Gavin said, shaking his head, as if he must've misheard. "Like that episode of *Courage the Cowardly Dog*?"

Harold smiled. "Yeah…"

"Thanks for your time." Noelle interjected before the conversation could get even more ridiculous. She stuck her handout toward Harold for a handshake.

He shook it, then said, "Hey, one more thing."

"Yeah?" Noelle said.

"Can you let me talk to my friend first?"

"Why?" Gavin asked.

"People on those forums are kind of, uh, reserved. They like their privacy. He might be a bit peeved that I gave you his info. If I soften him up for you, he might be more open to giving you info."

Noelle and Gavin exchanged a look, then shrugged.

"Sure. But talk to him ASAP and let me know as soon as you do. If you don't get back to me by tonight, I'll call him first thing in the morning."

"Aye, aye, captain." Harold said, saluting her.

Noelle nodded to him, then she and Gav headed out of the tavern. As they were pushing through the front door, Gavin leaned in close to her and said, "Man, that was one weird dude."

CHAPTER 29

He'd only partly told Noelle the truth about why he wanted to talk to his friend first. True, some of it was that Eli would probably be annoyed that Harold gave a stranger his contact info, but mostly he wanted to brag to his friend that someone came to him for info first.

Harold loved being seen as the source of information. His fondest childhood memories were when the teachers would ask him for the answer in grade school without him having to raise his hand. Those were treasured moments that rivaled playing freeze tag with the neighborhood kids and getting a Nintendo 64 for Christmas in 1996.

Harold hurried back into his apartment. As soon as he was inside, he opened his cellphone and dialed his friend. Eli picked up on the third ring.

"Yo, yo, what's the word?" Eli said.

In the background, Harold could hear plastic crinkling.

"Hey, so I just came back from an interesting meeting at the Green Lizard Tavern." Harold said, hanging his keys on the hook by the front door.

The jangling of his keys woke his Frenchie, Rosie, who was soundly sleeping in his bedroom. She came out into the living room, letting out small snorts to greet her human. Harold bent down to pet her, then led her into the kitchen for feeding time.

"Meeting? What are you talking about?"

"I'd been emailing with Emeril Dantes these last few days. You know, the YouTuber—"

"Yeah, I know who you're talking about. When's his documentary coming out? Dude's been ghost for months now."

"Funny you say that." Harold said, stepping into the kitchen. He flicked the light on, then went over to the pantry. He crouched down and grabbed a can of doggie food from the bottom shelf and a can opener lying next to it.

"Why?"

"Are you sitting down, Eli?" Harold said, standing up with the dog food and can opener in his hand.

"No. I'm actually kneeling, wrapping up my equipment for my set tonight."

"Oh. Well, brace yourself for what I'm about to tell you."

"Okay?"

"The old man and Molly got killed out in the woods filming for their documentary."

"Holy shit, dude!" The sound of plastic being wrapped stopped. "Wait, so was this meeting with detectives or something?"

"Juicier than that."

"What? How?"

"These people found Camp Slaughter at the same time that Emeril and Molly did."

"No fucking way."

"And guess what? They had an encounter with the cannibal."

"The… cannibal? You mean he's real?"

"Righto. He's the one who killed Emeril and Molly according to them."

There was a long pause on the other line. Harold took this opportunity to take the can of dog food and opener over to the kitchen counter, pressing the phone up to his ear to free up his hands. Rosie followed him across the kitchen, her tongue out and flicking around to lap up the drool dribbling out the side of her jowls.

"This is fucking insane, Harold."

"I told you you needed to be sitting for this." Harold said, working the can opener. "They're going back, too. They're apparently on some revenge mission to go back and kill the cannibal."

"What the fuck?" Eli more gasped it than said it.

"It's a whole thing." Harold said. "Neither here nor there."

"Yeah. Anyway, you know what this means, right?"

"No? What?"

"We have to go with them." Eli said. "We have to go see Camp Slaughter."

"Did you hear what I said, Eli? The cannibal *killed* the YouTubers."

"Yeah, yeah." Eli sighed. "But man, what an opportunity."

"Well, there's something else." Harold said. He stopped working the can opener, much to Rosie's chagrin. The lid on the dog food was half-opened, and he got a whiff of the processed meat and dainty vegetables. "I told them you have more info on Camp Slaughter."

"Why the hell did you do that?"

"I don't know. I guess because I wanted to seem important." Harold shrugged. "Also, I thought you told me you've been investigating it. I figured you'd have found *something* by now."

"Yeah, I have been. And you're right." Eli said.

"I am?" Harold said.

"Yeah. This is actually perfect." Eli told him. "The universe really works in mysterious ways."

"What on earth are you talking about?"

"I got maps from someone who's also been researching Camp Slaughter. They say they're different routes to get to the woods. Hidden paths if you will."

"Hm… how do you know it's not just bogus?"

"You sent Emeril some maps, right?"

"Yeah…"

"And he found the campgrounds, which means one of those maps led him to it, right?"

"Okay… I see where you're going with this."

"You sent them to me before, right?" Harold heard Eli breathing heavy as powerwalked through his house. "Hang tight. I'm gonna compare them right now while I have you on the line…"

Harold finished up opening the dog food and scooped it into Rosie's bowl. The Frenchie chowed down about half of her meal by the time Eli spoke into the receiver again.

"Yo, you still there?"

"I'm here." Harold said, leaning against the kitchen counter, watching his Frenchie let out little snorts as she finished her meal.

"These maps are legit." Eli said. "If they're indeed looking to hunt down the cannibal, this could help them.

"Uh-huh, yeah." Harold said, thinking of his strategies in tabletop games.

"I think I can bargain with them into letting us tag along on their return to the campgrounds."

"What do you mean *us*, Eli?" Harold said, shaking his head. "I'm definitely not going. For starters, it's way too scary. And secondly, it's way too cold and wet up north. I don't want to get pneumonia."

"Okay, well, whatever." Eli said. "I think they'll let me tag along if I use these maps as a bargaining chip."

"Man, it's kind of a crazy idea… you heard the part where they were attacked by the cannibal, right?"

"Of course it's an insane idea, but the magic happens outside of your comfort zone." Eli said, pausing to let that nugget of wisdom soak in. "Consider this, too. If these people are going there specifically to fight the cannibal, then it's like we have built-in protection from him. It'd be like going with bodyguards."

"I see your point." Harold said. "But I'm still not going, so you can drop the 'we' stuff."

"Yeah, yeah." Eli said. "Hey, do they happen to be from around here?"

"No, I don't think." Harold told him.

"I'm guessing they're heading back to wherever they're from after meeting with you?"

"Yuh, probably. Why?"

"I'm DJing tonight. Tell them I'd love to talk to them about this in person—and that drinks will be on me if they swing by for a chat."

"I'll see what I can do." Harold said, feeling good that his friend needed him as a liaison. This was almost as good as being the primary informant.

"Sweet, man. I'll send you the address."

"Sounds good. I'll talk to you in a bit. Probably, maybe."

"Alright." Eli said. "See ya."

CHAPTER 30

Noelle felt the phone vibrating in her jacket before the sound of the ring even hit their ears. She pulled it out without any hesitation.

"It's Harold." Noelle said out loud.

"Already?" Gavin said, glancing over at her phone screen from the driver's seat. "Must be our lucky day."

Noelle picked up. "Hello?"

"Hey," Harold said, sounding like he was out of breath. "I talked to my friend. Are you guys far from town?"

Noelle glanced at Gavin's phone, which was sitting in a holder in the middle of the dashboard. Judging from the progress on map on the GPS, they hadn't gone very far from the Green Lizard Tavern. Maybe ten miles or so at this point.

"What's up?" Gavin mouthed.

Noelle held up a finger. "We're not very far out, why?"

"My friend says he wants to meet with you guys. He's DJing at a local place tonight."

"I'm sorry, did you say DJing? Like playing music?" The fact that Harold had a friend who did something in that vein surprised her so much she couldn't help but ask.

"Yeah." Harold said. "I can send you the address. He told me he has something good for you guys. Said it'll help you guys defeat the cannibal."

Noelle looked over at Gavin, who kept alternating between keeping his eyes on the road and glancing over at her. She pointed her thumb to the grass on the side of the road.

"Pull over?"

Noelle nodded. Then to Harold said, "What does he have for us? Like a weapon?"

"Eh, I'm not sure if I'm supposed to say. Don't wanna step on his toes, you know?"

"Okay, well, what does he want in exchange for whatever this is? Money?" Noelle asked, her patience thinning.

"I think it's best if you meet him and discuss that." Harold let out a deep breath. "I'm just the messenger, Noelle."

"Fine. Send me the address." she said. "And thanks."

"Yeah, no problem." Harold said, his voice suddenly going somber. "I'll send it right over. I don't think the place he's DJing at is very far from the Green Lizard Tavern."

"Alright. What time does his thing start?"

"9:00 p.m."

Noelle looked at the time on Gavin's phone. It was only 8:15 p.m., which meant they had some time to kill. "Okay, we'll be there."

"Alright. Sweet." Harold said.

"We'll be in touch." Noelle ended the call.

"Okay, so what's going on?" Gavin said as soon as he saw Noelle take the phone away from her ear.

"Looks like we've got more business around here." Noelle responded, staring at her phone screen, waiting for Harold's message with the address to come through.

"That doesn't really explain anything." Gavin said, gazing out at the darkness beyond their headlights.

Somewhere in the trees, they heard twigs snapping underneath the weight of an animal—or maybe a person—walking. Because of the vastness of the woods on either side of them, it was hard to tell if the activity was close by or far away. Either way, it wasn't a sound they wanted to hear at this point in time.

"Harold's connection said he wants us to meet him tonight." Noelle turned in her seat toward Gavin, her phone an afterthought at the moment. "Tell me you have time for this?"

"Yeah," Gavin said, glancing at the hour on the dashboard. "I turned this into the most important thing in my life. Much to the chagrin of my girlfriend."

"Wait, you have a girlfriend?" Noelle said, then waved her hand through the air. There were more pressing matters to get to. "Never mind that."

Gavin laughed. "To answer your question, I do. Finish filling me in on what's going on with Harry or Dorko, or whatever his name is."

"Right," Noelle said, refocusing. "His friend is DJing a party or something. Wants to talk to us tonight. What Harold told me is that it'll help us in hunting down the cannibal."

"And he didn't say what it was?"

"Nope."

"I'm guessing this'll come with some sort of price tag attached to it."

"I'm guessing you're right."

CHAPTER 31

They both decided they weren't going to drive home tonight. They had no idea how long the meeting with Harold's friend was going to last, and it was about a four-hour drive back home, so they decided to book a hotel (two rooms, mind you) before driving to the place where they were going to meet "DJ Magic Mic."

They pulled up in front of a warehouse that looked like it'd been abandoned for at least a decade. The only reason they knew they were at the right location was because they could see flashing lights through the windows and that the lot in front of it had several cars in it. Mostly they were shitty, old beaters that looked like something a college-aged kid would be driving.

"You know that name doesn't even really make sense for a DJ." Gavin said as they watched a group of twenty-something year olds shuffle toward the warehouse. "A microphone isn't exactly what a DJ is known for. I feel like Magic Turntable would make more sense."

"Uh-huh." Noelle said, closing out the image of the flyer Harold sent her of the event on her phone. She'd opened it just to make sure the GPS address and the one on the JPEG matched up.

They got out of the vehicle just as the group of people walked past Noelle's Jeep. There were three girls with multi-colored hair, and they couldn't tell if it was permanent or if it was a dye-job for the night, but either way it was bright enough to attract attention even in the lowlighting of the darkened parking lot. They wore black skirts and fishnet stockings that showed off legs covered in tattoos underneath. There were multiple piercings on their faces and each of the girls had a lipstick color that was very much untraditional.

The guys they were with looked like a mixture of Calvin Klein models mixed with Edward Scissorhands. One guy had half his head shaved while the other half of his head was covered with jet-black hair that reached down to his shoulders. The smallest guy in the group was wearing shiny platformers and hair with massive volume, perhaps strategically chosen to appear taller, or perhaps just a stylistic choice. It was anyone's guess, really. The third guy, much like the women in the group, had colorful dyed hair. His hair was down around midback and a bright green—like the color of the surrounding wilderness in the spring and summertime.

The group's color of choice was black, and as such, they were all wearing mostly leather (or faux leather). Offsetting this, however, were the glow-in-the-dark accessories: bracelets, necklaces, and in the case of one of the women—a glow-in-the-dark choker.

"If I'd known it was this kind of party, I would've brought my light-up binky." Gavin said, watching the bunch go up the walkway toward the warehouse.

"Come on." Noelle said, leading the way as they followed behind the group of ravers.

The guy with the green hair opened the door for the rest of them, then saw Noelle and Gavin trudging up the walkway. He regarded them for a second, eyeing them up and down, the look on his face saying *you two look like you don't belong here.*

For a slight second, Noelle thought he was going to turn around and shut the door in their face now that his friends were inside, but he did no such thing. In fact, he did the opposite and smiled at them.

"Hey, you guys want some?" he said, reaching into one of the many pockets in his leather jacket. He held his hand out, palm flat and underneath the light coming from a fixture near the entrance, showing them a handful of bright blue pills.

"Depends on what it is." Gavin said, with a smirk on his face.

Noelle slapped him on the shoulder with a little too much force to be called playful. "What he means is, 'no thanks.'"

The raver smiled, shrugged, then put the pills back in the not-so-secret stash in his jacket. "Hey, no biggie. But if you change your mind, you know to look for the guy with the green hair. I'll give you guys a good deal on them.

"We'll keep that in mind." Noelle said.

The kid's smile broadened, then he waved them through. Noelle and Gavin walked past him, stepping into what felt like a scenic mixture of an EDM party and a goth party. Everyone who was here, which was only about sixteen people, was dressed in similar fashion as the group they'd came in behind. Black clothing, bright accessories, hair that was either jet-black or dyed a loud shade of a primary color. Some of the people had ninja masks covering their faces, some had chains dangling from several parts of their clothing, but almost everyone in the room had metal spikes jutting out from somewhere on their outfit.

Everyone in here, including the group they'd just seen come in, was dancing underneath dance lights hanging from the steel beams on the ceiling. The music that was playing through the loudspeakers was some sort of electronic music with slight hippie influences, something that might've been described as an "acid trip."

Something told Noelle that the type of music wouldn't be changing much throughout the night.

The kid who'd offered them the ecstasy slid past them and joined the dancefloor, throwing his arms up in the air and wiggling around so his green hair was flying all over the place. Noelle looked past the sea of dancing goths and saw the DJ at the back of the warehouse. His hair was up in spikes instead of a mohawk like in the event photo, and he was wearing 3D glasses on his face, but that was Magic Mic, alright. He was even wearing the same Space Jam jersey he had in the flyer Harold had sent Noelle.

He hadn't noticed them because he was busy staring down at his MacBook and moving sliders on a mixer up and down.

"There's our guy." Noelle said, leaning in close to Gavin.

"Yeah, I see him." Gavin said. "He's pretending to be doing something besides hitting play on a screen."

Noelle let out a courtesy laugh because, really, she was on a mission. Her sense of humor was dialed down to zero. She tugged on Gavin's sleeve, then led him through the dancefloor. They weaved through the goth kids, trying not to bump into them too hard so as to not disrupt their vibe. It was impossible not to come into contact with spike-studded shoulders and limbs shining with glowsticks as they traversed through the dancefloor, though.

They came out the other side and were at the stage where DJ Magic Mic was set up. The stage was nothing more than a few pallets bound together by packing tape and two pieces of wood laid on top to make the stage "floor."

DJ Magic Mic hadn't yet noticed them; he was still focused on his laptop and mixer. Noelle took the initiative here and stepped up on the stage, tapping him on the shoulder.

"Whoa!" he said, taking the cans off his ears and letting them rest around his neck. "Excuse me, can I—"

"Noelle Remington. I was sent here by your friend Harold Buckley."

"Oh, shoot! Right!" DJ Magic Mic used an index finger to flick the 3D glasses up onto the front of his head.

"Harold said you wanted to meet us."

"Yeah, yeah! Wow. Can't believe you guys actually showed up."

"Well, we're here." Gavin said, hearing his comment as he stepped up onto the DJ stage at Noelle's side. "So, let's get to talking."

DJ Magic Mic jutted a thumb toward a metal door a few paces behind the DJing booth with an emergency sign hanging over top of it. "Let's head out there so we don't have to yell over the music."

"What about DJing" Noelle asked, glancing toward the dance floor, which now had more people on it. It seemed like another five or six people had come in shortly after them.

Magic Mic shook his head. "Naw, it's all good. I just gotta click a few buttons and the music will play itself."

"See, I told you!" Gavin said, smirking at Noelle.

Magic Mic didn't hear because his attention was on the DJing software on his laptop. He clicked his mouse around a few times, moved some sliders on the mixing board, then grabbed a folded tie-dye hoodie that was sitting on the table.

"Alright. Music's on autopilot." He said, zipping up the hoodie.

Without any words, Noelle stepped off the stage and led them out of the warehouse.

The warehouse must've been a regular spot to party because there was a wooden picnic table set up out back that had a collection of beer can and an ashtray filled with cigarette butts. The back of the warehouse was dimly lit by a light fixture that flickered every few seconds. Out here, the music could barely be heard through the warehouse walls; it was nothing more than a gradual hum, and made it feel like they'd gone into another world.

The three of them sat down at the picnic table. The faint scent of old Marlboros hit their nostrils as they settled into their seats. Noelle opted to sit facing the warehouse. Gavin sat next to her, and Magic Mic across from them.

"Okay, so first off, my real name is Eli." Eli said, extending his arm over the table to shake their hands. "Nice to formally meet you guys."

"Yeah." Gavin said, shaking his hand after Noelle.

"Let's get to it." Noelle said. "Harold said you have something for us? Something that can help us with hunting down the cannibal?"

"Yup," Eli said, pulling his cellphone out. He flicked the screen with his index finger, then turned it toward them. "Look."

He scrolled through a collection of PDFs with maps that showed different routes. But the one thing that Noelle and Gavin both noticed was that at the center of these maps were the campgrounds.

"What exactly are we looking at?" Noelle asked.

"It's different routes leading to Camp Slaughter." Eli said, grinning.

"How do we know this isn't total bullshit." It was Gavin asking this.

"Well," Eli said, "Let me ask you this, you guys found Camp Slaughter, right?"

Noelle and Gavin nodded, wanting him to get to his point.

"Okay, and how did you guys find it?"

"From some old map that we found in Lakewood Cabin." Gavin said. "What're you getting at?"

"Where is that map? Do you guys still have it?"

"No, we were trying to scram out of there with our lives—" Gavin stopped, realizing what he was saying.

"To get back there, you're going to have to rely on one of the maps Harold emailed Emeril Dantes, right?"

"Yeah, but we already have access to those maps." Noelle said. "And going off memory, only one of the routes on the map matched up with the route on the map we found in the cabin."

"Precisely," Eli said, sitting back with a smug look on his face. "And I've compared my maps with the ones Harold emailed Emeril. Of my four maps, only one matches the one the old man got."

"How can we be sure that's it's the one that led the YouTubers to the campgrounds?" Gavin asked, narrowing his eyes.

"You can't be," Eli said, "until I send these other maps to you, and you compare them for yourself."

"You're asking us to gamble then because these maps could very well be nothing." Noelle said. "What's your price?"

"I think my price is pretty cheap, actually."

"We'll give you twenty-bucks." Gavin said. "I've got a crispy bill in my wallet right now."

Eli's eyes grew big and then he chuckled. "I don't want money, homie. I want something that's worth more to me than money."

"Alright?" Gavin said. He and Noelle exchanged a look, and both shrugged in unison.

"What is it? Don't keep us in suspense."

"I want you to let me and a friend tag along on your return to the campgrounds." Eli said, his eyes growing big.

"That's it?" Noelle asked, waiting for the other shoe to drop.

"That's it. Yeah." Eli said. "But you have to agree to let us join you even if the maps turn out to be bullshit."

"Fine." Noelle said.

Eli's eyes grew even bigger somehow, like he hadn't been sure the plan was going to work.

"Really?" he asked, his voice a pitch higher than previously.

"Yeah," Noelle said. "Just as long as you realize we're going there on a mission to find danger."

"Oh, trust me. I know, Harold told me all about it." Eli nodded. "That's why I want to go with you. It's like going with my own personal army, you know?"

"Uh, yeah, sure." Noelle said, not liking how that made it seem like they were nothing more than expendable grunts to him. "If you have access to these maps, why didn't you ever go try to find the camp yourself, though? I mean, you're not that far from Lakewood Cabin and you seem really eager to see the place."

"Because of the aforementioned danger." Eli said. "Me and all my friends are too chicken to go, but going with people who're taking weapons and ready to kick ass feels different. Like it's not as dangerous that way, you know?"

"Not really." Gavin said, then shrugged. "But whatever floats your boat."

"So, what's the verdict? Can we go with you guys?" Eli said, his eyes turning shiny. Shiny and pleading. "I promise we'll stay out of your way. It'll be like we're not even there."

"Yes, you can come." Noelle said.

"Oh," Eli said, glancing between the two of them. "You guys don't need to discuss it or anything?"

"She's the boss," Gavin said.

Noelle nodded.

"Okay, so my friend can come too, right?" Eli asked, his voice excited.

"Yes." Noelle said, waiting for the guy to jump up for joy. She was almost surprised when he didn't. "The more the merrier."

"Oh my God… thank you guys. Thank you!" Eli said. "You guys have no idea. This is like going to Disney World for weirdos like me."

"If Disney World were isolated and full of danger instead of a very populated amusement park filled with family fun." Gavin snickered. "So, actually nothing at all like Disney World."

"Well, when you put it like that…"

"Send us the maps ASAP." Noelle interjected before they could continue their banter. "And I'll let you know when we're going. But it'll be within the next two weeks, if not sooner."

"Yeah, yeah. I'll send it right over." Eli said. Then he reached into one of the pockets of his hoodie. He held his hand out, holding pills that looked similar to the ones the goth kid had been trying to sell them. "If you guys are staying for the party, you can take these as a token of my gratitude."

"No, thanks." Noelle said. "We're heading out as soon as we're done here."

"Alright," Eli said, putting them back in his hoodie, then standing up. "Well, I got a dance floor to rock. We'll be in touch?"

Noelle and Gavin stood up as well.

"Yeah," Noelle said. "Don't forget the maps."

"I won't. I promise." Eli said, sticking his hand out for handshakes.

Noelle shook his hand. Gavin didn't bother. He just gave him a big nod, then the trio headed back into the party.

Out of the silence and back into the noise of the party. But the next time these three would meet, it would be to head into the deep, isolation of the woods north of here.

CHAPTER 32

Tess was sitting at her kitchen table, the Yugioh deck she was working on deconstructed and laid out in front of her so she could really see the minutia of the cards. Her laptop was sitting on the other side of the table like a forgotten dinner guest. A lo-fi instrumental rap song played from its speakers.

Chrome was opened to multiple tabs: an eBay listing for a few cards she needed for her zombie deck, YouTube streamers playing the newest Pokémon game (which were currently muted), an Amazon cart filled with treats and toys for her two cats, a digital version of the latest Warhammer40k comic, and the last tab was opened up to Discord.

The *ding* of an incoming new message interrupted her concentration. Tess looked up past the three spell cards she had in her hands—the ones she'd been debating on putting into her deck—and saw the Discord tab flashing.

She set the cards down and went around the table, settling into one of the chairs. She spun the laptop around to face her, then clicked over to the Discord app. Her inbox was already opened, and the new message was at the top, waiting for her attention.

It was from her friend "MagicMic87." It read:

MagicMic87 [3:17am]: Yo. Guess what?

Jeez. It's past midnight already? Time really flies when you're building decks. Tess thought, looking at the timestamp of the message. He'd just sent it less than a minute ago, which meant he'd likely just gotten in from a DJing gig and messaged her right away.

"Guess it really is important." Tess whispered to herself, realizing these were the first words she'd spoken in hours. She typed back a message:

Raigeki12: You interrupted my deckbuilding. This better be good

MagicMic87[3:17am]: Oh shit. You're up

Raigeki12[3:18am]: Yeah, duh

MagicMic87[3:18am]: I forgot Tess never sleeps

Raigeki12[3:18am]: Hey! What did I tell you about using that name on here

MagicMic87[3:18am]: LMAO oh yeah, sorry

MagicMic87[3:19am]: Okay, I'm gonna call you

Raigeki12[3:19am]: Sure. My phone is… somewhere.

Only a few second after sending that message, Tess heard her phone ringing underneath a pile of her Yugioh cards. They were un-sleeved common cards she'd been shuffling through to try to find some she was considering for her deck that she'd cast off to the side. Tess moved them away and answered the phone.

"Hello." Tess said, putting the phone on speaker.

"Hey, Tess," Eli said, sounding both out of breath and drunk at the same time. "Are you ready for this?"

"I guess." Tess said, picking up a Yugioh card that caught her attention. "Hit me with it. What's it about?"

"Camp Slaughter."

"Okay… I'm listening." She put the card in her hand down and picked up another, wondering if it would work with her strategy, only halfway checked into the conversation with Eli.

"I met with some people that found the place over the summer. They're going back and they're letting me tag along. Do you want to come?"

Tess dropped the Yugioh card back on the pile, her deckbuilding going far into the back of her mind. It took her a few seconds too long to respond but she finally said, "Are you serious, Eli?"

"Dead serious." Eli responded, and she could practically hear her friend's smirk on the other end of the line.

"What's the deal? I thought you were too chicken to go?" Tess said, her own smirk forming. "Why the sudden change?"

"Look, there's a lot for us to talk about regarding this."

"It would seem so, my friend."

By the time their phone call was finished, it would be half past 4:00 a.m. And by the time Tess was crawling into bed to snuggle with her two cats, it would be early enough in the morning to say she'd pulled an all-nighter.

CHAPTER 33

IGNACIO WOKE UP, thrashing at the air, his massive hands swiping at the dark inside the tent. He'd had a bad dream. He couldn't remember what it was, but he could still feel his heart palpitating from the fear of whatever his mind had him living through while he'd slept.

Out the corner of his eye, he saw Papá's ghost standing by the mattress. He was staring down at the ground, a small frown on his face. "The nightmares are getting worse, aren't they?"

Ignacio nodded.

"There's something bad coming our way." Papá said. "I can feel it. You can, too, right mijo?"

Another nod.

"But you're fully recovered now?" Papá asked.

"Yes…" Ignacio responded.

Just then, his stomach grumbled. Loud enough that the sound seemed to bounce off the canvas walls. Ignacio threw the blanket off his body and got up. He had to walk through Papá to get out of the tent, as he did so, the ghost flickered like any other light in this world would.

Ignacio unzipped the tent flap and stepped outside. The campfire was still lit, which was lighting the tent area and warming it. Ignacio walked over to the brim of the firepit where he'd left a pot of soup.

There was a makeshift cooking tripod over the campfire. Ignacio had found it amongst the old woman's belongings. It was just three long sticks tied together at the top with thick tweed rope. Dangling from the point where the three sticks met was a chain with a hook attached to the end of it.

Ignacio put the pot of soup up on the hook.

Ignacio brought his face close to the top of the pot and watched the soup. The chunks of meat in it had come from the thighs of the girl with the glasses he'd killed earlier. There was also a mixture of vegetables: carrots, celery, peas, and potatoes. These he'd gotten from a can the old woman had stashed away in her tent.

It seemed the old woman had been properly prepared for wintertime out in the wilderness, but now Ignacio was reaping the rewards of her diligence.

After a few minutes of watching, steam started to rise from the soup. The broth started bubbling and moving vigorously. The bits of meat and vegetables started bumping into one another. It was hot and ready to serve.

Ignacio filled a bowl sitting by the campfire with a large wooden spoon inside of it, then sat down in the metal chair just outside of the tent. The chair was something he'd also gotten from the old woman, and Ignacio prayed her spirit was being well-taken care of in the afterlife.

Ignacio started eating the soup. Behind him, he felt Papá's ghost appear.

"When you were younger, I used to tell you to eat if you wanted to become big and strong." He heard Papá say.

Ignacio didn't respond. He just put a spoonful of broth and meat into his mouth. The flesh was tender, juicy, and full of flavor. The cold temperatures had properly refrigerated and kept the body fresh.

Ignacio chewed the meat down and swallowed it, then used two hands to put the bowl up to his lips. He drank some of the bone broth—which he'd made from the body of one of the guys he'd killed the first night he'd returned to the woods—and felt the warmness of the soup filling his belly.

"Now that you're all grown up, and embracing el Monstro, you need to stay satiated." Papá said. "You need to be prepared for whatever danger is coming your way, entiendes?"

"I could not see you before, Papá. Why?" Ignacio asked, ignoring the question. This was something he wouldn't have done before, but as his father had just said, he wasn't just Ignacio anymore.

He was more than that now. He was el Monstro.

"I told you I would always be there when you needed me, didn't I?"

Ignacio nodded.

"When that girl almost killed you in the junkyard, I knew you needed my help. Needed to see me and hear me to pull out the last bit of life you had in you."

"I understand." Ignacio said. "But I do not need you now. Why are you here?"

Papá's ghost appeared in front of Ignacio. He looked down at him while Ignacio slurped more broth from the bowl.

"Because, mijo, I want to witness you at your full potential." Papá said, smiling broadly. "I need to see just how strong my lineage is. Even in the afterlife, I need to know this."

Ignacio didn't understand the word "lineage" specifically, but he understood what Papá was saying. Because he understood that his father had always been about strength and power.

"Do you understand?" Papá asked.

Ignacio nodded, "Yes."

"Good." Papá said, disappearing and appearing behind Ignacio again, standing by his left shoulder. "Now, eat up."

Ignacio leaned back in the chair and did as he was told. He stared up at the half-moon in the pitch-black sky surrounded by stars while he downed the rest of the soup.

CHAPTER 34

THE MORNING WAS surprisingly warm. Noelle sat on the hood of her Jeep, staring at the sky. The sun was breaking through the horizon in the distance, making a mesmeric swirl of warm and cool colors. The hotel parking lot was silent, stoic almost.

In Noelle's mind, it was anything but peaceful, though. Since coming back from Camp Slaughter, she'd stop hallucinating Rachel. Or rather, stopped hallucinating her in the same way.

Out the corner of her eye, she saw Rachel running down the street. She knew it was a hallucination, knew how these ended, but she couldn't help but look. It was impossible not to.

Rachel ran through the street, splotches of blood all over her clothes, her Chuck Tayor's, and her face. She ran with a limp, like one of her legs was badly injured. A torn muscle or a gash Noelle couldn't see from this angle, perhaps. Rachel looked over her shoulder, and it was as if that action conjured up the second part of the hallucination because now Noelle saw Varias Caras chasing after her sister.

He had a chainsaw in his hands. A chainsaw that was revved and ready to shred through her sister but was silent.

It was no mystery to Noelle why it didn't make any noise. There wasn't actually a chainsaw there. Just like her sister and the cannibal weren't actually there.

It's just a hallucination. Noelle said, closing her eyes, but only for a second. Because she *had* to watch. The hallucinations felt like they'd never go away unless she watched them.

She opened her eyes and saw Rachel stumble, then fall down on all fours. Her sister craned her neck, watching the cannibal get closer to her. Closer and closer. Chainsaw raised above his head, ready to come down and chop her into pieces.

"You didn't get much sleep either, huh?" Someone to the left of her said.

Noelle took her eyes off the hallucination to make sure it was who she thought it was. Gavin was standing a few paces from the Jeep, holding onto two muffins wrapped in cellophane he must've gotten from the hotel breakfast bar.

"Hungry?" He asked, sliding onto the hood of the Jeep next to her. He didn't bother waiting for her response because it'd been rhetorical, anyway.

"Not really." Noelle said but took the muffin he was handing over to her. "I should probably eat something, though."

"It's banana nut." Gavin said, unwrapping his.

Noelle did the same, then broke off a piece. As soon as the sweet, fluffiness hit her tongue, she realized she hadn't eaten since yesterday morning.

In the corner of her eye, she saw Varias Caras standing over Rachel. Rachel was attempting to get up, but she couldn't get a good grip underneath herself. The blood smeared on her palms was making it impossible.

"You okay?" Gavin said, inching closer to Noelle.

Noelle peeled her eyes away from the hallucination for a second. Gavin had stopped munching on the bite of muffin and had it stuffed into the side of his mouth. It made him look comical, like a cartoon chipmunk, and Noelle would've laughed at him if not for the awful image her mind was conjuring up on the road.

Meanwhile, on the street, Rachel was crawling away, still slipping on her slick palms, but she'd managed to get a foot or so between her and the cannibal. The problem was that Varias Caras wasn't letting up.

They were in a spot where the sunshine came down in blinding spires, meaning part of Rachel was obscured. Noelle could only really see the bottom half of her body, could only see her sister kicking her legs to try to scramble away.

But just the same, she knew what was going to happen. Knew what the end result would be as Varias Caras hopped toward her and brought the chainsaw down on her.

"I'm okay… just didn't get much sleep." Noelle said, watching the chainsaw tear through her sister's back. She saw the blood spurting out into the air like a red geyser as Varias Caras pushed the chainsaw deeper and deeper into Rachels' body.

This particular hallucination was silent. But that somehow made it worse. It left it to Noelle's imagination to fill in the sounds of her sister screaming in pain as the chainsaw ripped into her.

"Really?" Gavin said, looking away from her. He used the hand not holding the muffin to shield his eyes as he stared out into the street. "Why does it seem like you're distracted by something happening out there, though? Are you seeing something I'm not?"

Noelle felt as if he'd read her mind or something and fidgeted her weight around. The movement caught Gavin's eye, and as he turned his attention back to her, Noelle gave herself even further away by gulping.

"Gavin, can I tell you something?" Noelle said, deciding it was time to tell someone her secret because deep down, she thought maybe this would be one of her last opportunities to ever tell someone.

"Yeah," Gavin responded, taking another bite out of his muffin.

"It's something I've never told anyone. Not my parents, not Fred, not even the therapist I saw for two months after we came back from Camp Slaughter."

"Okay. I'm all ears." He said.

The hallucination had disappeared, at least for the most part it had. Varias Caras and Rachel were gone, all that was left was a copious amount of blood on the street. Like the hallucination was leaving a reminder that she'd seen it. Or rather, imagined it.

Noelle blinked several times, and the blood went away, the street in front of the hotel turned back into nothing more than just a road shining gold underneath the morning sun.

"I—I have these vivid hallucinations." Noelle said, almost waiting for him to laugh at her. "It sounds silly when I say it out loud, but I hallucinate my dead sister."

She saw him turn to look at the street, then he turned back to her. "Did you just see her now?"

"Kind of." Noelle shrugged. "Ever since we returned from Camp Slaughter, I see her and the cannibal. The cannibal murders her brutally in these hallucinations. I just watched him shred her body up with a chainsaw."

"Jesus. That sound terrifying." Gavin's face soured, but he couldn't help to look out at the street again. "And here I thought my nightmares were bad. Here you are seeing this shit while you're awake."

"It's not a fun time." Noelle shrugged. "But I bring this up because it's how I know something weird happened after the car accident. As vivid as the hallucinations are, Rachel appearing on the hood of the car *felt* different. Her pulling me through the windshield… I don't know… it's like she was helping me cross some barrier between our world and the afterlife."

"Look, Noelle, whether it happened or not, whether I believe you or not, doesn't make any difference. All that matters is that our goal is the same, we're going back there to take this guy's fucking head off."

Noelle smirked. "When you're right, you're right, Gavin."

"Fredster used to say that, too." Gavin said, returning her smirk with a smile. He wrapped his muffin up and then set it to the side.

For a minute or so, they both stared out at the blue sky, at the radiant light shining from the bright sun. The cool air filled their lungs while they sat in silence. It was the closest either one had come to finding some semblance of peace since the encounter with the cannibal. And without having to communicate it to each other, they both knew it would be their last moment like this until this was all said and done.

"By the way, I've been meaning to ask you how your arm healed up." Gavin said, glancing over at the arm Noelle had broken in the aforementioned car accident.

Noelle held it up. It'd healed up fast and worked perfectly fine now; it was almost as if it hadn't happened at all. In fact, she didn't really remember it happened until now that Gav was asking about it.

"It healed just fine." She said, putting it back down. "It wasn't as bad as it looked."

"That's good." Gavin said, then slapped the hood of the Jeep. "You think it's about time we get this show on the road?"

"Yeah," Noelle said. "I'll drive this time."

Gavin nodded. "You're the boss."

CHAPTER 35

They stopped for an early lunch at a Panera Bread and to fuel up at a gas station before they got to Noelle's apartment. By the time they got back, it was midday. They had a quick chat out in the lot, nothing pertaining to Camp Slaughter or the cannibal, just some small talk to try to ease themselves back into the normalcy of their daily routines.

Noelle went inside her apartment. Despite that the sun was still shining bright and gold outside, her place was dark. The blinds were closed, and the lights were all off. But this was how she liked coming home nowadays, no matter the time of day. It was like returning to her personal cave. The one place in the world where she felt like she could embrace her obsession over Camp Slaughter without judging herself.

Noelle hung her keys up on the hanger on the wall, then went right to her research desk. Her laptop was sitting underneath it, leaning against one of the front legs. She grabbed it and set it on the desk. She powered it on, then impatiently waited for it to boot on.

There was something that had been sitting in her mind about the Camp Slaughter. Something that had been in the back of her mind, a missing piece in the jigsaw puzzle if you will, that she still hadn't found an answer to.

It bothered her even more than trying to figure out if the ghosts out in those woods were real (because deep down, she knew they were, despite her spiritual agnosticism). She wanted to know—and maybe even *needed* to know—what the origins of the campgrounds were.

As it were, the answer was all but about to fall onto her lap.

Noelle was punching in her password into the laptop when her phone started ringing. It was from an unknown number. She usually didn't answer these, but for some inexplicable reason, this time she picked her phone up and answered the call without thinking about it.

"Hello?" she said, watching the login screen on her laptop flash into the desktop, where her wallpaper was a picture of her and Rachel at Tyler State Park. One of the last pictures they'd ever taken together.

"Hi," a young girl's voice said. "You don't know who I am, but I got your contact info from Eli."

"Oh?" Noelle said. "Can I help you with something?"

"Yes," the girl said. She seemed to be short of breath. Like she'd just gone up and down a flight of stairs. Either that, or she was nervous about this call. "I'm the friend that Eli is bringing with him when you go to the campgrounds."

"Oh, okay. This call makes so much more sense."

"Yeah," the girl said, inhaling. "Okay, so what I wanted to ask is… would it be okay for me to film you and the others on this camping trip?"

"Film us? Like, for what? A blog?"

"Not quite."

"Then?"

"Well, after talking to Eli, I had this idea. He told me everything, about how Emeril Dantes and Molly Sanger were killed at the campgrounds. About how that documentary will never come out… and well, my noggin started joggin'."

"To make your own documentary?"

"Precisely." The girl said.

There was a pause in the conversation as Noelle considered things. She was going out into those woods with the goal of murdering someone. Putting the lead up to it on film wasn't exactly the brightest idea.

"By the way, my name is Tess. Tess Hall." the girl said, breaking the silence and attempting to continue the negotiations.

"Okay, Tess, but you have to promise me something if I allow you to come along."

"What's that?"

"My mission going out there is to hunt down and kill the cannibal. I'd like for you to omit anything that might incriminate me in your documentary."

"That should be doable." The girl said, letting out a small sigh of relief. "I'll make it look like it's just an expedition out into the deep, deep woods. Like those Bigfoot documentaries—only a lot less dopey, I hope."

"I'll hold you to that." Noelle said. "Also keep in mind I'll have to fly this by the others."

"Yes, yes. I was thinking that." Tess said. "Seeing how you're the ringleader of this whole operation, I was hoping maybe you could throw your weight around and get them to consent to being filmed?

"I'm doing lots of favors for you two, it seems." Noelle said, setting up to see if this girl could provide her with any new information. "I'll see what I can do, though."

"The favors don't go unappreciated."

Noelle let out a small laugh. The girl had a pleasant voice, a certain cadence of speaking that was somehow relaxing. "How much do you know about these campgrounds?"

"I'm a fanatic." Tess said. "It's the reason why I want to make this documentary. When Paranormal Talk first announced they were working on a Camp Slaughter documentary, the weirdo community was beyond excited."

"Okay, so, given that they were killed, no one questioned why they'd suddenly gone silent or why the movie hadn't come out?"

"No, not really. We all just assumed they were hard at work on their film." Noelle heard something like plastic being unwrapped, then the girl spoke again. "I've been doing nothing but researching Camp Slaughter since talking to Eli last night."

"I've been doing that since returning home." Noelle said. "Haven't found all that much, to be honest. Place seems to be a… ghost on the internet."

"Well, I've been researching it for a while now. It's kind of a big deal amongst us weirdos here in PA." Noelle heard the candy clatter against Tess's teeth as she passed it from one side of her mouth to the other. "But I'm going even deeper now."

"What do you mean?"

"There's certain sources information I'm privy to that normies wouldn't know about. I haven't tapped into them because I figured I would get all of this information when Paranormal Talk put out their film, but, well… we both know that's not ever coming out."

"Like what? I have access to Emeril Dantes's Google account. Maybe I have it on hand already."

"Wait, really? How did you get access to that?"

"That's a story for another time. Tell me what you're looking for specifically?"

"The origins of the name Camp Slaughter. I've never gotten to the bottom of it, and there are tons of rumors floating around the internet. As you may imagine."

Noelle went through the files she'd seen in Emeril's Google account. Nothing that could've had that information stood out to her, but maybe it was in one of those videos she didn't feel comfortable watching.

"Hm, I don't think I saw anything like that in the files when I was snooping."

"Drats." Tess said. "Well, I'm going back to researching. Will you let Eli know when exactly you're heading up to Camp Slaughter?"

"I will." Noelle said. "Actually, I'll make a group chat with everyone going and keep everyone posted."

"Stellar." Tess said. "Except, this is a burner number I'm calling from. I'll text you from my real phone once we end the call."

"Uh, okay." Noelle said, a bit weirded out by this. "Talk to you soon."

"Right on." Tess said.

They ended the call. A few beats later, a new text message came in from a different number. Noelle opened the text message. It read:

> Hey, it's you-know-who. Through text, can you call me Raigeki?

Noelle replied back:

> Sure.

She saved the girl's contact info under "Tess" and locked her phone screen.

Noelle sat back, thinking about the merry band of misfits that had formed— "weirdos" as Tess might've put it. There was her, a girl who hallucinated. A depressed former sheriff with endless sadness. A guy who was a DJ at a rave for goth kids. And now a strange girl who wanted to be called "Raigeki" had joined the squad. The only one with any sort of normalness to them was Gavin, which in some way made him the oddball for being associated with this group at all.

Life really is strange. Noelle thought, staring out into nothingness. Then, behind that thought came another one. A morbid thought that crawled out from the dark, cavernous parts of her mind like a demon. *Maybe this life is almost over, though. Not just for me, but for all of us.*

She hoped not.

About forty minutes later, it was done. Noelle had made the group text and coordinated with everyone to figure out a date when they were available. As it turned out, everyone was ready to go within the next two days. Noelle booked Lakewood Cabin and touched base with everyone to make sure they were all good to go one last time..

Everyone was on board. Locked and loaded, so to speak.

There was only one reason they were going into the woods: to hunt down Ignacio Calderon/Varias Caras. But it would serve them to have a "homebase." A refuge point where they could store their extra ammunition and retreat to if need be. Especially since most likely by the time they made it there, they'd only have a few hours of sunlight.

The plan was to meet at Eli's home. From there, they would drive together. It added some time to their trip to do it this way, but it was the safest way possible. They wanted to enter what could be constituted as the cannibal's territory together, just in case one of the vehicles suddenly broke down or something along those lines happened.

Everyone had agreed to all of this. Somehow, though, Noelle could sense the collective nervousness of the group. She stared at the thread as the responses to her confirming the booking came through.

Two days, and they would be in the northern woods of Pennsylvania. Hunting for a cannibal that had damn near killed her and Gav just months ago and had killed multiple people just a few weeks ago.

It was really done, though. There was no turning back now. At least, not for her. The others might bail at the last minute, but she wouldn't.

There was no chance. She was fully committed.

All roads lead back to the camp. The phrase popped into her head like a mantra. She wasn't sure where it came from, but it felt right.

III

CHAPTER 36

THEY WERE GATHERED inside of Eli's apartment, which was as odd as one could imagine. One corner was cluttered with his DJing equipment: a turntable, a computer with an uncountable amount of cables plugged into it, outfits and hats (one jacket looked like an astronaut suit) that he wore for his gigs hanging on a hook, a number of microphones, and several other pieces that most people wouldn't have been able to name unless they did some sort of audio engineering or DJing themselves.

There were lava lamps decorating the end tables and shelves, all of them plugged in, which gave the living room a feeling that it was alive and breathing. Statues of animals made of wood and faceless women in vaguely seductive poses were strewn about. These statues had an interesting artistic choice about them, though, as they looked like they'd been sawn in half. Not in a morbid way, but more like something that had come out of Willy Wonka's room at the end of *Willy Wonka and the Chocolate Factory*.

A massive painting of a group of clowns hung over one of the couches. It was done in a style reminiscent of an old circus advertisement, with purposeful deterioration and wear on it.

Across from the couch was the broom closet door decorated with a poster of *Zombies Ate My Neighborhood.*

All-in-all, the feel Eli's apartment gave Noelle and Gavin as they came into it was a strange one. Independently of one another, they both thought this was appropriate given what they were here to do.

"Welcome, welcome." Eli said, leading them to where the couches were.

Tess was already here, and she wasn't anything how Noelle had imagined her. She had fire red hair and skin the color of milk. She was sitting on the floor, cross-legged, striped socks going up all the way past her knees. In front of her was a shiny Yugioh tin box and several cards splayed out on the carpet.

"Hello," she said, putting the cards she had in her hand down on the floor and standing up. "Glad you could join us."

Noelle and Gavin shook her hand, formally introducing themselves to her.

"Make yourselves at home." Eli said, as he walked over to a fish tank with several clown fish in it. He grabbed a container of fish flakes from the shelf space underneath it and started unscrewing the cap. "We're waiting on one more, right?"

"Yeah," Gavin said, sitting down on the couch facing the fish tank.

"Mr. Olmos should be here soon." Noelle said, sitting down next to him. "He said he's only an hour away from here and he texted me about an hour ago that he'd left his home."

"Crazy what happened to his daughter, huh?" Eli said, opening the top of the tank and shaking flakes into it. The school of fish quickly swam to the top and began feeding on the food sinking into the water.

"Is that thing on?" Gavin asked, noticing the camera on the tripod in the corner of the living room for the first time.

"Not yet." Tess said, glancing that way. "I was waiting for the whole band to be here before I start recording anything."

As if on time, Noelle's phone went off. She picked it up without looking at the screen because she knew who it was. "Hello?"

"Hey, Noelle. I'm outside. I couldn't figure out whose number was who in the thread, so I just rang you."

"I figured." Noelle said.

"That him?" Eli asked, shelving the fish flakes in their spot and crossing the living room over to the intercom system where he could control the apartment building's front door.

"Yeah, it's him." Noelle said.

Eli gave her a thumbs-up, then hit the button. "Tell 'em to come on up."

"Eli says to come up." Noelle said.

"I think maybe you guys should come out here." Greg said. "We can't waste any more time."

Noelle glanced at the watch on her wrist. It was mid-afternoon. It'd taken her and Gavin about three and a half hours to get to Eli's apartment. From here, the drive would be another two hours until they were at Lakewood Cabin. Given that the sun set around 5:00 p.m. this time of year in Pennsylvania, that would only give them a few short hours of daylight once they made it to the woods.

Not ideal, but it wasn't like the sunlight was going to make this plan any less dangerous, anyway. Either way, Mr. Olmos was right. They should get there sooner rather than later. There was no point in delaying the inevitable.

"Are you guys all packed up?" Noelle asked Tess and Eli, while still having the phone pressed up to her ear and Mr. Olmos was still on the line.

The two of them exchanged a quick glance, then Tess said, "Yeah. I'll just have to pack up my camera and we're good to go."

"We're leaving already?" Eli asked, knowing the answer already and beginning to cross the living room in the direction of the bedroom, where his and Tess's bags were waiting.

"Yeah. Mr. Olmos is waiting for us outside." Noelle felt Gavin look at her, as he was taken aback by this abrupt departure as well. At the same time, though, she knew he understood it.

There was a collective murmur of acknowledgment from the rest of the group, then everyone started moving at the same time. Noelle and Gavin went to grab their coats and winter accessories hanging on the old school coatrack by the front door. Meanwhile, Eli went into the bedroom to grab the bags and Tess went into the living room to grab the food they'd packed.

"We'll be outside with Mr. Olmos." Noelle called out into the apartment as she finished putting on her leather gloves. She heard them both respond back in some form, then Noelle grabbed the doorknob, twisted it, and pulled the door open.

"We're really at the endgame now." Gavin said, zipping up his Carhart jacket. "Only hours away from returning to the cabin."

Noelle didn't respond, just turned to look at him to gauge his expression. There was a mixture of fear, nervousness, and determination on his face.

"It's almost hard to believe, huh?" he asked.

"Not for me," Noelle said. "I've thought of returning to the woods countless times."

"You know," Gavin started, then paused. Perhaps to search for the right words instead of blurting out what was in his mind for once. "I really hope you keep this same energy if we end up fighting the cannibal again."

Me too. She thought but didn't dare vocalize this. Instead, she ignored his comment and headed out of the apartment. Gavin followed.

CHAPTER 37

Mr. Olmos was waiting for them in the parking lot. The truck of his bed was opened, and he was sitting on the edge of it with a half-eaten powdered donut in one hand and a heavy-duty thermal in the other. Next to him was a bag filled with more donuts and two carry-out trays filled with Styrofoam cups containing coffee.

He waved at Gavin and Noelle as they came out of the apartment building with the hand holding the donut, shaking some of the sugar off the donut in the process.

"Where's the film crew?" Mr. Olmos asked as the duo neared him.

"Inside," Gavin said, jutting a thumb over his shoulder. "We've got time to comb our hair and powder our noses."

"You must be Gavin," Mr. Olmos said, extending a hand.

"Pleasure to meet you in the flesh." Gavin said, shaking his hand.

"Looks like you've brought some weapons with you." Noelle said, bringing attention to the metallic cases sitting in the truck bed behind Mr. Olmos. One was small, like the one she used to carry her own handgun, the other was long and wide and likely contained some sort of rifle.

"Oh, yeah." Mr. Olmos said, twisting around and tapping the tops of the metal cases with his thermal. The small *clunk* resonated through the quiet of the parking lot. "I hope you've brought yours?"

Gavin lifted his jacket up to show him the handgun holstered to his hip underneath it. "Got my trusty sidekick right here."

"I've got mine on me. These are just extras." Mr. Olmos said.

"Mine's in there." Noelle said, pointing at the blue Jeep parked two spots down from Mr. Olmos's Ram truck.

All three of them heard the apartment building's front door open. Noelle and Gavin turned to see Tess and Eli coming through the door. Eli was at the front, carrying the tripod, camera bag, a Nike duffle bag, and a third object that none of the others could figure out what it was from where they stood. It was a long object in a black casing with a golden rope dangling from one end of it. He also had a camping backpack strapped to his back, the kind you would take when you knew you were going to be out in the wilderness for several days. It seemed a bit unnecessary, but perhaps there was no such thing as being too prepared when you were going as far away from civilization as they would be.

Behind him, Tess was carrying two tote bags stuffed to the brim with food. There was an Italian bread poking out from the top of one. The leafy parts of a pineapple and the head and neck of a clear bottle could be seen sticking out of the second one. Her other hand was holding a set of keys.

"The band is all here!" Tess shouted as the apartment building's front door closed behind her.

Eli and Tess joined the other three by the truck and set their belongings down on the ground. They huddled in a loose semi-circle in front of Mr. Olmos, who stood up to introduce himself and offer coffee and donuts to everyone.

They all grabbed a coffee and passed on the donuts. All except Tess, who chomped down a chocolate one in three quick bites. The others stared at her, surprised by this given her slender frame.

"I didn't eat breakfast." Tess said, using an index finger to push her glasses up the bridge of her nose. "Also, as my parents described it, I have the appetite of the Big Bad Wolf."

"No judgment." Mr. Olmos spoke for the group. "Eat to your heart's content."

"Okay, no judgment on how much you eat, yeah." Gavin agreed, then pointed at the mystery object with the gold string. "But what the hell is that thing?"

"Oh!" Tess nearly jumped up in excitement. "Do you want to tell them or can I?"

Eli's face flushed red, and his eyes dropped to the ground. He grumbled something under his breath that Tess took to mean she could tell them.

"Well, since it's possible we'll be in danger, Eli brought his mid-15th century katana."

"Mid-17th." Eli said, his face getting a shade redder at having to correct her. He glanced past Mr. Olmos to where the metal cases were sitting in the truck bed. "I'm guessing there's some sort of rifle that makes my sword look like a child's toy in there, though."

"Yeah, probably." Gavin answered for Mr. Olmos. "You guys aren't bringing any guns?"

"No." Tess said. "I have my cricket bat in my vehicle, though."

"Great." Gavin said.

"Hey, don't be mad at us." Eli said. "Your fearless leader here agreed to let us come along."

"I know, I know." Gavin said.

"What do you think of the map, by the way?" Eli asked Noelle.

"The routes will come in handy." Noelle said, giving him a small nod. "Thanks."

"You know about the map?" Gavin said, turning to Mr. Olmos.

Greg nodded. "Yeah. How I understand it, it's the reason the film crew here is coming along with us."

"Oh!" Tess said, walking out of the group and going over to her camera bag. She unzipped it and pulled the camera out. Then, she grabbed the tripod, which Eli had set a little behind him.

She walked a few paces away from the group and set the tripod on an angle that would put Noelle facing the camera. It was the perfect shot, given that she was—as Eli had put it—their fearless leader in this whole thing.

Satisfied with the camera's setup, Tess left it recording and hurried back into her spot in the huddle.

"I hope everyone is OK with me recording."

"They are." Noelle said, a tinge of annoyance in her voice because they'd all consented to Tess recording their trip in the text thread.

Perhaps the girl needed in-person confirmation, but it was also the least important part of this whole operation. At least, to Noelle and the others it was.

"A-OK." Gavin echoed, holding up his three fingers to emphasize the point.

"Now, before we get going, I want to establish some ground rules." Mr. Olmos said, reaching behind him for the larger of the metal cases. He punched in a combination into the lock at the top of it, then popped the case open, revealing the hunting rifle sitting inside of it.

"That looks… menacing." Eli said, staring at it like it was about to come alive and start shooting bullets through the apartment complex.

"It is." Mr. Olmos said, taking the rifle out and laying it across his lap. "It's a high-powered hunting rifle. Nothing in the human body can stop one of its rounds. It'll pierce even through the thickest bone like it's made of margarine."

"Whoa." Tess whispered under her breath.

"This will be my weapon. No one except for Noelle is to touch it. The only circumstances where it will be acceptable for anyone else to wield it is if it's life or death. Do I make myself clear?"

"You mean no one except me and Noelle." Gavin said, his hand half raised.

"No, I mean what I said. Only Noelle has my permission to use this weapon at her discretion." Mr. Olmos said, his voice stern. "We cannot risk any accidents with this weapon; do you understand?"

"Sure." Gavin said, crossing his arms, his big biceps slightly bulging out from the thick sleeves of his jacket in this position.

"Understood." Tess said. "Big weapon. Very dangerous. Stay away."

"Yeah, I got it." Eli grumbled.

"Good." Mr. Olmos said. "Now that that is out of the way, what's the arrangement of how we're getting there?"

"I say we take as many vehicles as possible." Eli suggested.

"I don't think so." Noelle interjected. "There are only five of us, that means if we take three vehicles, one person will have to be by themselves. I don't think anyone should be by themselves at any time once we're in the woods."

"So only two vehicles?" Mr. Olmos asked.

"It'll only give us two escape vehicles, if it comes to that, but it's safer as we enter the woods that way."

"Right. I agree." Gavin said.

"We can't risk a solo person getting lost or their vehicle breaking down." Noelle said. "Two vehicles will allow us to travel more safely."

"Okay, then the question becomes which vehicles." Mr. Olmos said.

"My bus has plenty of space for three people plus bags." Tess volunteered, a big grin on her face.

"Bus? Like a school bus?"

Tess snort laughed and shook her head. Her red hair flailed about underneath the knit cap she was wearing. "No, no. A VW Bus."

She pointed them to the VW Bus across the parking lot. It was tan with green trim and looked old school enough that it might've been at Woodstock.

"Oh, *that*." Gavin said, then his expression turned forlorn. "I knew a friend that would've loved it. Guy had the best weed I've ever had—"

Gavin stopped himself and looked over at Mr. Olmos, realizing what he was saying in front of a former sheriff.

"Don't worry, kid. I've smoked a joint here and there in my heyday." Mr. Olmos laughed. "So, we take Tess's bus and my truck?"

"Negative on that. No offense to anyone, but my Jeep is the only vehicle I trust." Noelle said.

Mr. Olmos shrugged. No one else had any objections to that.

"Mr. Olmos, you go with Tess and Eli." Noelle said.

"You want me to drive, Noelle?" Gavin asked.

"I'll drive. Last time you drove in the woods you almost took out a small bush with your car." Noelle said, smirking at him. Gavin laughed.

Noelle turned away from Gavin and addressing the other three said, "I'll be leading the way. Follow me close. If you happen to lose me, call me immediately. Understood?"

"We got it." Eli said on behalf of the group.

"Alright. If there's nothing else, let's get going." Noelle said. "And if anyone wants to bail last minute, this is your last opportunity.

She saw Eli take in a deep breath and the color drain out of his face, like he'd just seen a ghost sleeping with one of his ex-lovers. To his credit, though, he didn't back out.

No one did. They were all in.

"Full steam ahead, gang!" Tess shouted, as she ran over to her bus to bring it closer to the truck so they could begin transferring Mr. Olmos's belongings into it.

Noelle and Gavin broke away from the others as they loaded up the VW Bus. As they neared Noelle's Jeep, and were out of earshot from the others, Gavin turned to Noelle and said, "You're really all in on this, aren't you?"

"What do you mean?"

"You won't stop until one of you is dead. You or the cannibal."

"Correct," Noelle said. They reached the Jeep, she hit the unlock button on her keys. The alarm system chirped to let her know it was unlocked, but she didn't open the door just yet.

"I thought maybe you were just talking a big game before," Gavin said, stopping next to her. He started fishing in his jacket pocket for a pack of cigarettes. "I really thought your determination would've wavered by now."

"How do you know it hasn't?" Noelle challenged.

"I can see it on your face." Gavin said, sticking one of the cigarettes in his mouth and lighting it up with a lighter he grabbed from his other jacket pocket. "It's the same look my pops and my uncles had when we would go hunting. Seconds before pulling the trigger and taking out a buck, they looked how you look right now."

"I see." Noelle said.

"Yeah, except you look a little more pissed off." Gavin said, taking a drag of the cigarette.

"The cannibal's responsible for my constant anxiety, the sleepless nights, the nightmares, the guilt… all of it. Of course I'm pissed off."

"Yeah," Gavin said, taking a few steps away to blow a cloud of smoke.

"I thought you were turning a new leaf?" Noelle said. "Last time you were drinking. Now you're smoking?"

"Yeah, well, I thought about it. And I think only the old me has a chance of surviving out there." Gavin shaking the ashes off his cigarette with a flick of the two fingers he was holding it with. "The one that's sober and comfortable with a great girl would get chewed up out there, so he stays here with civilization."

"Smart decision."

"I'll pick his ass back up if I make it back from the woods alive." He put the cigarette to his lips, inhaled and then exhaled a perfect circle of smoke into the air. "Even if I come back missing pieces of me."

CHAPTER 38

THEY DROVE AND drove, the highway getting emptier as they neared the woods where Camp Slaughter was located. As they'd planned, Noelle was leading the way in the Jeep, while Tess chugged along behind her in the us.

Miles of farmland were quickly turning into nothing but wilderness. Into nothing but dead trees, cliffs, mountains, and the occasional field of dead grass.

Eli had his head rested against the passenger window, half asleep. The reflection of a seemingly endless row of thin trees whizzed past his glasses as the VW Bus went by them.

It felt like a normal camping trip, like the family ones he'd taken with his mom and dad and older brother to the Poconos on breaks from school. The kind that he'd sometimes looked forward to, but he knew this was no such thing.

All he had to do was turn his neck a few inches and see the rugged older man sitting in the seat behind him with a rifle across his lap to remind him this was no family trip.

Tess had been playing music that sounded like Stevie Nicks the entire car ride. Or maybe it was someone trying to sound like her. Eli wasn't sure because he wasn't very familiar with that type of music; all he knew was that it was making him feel like rolling a joint. That, too, was another hint that this was nothing like his family trips.

Eli took his head off the window, realizing the oils from his hair had left a smudge, and silently apologized to Tess for it before turning to her. She unwrapped another lollipop with a single hand. Her other hand she kept on the steering wheel.

With the grace of someone who'd practiced a motion countless times, she stuck the candy in her mouth and placed the wrapper in the small container she had glued in the middle of the dashboard. The plastic container was filled with wrappers and sticks from the other seven lollipops she'd already eaten on this trip.

"How long until we're there?" Mr. Olmo asked from the backseat. His voice was croaky, like he'd just woken up from a nap.

Tess almost jumped out of her seat, as if she'd forgotten Mr. Olmos was there this whole time, then relaxed when she looked in the rearview mirror and saw him.

Eli looked behind him. Mr. Olmos was laying back on the long seats of the bus, his hands tucked behind his head and his elbows flared out. The rifle was on the ground, only inches away from him. And even though the former sheriff was an ally, there was something menacing about the sight of this, about a man so relaxed while being only inches away from a killing machine.

Mr. Olmos had insisted on getting the rifle out of the case and having it ready in case they needed to jump into action the moment they got out of the vehicle. Neither Tess nor Eli liked the idea, but it was better to be safe than sorry.

"About an hour." Tess informed him.

"Guess I better start shaking the cobwebs off." Mr. Olmos said, picking himself up and sitting upright in the seat. "I have to ask something."

"Ask away, good sir!" Tess replied.

"Why are you two going on this trip? I know it's to make a movie, Noelle mentioned that to me in a conversation, but why about this place? What is it about this dreaded place that draws you in?"

"Because for years no one was sure if it was even a real place." Tess answered. "And knowing that Noelle and Gavin actually saw it…well, it kind of sparked something in me.

"See, there's a certain mystery to places like the campgrounds that is like nothing else. I mean, sure, there's mysteries in things like the pyramids in Egypt and the ruins in Latin America and Asia, but there are entire fields of study dedicated to those locations and landmarks. Places like Camp Slaughter, though, Mr. Olmos… well, only weirdos like Eli and I are drawn to it."

"It's almost like if we were on our way to go see Atlantis or something."

"Except Atlantis is mythicized as a beautiful city with rich architecture… where we're going is just an abandoned campsite." Mr. Olmos countered.

"Oh fooey! Where's your sense of adventure?" Tess said, taking the lollipop out of her mouth and waving it around like it was a wand.

"I'm in this because the cannibal killed my daughter. And you two are in it for adventure." Mr. Olmos sat back in his seat, groaning. "Dear God, help us."

"We won't get in your way, Mr. Olmos." Tess reassured him. "Promise. It'll be like we're not even there."

"Sorry, I didn't mean to come off so blunt." He said, sighing. "It's just that I've spent my whole life trying to protect people from danger. Now look at me. I'm diving headfirst into danger with a group of people young enough to be my kids."

"Everything's changed, though, right?" Eli said.

"What do you mean?" Mr. Olmos asked.

"Like, after your daughter died. Nothing really seems to matter anymore." Eli felt a wave of embarrassment go through him, like maybe he'd said too much, and maybe what he'd said was stupid and hurtful.

To his relief, though, he saw Mr. Olmos's shoulders relax. "Yeah, something like that."

"I'm a nihilist by nature." Eli said, turning in his seat to look back out the window at the endless trees surrounding either side of the narrow highway they were on. "I sort of get it."

Noelle and Gavin had been driving in relative silence. They'd had some small talk here and there. Mundane stuff, like Noelle asking him if she should make a stop for a bathroom break and Gavin saying no. Noelle asked him some quick question about his girlfriend, which Gavin answered with short replies.

"It doesn't feel the same, does it?" Gavin said, breaking the silence as he kept his eyes out the window, looking at the trees.

Trees that made up the woods where his best friend and little brother had been killed. He swallowed, feeling a knot of emotion in his throat, and fought back the tears threatening to come out of him.

Because the old Gavin would never cry in front of anyone. Maybe not the new Gavin, either. He wasn't sure about that one because, as he'd told Noelle, he was leaving that version of himself behind.

"No, not at all." Noelle said.

"Okay, so it's not just me being dramatic." Gavin said, leaning back, bending his knees to bring his legs closer to the seat. "We're at the point of no return now, huh?"

"Yep."

Gavin nodded. Then thought about the phrase he'd just used. *Point of no return.* In this context, there was a certain morbidity to it that wasn't usually in the expression because, indeed, if the cannibal was there waiting for them, there was a good chance not everyone on the trip would be returning.

"Damn," Gavin said, shaking his head. "Maybe I should've picked my words better."

He meant it as a joke, but Noelle didn't laugh. And now that he'd shared the thought, he wasn't sure it was that much of a joke after all.

CHAPTER 39

AN HOUR LATER, they were driving down the dirt path that would lead them to Lakewood Cabin. It was daytime, but this deep in the woods, even though the trees were dead, they were packed so tightly Noelle had to turn on the headlights.

Gavin felt his bowels moving, but they were empty, which meant this was just his body's primal reaction to the ever-increasing unease that was slowly—slowly but surely—turning into raw fear.

Noelle had also cut the radio off a few miles back—it'd been playing a repeat episode of NPR from her phone the whole ride—in the silence they could hear every creak and croak in the car. Parts that needed their screws tightened, metal pieces that rubbed and squeaked against one another, and springs that were old and beginning to rust. Somehow, all these sounds added an extra bit of eeriness to the situation.

"Hey, Noelle, maybe a dumb question, but have you seen any ghosts yet?"

"No, not yet." Noelle said, glancing over at him to see if he was asking a serious question and not just ribbing her. When she saw he was serious, she continued. "But I feel a bit funny."

"Funny how? Like you have to take a dump?" Gavin said, grinning—knowing deep down he was making this wisecrack to hide his discomfort.

"Huh?" Noelle said.

"Nothing. I'm just being a bozo. What're you feeling, exactly?"

"Like a part of me has woken up and is screaming at me."

"Damn." Gavin responded.

A few minutes later, the dirt road gave out to several yards of gravel and Lakewood Cabin came into view. It was a lot smaller than they remembered it, and maybe that had to do with how much they built the place up in their heads all this time away from it.

Noelle parked the Jeep a few feet away from the porch by the area where the firepit was located. The VW Bus pulled up behind them and parked next to them.

Gavin looked over at the rest of their party. All three of them looked exhausted and nervous. Even still, Tess gave them a thumbs-up with a big grin on her face. The goofy look on the girl's face reminded him of his little brother, and for a second, his mind superimposed Wayne onto her.

Tess was about their age, in her early twenties. And for the first time since his little brother had been killed, Gavin realized he would never grow old enough to be that age. A pang of sadness hit him, and he almost came close to letting the tears flow.

But he remained strong. He brushed the thoughts away and sliced his hand through the air to give Tess a half-assed wave.

Inside the bus, everyone started moving. Next to him, Noelle shut the engine off the Jeep, and she too started getting out.

"Come on," Noelle said, opening the car door. "Let's start unpacking. I have some setting up to do before it gets dark."

"Setting up?"

"I brought things. You'll see." Noelle said as she got out of the vehicle.

Noelle stopped at the side of the vehicle and took a second to glance at Lakewood Cabin. The expression on her face was like a boxer sizing up their opponent on fight night. A few clouds rolled past the setting sun, turning the area dark.

And she wondered if perhaps this was a premonition of things to come.

CHAPTER 40

The heat woke Ignacio. He opened his eye and saw his tent was ablaze. He tried to move, but he couldn't because his limbs were bound to his torso by rope. The rope was so tight it was cutting the circulation of his blood.

The fire raged all around him. Parts of the tent walls had melted away, leaving holes large enough that he could see the woods beyond them. Smoke was filling up the tent space.

Ignacio felt his heart beating faster than ever in his chest. Then, he heard the front of the tent being unzipped.

He craned his neck and saw the outline of someone standing outside the tent. They carried a long, sharp object in their hand. With their freehand, they pushed past the tent flap and stepped inside.

Ignacio didn't recognize the person, but it was someone he'd encountered before. The person moved toward him. Gliding across the tent, like they were a ghost. Or more accurately, a spirit.

Even as they neared, they remained a shadow. The machete did, too. But now, the person rose the weapon up over their head, ready to drive it down at him. Ready to plunge it into his heart—

Ignacio had fallen asleep in the chair after a large meal of chunks of meat, but he awoke from the nightmare now. Sweat dripping down his back despite the low temperatures.

It was twilight, but the sky was still mostly bright and blue. Birds chirped in the trees and the sound of a rodent building a nest could be heard somewhere behind the tent.

"They're here." Papá's ghost said, appearing next to him. "Focus your hearing."

Ignacio did as he was told. Immediately, his super hearing picked up on doors opening and closing. There were at least two vehicles, which meant there would be several of them.

"They've come to try to kill you." Papá continued.

"Kill me…" Ignacio muttered. Now that the fear of the bad dream was beginning to subside, the idea of new victims in the vicinity excited him. "I'll kill them first."

Papá smiled at this. "That's my boy."

"I'm not a boy," Ignacio said, standing up. "I'm a monster."

With that, he headed into the tent.

He went to the wall with his masks and selected his newest one. It was a mask made from Madison Charleston's skin that he painted dark red. In the middle of it, he'd painted a black swirl, like something a villain in an old cartoon would use to try to hypnotize the protagonists. The mask had only a single eyehole, as his disfigured face only required one now.

Next, he went over to the wooden table, where underneath it sat his chainsaw inside of its metal case. He popped the lid open and pulled the chainsaw out. A chain he found in the back of the Bronco dangled from its handle. Ignacio strapped the tool to his body from this chain, the chainsaw hung from his back like a bookbag.

Then, he grabbed his hunting knife sitting on the wooden table and headed out of the tent.

Mask on. Weapons equipped. It was killing time once again.

CHAPTER 41

It was twilight by the time Noelle was done setting the last bear trap. Gavin had come with her to the back of the cabin because the plan was that at no point was anyone allowed to be alone while they were out here.

Noelle figured that at some point that would be impossible to adhere to, especially if the cannibal came. Or rather, *when* the cannibal came because now, she was convinced he was here in these woods. There was a sense of danger in the air that felt like something more than just discomfort from the memories of the summer slaughter.

Noelle scooped up leaves from a pile next to her and dumped them over the bear trap. Carefully, she brushed them over until they were flat, yet hiding the metallic jowls of the contraption. The leaves were soggy from the snow that had fallen on them and melted from the sun, but they got the job done. Satisfied with how the beartrap was hidden, Noelle stood up from the crouch.

Gavin had been looking around, looking through the trees constantly as she'd been setting the last bear trap, but now that he saw her standing, he focused on her.

There was still a sliver of sunlight poking out from the horizon, but he'd turned on the flashlight in his hand on already.

"Done?" he asked. Then glanced over at the spot where the second beartrap lay underneath an inconspicuous pile of leaves. "Why so close to each other?"

Noelle shrugged. She didn't quite have an answer except that it felt right to keep these two traps about four feet from each other.

They'd set up six bear traps around the cabin. Two in front, two in the back, and a single one on the left and right sides of the cabin. They were placed about ten paces into the woods surrounding the cabin, in spots that Noelle hoped the cannibal would travel if he were approaching their cabin.

She wasn't sure if he would fall into any of them or if they would even damage him and hold him long enough, but she felt better having them set now.

"You think Tess has that coffee ready for us?" Gavin said, switching the flashlight from his right hand to his left hand, then back again. Its light flashed through the air.

"Hopefully." Noelle said, slapping her hands together to get rid of the dirt on her gloves from the leaves. "I could use a warm drink right about now."

Gavin nodded in agreement, then they started making their way to the front of the cabin. Twigs and pieces of acorns crunched underneath their boots.

"I don't know if I'm ready to go in there yet." Gavin said.

He said it like they'd been talking about it just a second ago. Noelle was thrown off for a second before she realized he was referring to the rec room. The room where the cannibal had left his little brother's severed head after chopping it off his body.

"You know, you don't have to go in there." Noelle said.

"I feel like I *do*, though." Gavin exhaled. His breath shot out in a big, white cloud. The sight made him want a cigarette. "Maybe partly for my own ego. But mostly because I feel like it would be disrespectful to my little brother not to."

"I thought you didn't believe in things like ghosts and the afterlife?"

They turned the corner and were at the front of the cabin. Through one of the windows, they could see someone moving about the living room. From the size of the outline, it looked like Mr. Olmos, but for a second, they both had this quavering feeling that it was the cannibal.

Of course, it wasn't him. There would be screaming and blood when the cannibal showed up, so they both turned back to the conversation at hand.

"I feel crazy for even being here. I don't know what the hell I believe anymore." Gavin said, then started up the short porch steps. "But I'd rather make my decision inside where it's warm."

Noelle followed. At the top of the steps, the feeling that they were being watched made her stop. It felt like someone had just breathed on the back of her neck. Noelle looked over her shoulder into the woods and searched as far as her eyes would let her, but she saw nothing. Nothing except the endless expanse of trees and a few spires of the last winks of sunlight piercing between their branches.

No cannibal. And if he was out there, hiding and waiting for his moment to strike, then so be it. She would be ready for him.

She hoped the others would be, too.

CHAPTER 42

Ignacio watched the two of them stop in front of the cabin. He recognized both of them. The girl's hair was different than it had been months ago. It wasn't silver-blond anymore, no. Her natural light brown hair had grown out, and now it looked more like highlight. But there was no doubt in his mind. It was the same girl who'd hit him with the ax.

The girl who was responsible for the scar right under his collarbone.

The guy she was with was the muscled-up guy Ignacio had almost killed with the chainsaw—the same one who'd smashed him over the head with a rock.

These two were the same people that had almost killed him back in the summer. That explained the bad dream he'd had earlier. And the persistent sense of danger he'd felt in the woods recently.

Ignacio licked his lips, feeling the roughness of his mask on his tongue as he did so.

He heard them talking in front of the cabin for a few seconds. Something about the guy not knowing what to believe anymore—whatever that meant—before the muscled-up guy headed up the wooden steps. The girl followed close behind him, then stopped at the top of the steps. She started turning her head to look behind her, in the direction of the tree Ignacio was standing behind.

Before she could see him, Ignacio ducked his head behind the tree. The fact that she didn't scream and he couldn't hear her approaching him told him she hadn't seen him. A few seconds later, he heard the cabin door close behind her.

Ignacio poked his head out from behind the trunk, just enough for him to see the cabin with his good eye. He tuned his hearing up as high as he could.

He would watch and listen… watch and listen as long as he needed to before it was time to strike.

The whole time, his hands would be itching to grab the machete from his back. But this was a different Ignacio. A more patient Ignacio.

And as he would come to find out, a more ruthless one, too.

CHAPTER 43

Gavin stopped in front of the rec room and took in a deep breath. Someone in their party had had the decency to close the door for him. Either that, or they'd all had the decency to have not opened it. Whatever the truth was, he was grateful the room wasn't wide-open.

He needed a second to collect himself.

Gavin grabbed the knob and twisted it. He pushed the door open, waiting for the stench of death to fill his nostrils. Instead, what he got was a blast of lemon-scented cleaner. Gavin stared into the room where his little brother had died.

But it was nothing like it'd been that day. There wasn't any blood anywhere. In fact, there weren't even traces of blood whatsoever. The room was as neat as could be.

On the ping-pong table, the balls were lined up against the net. The paddles were beside them, their handles neatly crisscrossing one another. Similarly, the balls on the pool table were placed in the triangle, and the sticks were leaning against the edge of it as if waiting for someone to pick them up for a game.

The entertainment stand in the corner had gotten an upgrade on both the television and the console. Instead of an old school tube television, there was a 55" HDTV in its place.

And instead of the Super Nintendo Entertainment System, there was a Nintendo Switch and two controllers in the cubby underneath the television.

On the wall, near the window where his little brother's head had been lying, was a poster of *The Fifth Element* starring Bruce Willis. There were other posters that hadn't been there before too. A poster with Samus Aran, a *Batman Returns* poster, and a *Stranger Things* one were the three that caught his eye. It seemed they'd decorated the place to try to make it look more "fun," and something about this made Gavin's stomach turn sour. Because there was no doubt in his mind the same person who'd updated the place knew about his little brother's death.

And Brooke's cousin's death, too.

Gavin took two steps into the rec room. To his surprise, there wasn't any sadness. Only disgust that was beginning to turn into anger. He could feel his blood beginning to boil, his ears getting hot.

Staring at the spot where his little brother's head had been, his stupid shaggy hair drenched in blood and flailed out on the floor like a mop top, he knew he'd made the right decision to come out here.

He realized that Noelle had been right about everything, more than ever now.

The only way they were going to get over this was seeing the cannibal dead. Whether it was by his hand or Noelle's or Mr. Olmos's made no difference to him.

But he hoped that the kill shot would be his.

CHAPTER 44

Tess and Noelle were in the kitchen. Tess sat the table, Noelle's laptop in front of her. The glow of the screen was reflecting off her glasses, the file names scrolled past her eyes as Tess moved through the page.

Noelle was standing next to her, arms crossed, looking at the screen. She wasn't as fascinated by the files because she'd had possession of them for a while now, but she knew she must've had a similar expression as the one Tess had on her face the first time she'd logged into Emeril Dantes's Google account.

Noelle had downloaded every single file in the man's account to her laptop and saved them into a folder that she was showing Tess. The files were mostly footage Molly had captured, but there were also notes on the overarching story of the documentary and a boatload of information on Camp Slaughter and the theories surrounding it.

"And I can… I can have all of these?" Tess said, looking up at Noelle. Her eyes were wide behind her frameless glasses. Wild almost. Like someone who'd been starving stumbling across a feast.

"All yours." Noelle said. "You just have to find a way to get them to yourself."

"I have a thumb drive in my bag." Tess said, flicking her eyes back to the screen, as if not doing this would cause them to disappear. Then she reached down for the bag resting against one of the tables and unzipped a side pocket. "Did you watch all of the footage?"

"I watched none of it." Noelle said. "I only looked through the text files."

"I see." Tess said, reaching for the bag of lollipops sitting next to the laptop. She grabbed a mango one, unwrapped it, and shoved it into her mouth. "How'd you get access to his Google account?"

"That, the world may never know." Noelle said, grinning. She started heading out of the kitchen. "Where's Eli?"

"He's outside. Said he got hungry, so he started cooking up some sausages for everyone."

Noelle checked the time. It was pushing 4:30 p.m. The sun was all but down at this point. Nighttime would bring another element of danger to this whole ordeal, but if they were close to each other, it was OK to split up while at the cabin. It was when they would wander out of the cabin that they would need to stay in pairs.

Besides, the way the cabin was built, the porch was just outside the kitchen windows. If anything happened, Tess would hear it. Or vice-versa. At least, Noelle hoped so.

"Alright. Do me a favor?" Noelle said, stopping at the doorway.

"Yeah?" Tess turned to face her. Noelle could see it on her face that she really wanted to get to these files.

"Can you check up on Eli every fifteen minutes or so?"

"Sure." Tess said, getting up. She went over to the window that overlooked the porch. Eli had his back to her, but she saw him grilling away in a cloud of smoke. She turned to Noelle and gave her a thumbs up.

"Great. Thanks." Noelle said. "I'm going to go see what Gav and Mr. Olmos are up to. I'll be back, hopefully shortly."

CHAPTER 45

Darkness surrounded the cabin. But inside, the lights on. Ignacio knew the cabin well enough to know which rooms were lit. The bathroom upstairs, the living room, the kitchen, and one of the bedrooms.

Ignacio stood behind the same tree, still watching the movement inside the cabin. There was activity in all the rooms except the living room and the kitchen, but he could hear the heartbeat of someone inside the kitchen.

The person in there wasn't moving, but their heart was beating fast from some excitement that whatever activity they were doing was bringing them. The other heartbeats inside the cabin were normal. They were relaxed. Their defenses down.

It was time to strike. Not a full-on slaughter, but it was time for at least one kill.

There was a guy outside by himself. On the porch, wearing bright white shoes with bright purple on them and a sweatshirt with various colors on it. Clothing that would make him easy to hunt down even in the darkened woods. Under the porchlights, though, he may as well have been begging Ignacio to kill him.

"You're going to have to make it quick." Papá's ghost said, appearing next to Ignacio. He was looking out at the unsuspecting kid with the colorful clothing, index finger on his chin. "Quick and silent."

"But painful." Ignacio responded.

He unstrapped the chainsaw from his back. He didn't need it at this moment, and it would only slow him down some and possibly make too much noise by clattering against his body. He set it on the ground and instead reached for the knife in his back pocket.

"I like how you think, mijo." Papá said, a smile across his face.

Ignacio crouched down and started moving through the trees, trying to find the best angle to approach from.

Eli was as high as the Hubble telescope. He'd smoked a bowl in the upstairs bathroom because now that they were here, he was terrified. He'd underestimated just how damn *dark* the woods would get, how damn claustrophobic the isolation would be.

Even still, the weed had made him hungry. And no one was taking the initiative to cook up food, so he'd taken Tess's camping grill and set it up on the small picnic table on the porch to cook up sausages and burgers for everyone.

His stoned mind was wandering at the moment, making him forget to watch the food. The burgers and sausages were beginning to burn as he gazed out at Tess's bus.

It was parked only a few paces away. All he had to do was go inside, grab the keys from Tess's jacket hanging on the coatrack by the door, and he could drive home.

But first, he'd have to drive into the woods…into the darkness.

Eli's glazed eyes fixated on the near pitch-blackness past the cabin's outside lights. The trees and bushes were nothing more than amorphous shapes in the distance, moving about as the wind rustled them together. Their bare branches clattered together. There was a certain hypnotism to it, like Mother Nature herself was trying to talk to him. Like the wind was whispering a warning to him while the branches were screaming at him to run.

Run, Eli! Run! He smiled at the absurdity of this, and his smile grew bigger when he realized his new weed guy had the best shit he'd ever smoked.

Then, the smell of burning meat hit his nostrils and ruined his mood.

"Ah, fuck!" Eli scrambled to grab the tongs and piece of tinfoil from the box sitting behind the grill.

Using the tongs, he placed the burned-up hamburgers and sausages in the tinfoil and set them out. He rolled them around, slowly to inspect them, to see if they were salvageable or not.

An admirable thing to do, but it would be the last good deed Eli would ever do.

Ignacio saw the kid's eyes were focused the food he'd put on the tinfoil. He was using the tongs to roll one of the burned sausages over and over, as if this motion would make it less burned.

His movements were slow. Like he was underwater, or like his muscles were weak from lifting heavy objects all day. The physical act of killing him was going to be easy; the tricky part would be making sure he could be quiet about it.

Ignacio readied the knife. He'd made his way out of the trees and was crouched behind the blue Jeep, only a few paces away from the porch. Ignacio estimated he could clear the steps and be on the guy in a matter of seconds even going slowly. The problem was there was plenty of light between the vehicle and the cabin, and he would need luck that no one would be peering out of the windows.

He did a quick sweep of the windows in his view. No one was currently at them at all. That was good.

It was time to move.

Staying crouched, Ignacio stepped from behind the Jeep and started cutting across the gravel driveway. Stepping slowly and quietly. The pebbles shifted slightly underneath his boot with each step, but the movement was subtle enough that the kid on the porch was unaware of Ignacio approaching.

Ignacio made it to the bottom of the porch steps, then in one big motion planted his right foot at the top of the steps. The wood creaked underneath his weight, but the boy was muttering to himself and didn't notice it.

Ignacio brought his other foot up to the top step, but this one he could step lighter with since his other foot was set in a solid position.

He was on the porch now. The guy to his side, still staring at the food and mumbling at it, almost as if he was having an argument with the food. His glazed eyes were glued to the burger he was holding with the tongs. He smiled at it and then brought the burger up to his face.

Ignacio saw him opening his mouth and saw this as his signal to attack. He sprung out of the crouch and took a light half step toward the kid. He used one hand to slap the tongs and burger out of his hand, then quickly clapped it over his mouth to keep him from screaming. The burger and the tongs went flying over the porch railing and landed somewhere in the grass a few feet away.

Meanwhile, Ignacio used his other hand to drive the knife into the back of his thigh. The kid's knees buckled from the sudden pain, and Ignacio used the hand over his mouth to bring him closer. Then he switched that arm lower and put him in a chokehold. He flexed his bicep, pinching the kid's windpipe closed.

Using brute strength, Ignacio lifted him up into the air so he couldn't stomp his feet to make noise, effectively tightening the choke at the same time. The kid flailed his arms, alternating between trying to find Ignacio's eyes (or rather, eye) to rake them and scratching at his arms, but it was futile.

Ignacio felt the boy's body getting weaker and weaker with each passing second. His struggles becoming more and more fruitless, until finally, his body went limp.

Ignacio eased him down onto the ground. The kid wasn't dead. He could still hear his heart beating, ever so slowly, but it was present.

This was good. Ignacio wanted him to be alive. He needed him to scream. Just not yet.

Not until Ignacio had the chance to get into position.

CHAPTER 46

Tess had opened a video file—the last one Molly had ever recorded and uploaded into their shared Google Drive.

It was them driving. Judging from what she could tell through the car windows, Tess figured they were on their trek up into the northern parts of Pennsylvania.

The camera was focused on Emeril, who was at the wheel. A lush hill with a herd of cows and a massive mill rolled past the window behind him.

"*We're about three hours from the supposed location of Camp Slaughter,*" Molly said to the audience. "*Tell everyone how you're feeling, Emeril.*"

Emeril shifted uncomfortably in the seat, glanced over at the camera, and gave it a slight frown. "*Feeling like a million bucks.*"

"*We'll make a million bucks if we find this place and capture it on film. That's for sure.*"

Just as Tess let out a small laugh at Molly's retort, a few feet away, unbeknownst to her, Eli went limp in the cannibal's chokehold. It didn't matter that Tess had the volume set so low that she could barely hear it, Varias Caras's ambush had been that much quieter.

Oblivious that her friend needed help, Tess continued to watch the video of Molly and Emeril driving into the very same woods she was in now.

Noelle didn't hear anything either. She was upstairs, captivated by the darkness beyond the cabin. It looked as if, in the last hour or so, the endless woods back there had been replaced by an endless blackness. As if an abyss had swallowed the entire world around the cabin.

Really, though, she knew what she was staring at was the shadows of the woods she'd run into like a coward when she'd left Dalton and Wayne to fend for themselves.

Guilt tried to work its way into her. Guilt that wasn't just about Dalton and Wayne. No, she was starting to feel guilty for bringing everyone here because now she was letting herself accept the whole truth of why she'd brought them.

She didn't *actually* care about Mr. Olmos avenging his daughter's death. She didn't care about Gavin getting another chance to kill the cannibal. She didn't care about Eli's maps or Tess's documentary.

She'd brought those people with her because the more bodies there were, the better chance she had at killing the cannibal.

Strength in numbers and all that. Noelle thought.

Really, though, it was more like the bigger the group, was the more protected she was.

Noelle brushed the guilt away. This was no time for any sign of weakness. Afterward, if she lived through this, she would allow herself to feel whatever she needed to feel. But right now, there was no time for that.

Right now, she had to be as cold-hearted as possible. The mission was the only thing that mattered.

Noelle touched the butt of the gun holstered to her hip just to make sure it was still there and moved away from the window.

In the place where one felt their gut instincts, she felt the cannibal was out there. Which meant all her energy had to be focused on one thing: murder.

CHAPTER 47

ELI WOKE UP to the world being upside down. Upside down and wobbling left and right. The disorientation made him want to vomit.

There was a terrible throbbing pain in the back of one of his thighs, and his pants were wet like he'd somehow pissed out of his ass.

What the hell? Where the hell?

Eli looked down, which was actually up, and by the moonlight coming in through the trees, he saw both his feet were tied together with a belt that had then been wound around and tied to a tree branch.

The belt was studded with bottlecaps of different beers, easily distinguishable as his own. Someone had taken his belt off and tied him upside down from a tree. Eli squirmed, realizing his arms were bound to his torso by a thin rope or a cord or—his eyes went back to his feet, and he saw the laces on his Osiris shoes were missing.

"Wakey, wakey…" Someone that was outside of his view spoke. The voice was somehow gruff and somehow high-pitched at the same time.

Eli saw the cannibal come into his view. He was as massive as the myths on the internet had described him, built like a fucking refrigerator. He was holding a lantern in his hand and wore a dark reddish-brown mask over his face. A color that made Eli think of the way blood dried on a paper towel. There was only one eyehole on the mask, and the dark eye behind it stared at him. It made Eli feel like he was transparent, made him feel like the cannibal was staring right into his soul.

The moment was so terrifying, Eli couldn't even bring himself to scream.

"You are afraid…" The cannibal said, setting the lantern down on the ground. "But you are not screaming yet."

Eli's head felt heavy with the blood, a combination from hanging upside down and the sudden surge of adrenaline. He started thrashing against his constraints again, but his brain still couldn't send the signal to make him scream—it was overloaded.

The cannibal reached for his back pocket, pulling out a hunting knife covered in coagulated blood.

"You will scream now." The cannibal said, holding the knife horizontal and aiming it at Eli's lower body.

The point of the knife was way too close to his balls, and this did the trick.

"NO! PLEASE!" Eli screamed and then tried even harder to burst out of the laces.

But it did him no good. There was no give, not even the slightest hint of a budge, the laces were bound too tight around his body. He was a sitting duck—hanging duck, if you will—and had no option but to accept what was to come.

More than likely, it was death. Somewhere in his frenzied, panicked mind, Eli was sure of his fate. Given enough time, and the proper mental acuity, he would've debated whether seeing Camp Slaughter was worth being in this position.

He had neither of those, though, as he hung from the branch by his ankles like a chicken carcass at the window of a meat shop. His mind was flooded with sheer panic and fear.

The cannibal cocked his arm back and stabbed the knife into Eli's thigh. Blood spurted out from the wound as the blade gashed several veins open. Eli felt the cannibal pull the knife out and then stab it into him again.

And then he did it again, and again, and again.

Meanwhile, Eli's screams and the cannibal's maniacal laughter resonated through the trees like a macabre song playing in the dark woods.

CHAPTER 48

They met in the upstairs hallway just outside of the rooms. Mr. Olmos slapped the light switch that turned the single ceiling panel on. Noelle and Mr. Olmos stared at one another.

"You heard that, too? I'm not imagining things, am I?" Mr. Olmos asked. Noelle couldn't help but notice that his lips quivered as he spoke.

The question was rhetorical, of course, but Noelle answered anyway. She shook her head. "Those were definitely screams."

Another scream pierced the night. This one was the last pained howl produced by a dying being.

Noelle gulped.

"It's not an animal." Mr. Olmos said.

"No." Noelle agreed. Something about the emotion behind the harrowing sound solidified this in her mind as well.

"I'm going to get dressed. You find out where everyone else is." Mr. Olmos said.

Noelle hadn't noticed until now that Mr. Olmos was standing in only a red t-shirt and boxers. His hair drenched, and parts of his shirt were soaked from when he'd thrown it over his head as he'd rushed out of the shower.

"On it." Noelle said, pivoting to face the stairwell.

Tess was at the bottom of the stairwell, staring out at the open cabin door. The darkened woods beyond the cabin never looked more dangerous. Cold wind from outside whipped through the cabin, making the curtains on the windows flutter.

"I'm scared, Noelle." Tess said, looking up at Noelle as she raced down the stairs two steps at a time.

Noelle was at her side within seconds, gun drawn, safety taken off. "Where're Eli and Gavin?"

"Gavin ran out the door." Tess said, grabbing onto Noelle's arm and pulling it close to her. "I—I don't know what happened to Eli—Tell me everything will be okay, Noelle. Please."

Noelle felt Tess bury her head on her shoulder and begin to cry. Noelle's emotions remained steadfast, though. She took a few steps forward and yanked her arm away from Tess's hold.

"Tess, I need you to stay put." Noelle said. "Mr. Olmos will be right down—"

"What's going on?" he asked, standing on the last step.

He'd thrown on a brown flannel, a pair of jeans, and work boots. His rifle was strapped around his shoulders, and a pistol hung from his hip. He stared out at the open cabin door as he waited for an answer.

"Eli's missing and Gavin ran out." Noelle informed him.

"That was Eli screaming, then." Mr. Olmos said.

"Yeah, I think so."

"No!" Tess screamed and threw herself onto the ground, head hanging low. "No, no, no. We weren't supposed to be in danger, we were only here to make the stupid movie…"

The end of her sentence trailed off, turning into full on sobbing as she buried her face in her hands.

"I'm taking her out of here." Mr. Olmos said, looking down at Tess.

Noelle nodded. "I'm going out there to find Gavin. Take her bus."

Mr. Olmos nodded, then both ran over to the coat rack to put on their coats.

Noelle threw on a black neck gaiter, a pair of leather gloves and then she was out the door with her pistol in hand. She raised the gaiter up above her nose, ready for the cold. More importantly, though, she was ready for this next confrontation with the cannibal.

Because now, after hearing those screams, there was no doubt. Varias Caras was out there somewhere, with murder on his mind, too.

CHAPTER 49

The age disparity between Gavin and his little brother made it difficult to have very many serious conversations with Wayne, but there was one that always stood out to Gavin. It'd been after Gavin had flipped off a guy that cut them off when they were driving back from GameStop (their parents had preordered the latest *Call of Duty* for his little brother).

The guy in the pickup had seen the middle finger and switched back to the lane next to them. He'd rolled down the window and jutted his index finger over to the side of the road, daring Gavin to pull over, presumably to get into a fistfight with him.

Gavin had rolled down the window and yelled, "OK, let's do it asshole." Then he'd promptly cut the guy off and pulled off onto the shoulder. The guy drove his pickup truck onto the shoulder as well, but when he saw Gavin get out of the car, with the sleeves of his baseball tee rolled up, ready to fight, the guy got cold feet and drove off. He flipped Gavin off as he drove past, and Gavin returned the gesture with two middle fingers of his own and called him a "pussy."

After that, Gavin slid back into his car. Wayne was in the passenger seat, holding onto the video game case with his mouth agape, staring at Gavin like he was Superman. Gavin looked at him and said, "What?"

Wayne had asked him how he was always so confident and was never scared of anyone. Gavin sat back in the seat, thinking about how to answer that.

Because the truth was, he *was* scared. He just didn't realize it until the moment had passed. He'd been scared that the guy would pull over and shoot him or stab him or even just kick his ass in front of Wayne. But his brashness and anger always overshadowed the fear.

That was the truth, too, as Gavin ran through the woods in the direction of where he thought the screams had been coming from. He held the flashlight on an angle in one hand, shining the ground ahead of him. In his other hand, he held the gun pointed in front of him.

Up ahead, several feet through some trees, he saw the glow of a lantern hanging from a tree branch. He knew this was bait. Knew the cannibal was using Eli's screams as bait, too, but Gavin didn't care.

He knew that at the end of the bait he'd find the cannibal, and he was ready to end this motherfucker. Even though he'd have the jump on him because he was walking right into the cannibal's trap, he had the handgun. One properly placed bullet was all he would need to get the advantage.

And this time, he wouldn't run away. This time, he was going to end things for good.

Gavin got to where the lantern was hanging. At the edge of its glow, which was nothing more than about a three-foot radius, he saw a lump on the ground in the shadows. He shined his flashlight beam on it and saw it was a wide skateboarding shoe that had no laces and was smeared with blood.

Gavin moved the beam along the ground, past the shoe, and saw the leg attached to it. He continued shining the light over it and then the leg ended. At the end, where the shin had once been attached to the knee, was a large wound that was pumping out blood all over the ground.

It was like seeing the blood made his olfactory senses pick up on the scent because now all he could smell was the coppery stench of blood. Gavin felt his stomach turn sour.

And then he realized that the bait had worked better than he thought it would because the sight of the severed leg had caused him to lower his gun and lower his defenses. Behind him, he heard something clattered through them like something had just fallen from one of the higher branches.

Gavin whirled around, gun aimed and finger on the trigger, ready to shoot at anything that moved whether it was a cannibal or a fucking racoon. He shined the light all over the trees in that direction and saw nothing, only their branches moving from the wind.

"Over here, idiota!" The cannibal screamed from behind him.

Gavin whirled back around in the direction he'd been facing, but before he could find the cannibal with his light and fire off his gun, Varias Caras was barreling toward him.

The cannibal lowered his stance, then crashed his shoulder into Gavin's midsection. One of his lower ribs shattered on impact. The pain was so sudden and excruciating that it forced him to drop the gun and the flashlight.

Varias Caras continued to drive him backward; the momentum seemed unstoppable. As strong as Gavin was, the cannibal possessed a superhuman strength. Out of pure instinct, Gavin smashed one of his elbows into the back of the cannibal's head. It was like striking a bowling ball, though, and did nothing to stop the cannibal's momentum.

Gavin crashed against the tree trunk, pinned between it and the cannibal. Gavin raised his arm to drop another elbow, but by the time he brought it down, Varias Caras had already taken a half-step back.

Worse, though, Gavin saw him take out a knife from his back pocket in a fluid motion.

Varias Caras drove the front of the knife through Gavin's chest. The blade pierced right into his heart.

With one of his last breaths, Gavin threw a haymaker at the cannibal's face, aiming for the exposed eye. Varias Caras was too quick, though, and ducked under it. At the same time, he pulled the knife out and stabbed him in the chest again. A new wound opened near the first one.

Blood flowed out from both wounds, and Gavin's weakening body slumped forward. He tried throwing another punch, but with his life quickly escaping him, by the time it struck Varias Caras, it was more like a weak push with his hand.

Varias Caras took the knife out once more, using his other hand to keep Gavin standing, then stabbed him in the chest again. Just for good measure he twisted the knife, turning all of the stabs into one giant gash.

Varias Caras pulled the machete out one last time and let Gavin drop to the ground, now a lifeless corpse.

As much as Varias Caras wanted to take a second to admire the dead body, there wasn't much time. He could hear the footsteps of another person running into the woods. Behind that, closer to the cabin, he heard vehicle doors opening and closing. Then, the sound of an engine starting up.

It seemed at least one person was planning to escape. But tonight, Varias Caras wouldn't let there be any survivors.

CHAPTER 50

Someway, somehow, Tess had managed to find her composure and get her coat and winter accessories on. She was in the passenger seat of her VW Bus now, which felt strange. She'd never been inside the vehicle in this seat; it felt a bit like when you accidentally put your foot into the wrong shoe.

"Stay close to me at all times." Mr. Olmos said, shoving his key into the ignition. "And if I tell you to run, you run like hell. You understand me?"

Tess nodded.

"We'll make it out of this alive, honey." He said, reaching out and rustling the top of her hair. "You just have to stay strong until it's safe, OK?"

"OK," Tess said, feeling younger than she ever did.

Mr. Olmos fired on the engine and then began reversing the bus out of the gravel driveway. Once they'd cleared Noelle's Jeep, he U-turned and headed down the narrow road leading into the woods.

Tess watched the cabin get smaller and smaller in the passenger side mirror. The cabin sat in the yellow glow of the outside lights. In their haste, they'd left the door open, and Tess could see the living room, sitting still. The glow from the flames in the fireplace, which Tess herself had lit, made the lighting in the room appear to be flickering, as if at any moment the room might disappear like an apparition.

Tess looked away, the skin on her arms and neck raised into gooseflesh. She never wanted to return to this place, and as this thought hit her, she realized just how valiant Noelle truly was.

The VW Bus entered the woods just as snow began to fall from the sky. It made Tess feel like they were entering a void.

Mr. Olmos turned on the high beams, but that did nothing to alleviate her nerves.

CHAPTER 51

Noelle found the spot the same way Gavin had, by seeing the glow of the lantern, which was still hanging from the tree branch.

The first thing the flashlight fixed atop of her pistol shined on was Gavin's body. He was face down, head turned away from Noelle, but she knew he was dead. A copious amount of blood had leaked out of his body and was pooling all around him.

Noelle walked closer to him. The snow was coming down heavy now, and she walked through a curtain of frozen flakes that left their icy touch on the parts of her face that the neck gaiter left exposed.

Noelle got to Gavin's side and crouched down, feeling a surge of loneliness strike through her. The person who'd been by her side during her first encounter with the cannibal was now dead.

The cannibal wasn't around this space anymore. Noelle wasn't sure how she knew this, but she did. It was as if he'd only left behind the stench of death and then went elsewhere into the woods. It was like she could feel him waiting for her somewhere deeper in the darkness.

She allowed herself to drop her defenses for a brief moment to mourn Gavin Briggs's death.

"Rest in peace, my friend." Noelle said, patting him on the shoulder.

Even in death, Gavin felt as solid as a slab of concrete. It reminded her just what she was up against that even someone as strong as Gavin had been slain by the cannibal. It reminded her that she was going to need to be on her A-game for the second confrontation with Varias Caras.

But more importantly, it motivated her.

Noelle rose, then turned around, sweeping the light over the rest of this area in the woods. She found the same severed leg that Gavin had. The leg had been chopped off the body and the bone broken off the rest of the body, but the Osiris shoe told Noelle it'd belonged to Eli. Likely, Eli was chopped up in pieces somewhere in the woods.

Which meant only three of them remained alive.

Noelle wasn't sure what to do next. As far as she could tell, there wasn't anything hinting at where the cannibal might be. He may very well have gone back to the campgrounds to regroup.

Maybe I should start there. Noelle thought, reaching for the printed-out map she had stashed in the pocket of her jacket that would lead her back to Camp Slaughter.

But as her fingers grasped the piece of paper, she stopped. Because somewhere in the short distance, she heard a chainsaw revving.

Her defenses went back up. Noelle pivoted on the balls of her feet, gun aimed in front of her, waiting for the cannibal to come out of the trees in an attempt to ambush her.

To her surprise, though, the sound of the chainsaw's motor started getting fainter. The cannibal was moving *away* from her, gunning elsewhere.

Gunning for the VW Bus, no doubt. The cannibal's sight was set on Tess and Mr. Olmos, which meant he would be distracted.

If she was going to kill him, she needed to take any opportunity presented to her. Clutching the gun tight, and pushing away the sadness of seeing Gavin dead, Noelle sprinted through the woods, trailing the sound of the chainsaw.

CHAPTER 52

IGNACIO CAME CHARGING out of the woods, chainsaw revving over his head, and stopped at the side of the road. The VW Bus was barreling up the road, only a few feet away, coming perpendicular toward him. It wasn't far away enough for him to hop out and scare the driver into hitting the brakes, which had been his original plan, but there was enough distance that Ignacio still had time to disrupt their getaway.

He squeezed down on the button to give the chainsaw a good boost of juice, the motor let out a roar; the chain began spinning faster around the blade. Ignacio pulled his arms back and waited for the VW Bus to pass him.

His aim was going to have to be perfect in order for this to work. It was going to be difficult, but he knew he could do it even with one eye. All his senses were firing at a different level now that he had control of el Monstro. His body and mind were in perfect synchronization.

The bus came within touching distance. Ignacio launched the chainsaw at it. It flipped through the air before the motor smashed through the passenger window. That was all he saw for now because the VW Bus continued up the road, whizzing past him. Ignacio had been so close to the vehicle the wind from it rushing past him sent his hair back.

He watched the VW Bus fishtail as the brakes were slammed on and the driver attempted to keep the vehicle from running off the road. It was going to come to a stop one way or another, though, which meant the plan had worked.

Ignacio grabbed his knife from his back pocket and sprinted toward the bus.

The chainsaw had gone through the passenger window, spinning through the air as the engine continued to rumble. By some miracle, it missed Tess entirely, but Greg wasn't so lucky. The chainsaw landed on top of his right thigh with such force and on the perfect angle that some of the teeth bit into his leg.

Blood squirted out from the wound like a drinking fountain. Greg screamed and stepped on the brake pedal even harder. At the same time, he took one hand off the wheel and grabbed the chainsaw by the handle and pulled it out of his leg. With the wound exposed, more blood jetted out from his leg. It splattered all over his lap, the center console, the face of the radio, and even reached all the way up onto the dashboard.

He tossed the chainsaw into the back of the vehicle. Meanwhile, the bus started fishtailing on the inch of snow covering the road. Greg brought back his other hand, which was covered in blood now, back onto the steering wheel. Using his injured leg, he pumped on the brakes. Each stomp sent a hot flash of pain through his leg and caused more blood to squirt out, but he knew if they crashed, this would get much, much worse.

The VW Bus came to a stop, just short of smashing into a tree. Greg took a second to recompose himself. He closed his eyes and squeezed the steering wheel. Next to him, Tess was crying her eyes out.

Greg inhaled, realizing that he was about to go another round with the cannibal. This was his second chance to avenge his daughter's death.

"Run!" He screamed.

Tess recoiled from him yelling but then complied. She pulled the silver lock pin upward and flung the bus door open. She hopped out of the vehicle and turned to look at Greg. Her cheeks were streaked wet with tears and her eyes were full of horror.

"Go!" Greg said, waving his bloody hand through the air. "Get away."

Tess let out a small sob, then darted out into the darkness.

He watched her disappear into the trees. She was faster than she looked, and he hoped that her quickness would discourage the cannibal from chasing her.

Greg undid his seatbelt, then reached into the back for his rifle that was laying on the long seat behind the driver seat. He strapped it around his shoulders, then unlocked the car door and pushed it open. Dragging his injured leg behind him, he climbed out.

"Come on, motherfucker! Come after me!" he screamed, pointing the rifle in front of him. Ready to blast a round at the sight of Varias Caras. "Show your face, you goddamn coward!"

As much as he was trying to entice the cannibal, he knew this was mostly posturing. He was starting to feel woozy from the blood loss, and the weight of the rifle wasn't helping matters. Each step he took, he could feel more blood oozing out. His right pantleg was soaked and hot, yet the cold temperature was drying the blood fast at the same time. The feeling was disgusting and uncomfortable in a way Greg had never felt before.

To his right, he heard footsteps crunching in the snow. Greg whirled that way, finger on the trigger, and waited. He could see a shadow cast from the full moon's light casting down on the snow. The shadows of the trees made it difficult to tell what size the person was or even what shape the person was.

If it was a person. For a split-second, perhaps a thought caused by the deliriousness of the blood loss, he wondered if maybe the cannibal was actually a demon and he'd reverted back into his true form.

Then, out the corner, from behind the bus, Tess stepped out, holding the katana in her hand.

"Mr. Olmos!" Tess screamed, pointing into the shadows of the trees to his left.

Greg pivoted on his feet, the wound on his leg making it a jerky motion, and saw the cannibal's dark red mask, a single eye peering back from behind it. He was crouched down like a snake coiled up to pounce on its prey, a knife covered in blood in one hand.

Greg moved the rifle, intending to aim it at his face. The weapon felt heavier than ever, like he was trying to move a free weight in an awkward motion. He had his trigger on the finger, but by the time he had the barrel lined up with where the cannibal had been, he was gone.

He'd jumped back into the shadows.

"Fuck," Greg muttered.

Ice water shot through his veins. It wasn't fear of the cannibal, exactly. But the fear of failure.

Fear that he was going to fail Sharon. Fail Judy. Fail all of Hilltown.

Again.

The old man shot his rifle into the darkness, bullets scattering through the woods, hitting nothing but air because Ignacio was ducked behind a tree several feet away. The flash from the nozzle lit the old man's face up as the bullets fired into the empty air. An expression of panic and terror covered his sweaty, pale face.

The effect of seeing the man firing the rifle in the darkness of the woods was like watching someone underneath a flicker light. On. Off. On. Off. Except, in the intermittent, there were loud bangs.

Bangs that rang through the woods, sending the nocturnal wildlife scattering about. The only beings left in the vicinity were the ones about to engage in a fight to the death.

The shots ceased. The last bang of the rifle echoed through the woods for a few seconds that felt longer and then silence blanketed the night once again. Darkness, too.

In the distance, he could hear two sets of footsteps. One running toward this area, the other running away from it. He could guess which was which, but right now, he wasn't worried about either of them.

Right now, his target was set on the old man.

He could hear him breathing heavy. Could hear his heart thumping in his chest. He started moving away from the vehicle as he reloaded his rifle, probably to inspect the area and see if he killed Ignacio. The snow crunching underneath his feet.

Even though it was dark, enough moonlight was seeping down through the leafless treetops that he could make out the old man's outline, and saw he was moving with a limp. The sight energized Ignacio, like a shark smelling blood.

Staying crouched, and stepping as lightly as he could, Ignacio approached him. With the direction they were moving, Ignacio would end up behind him if he walked in a straight line.

"Come out, you coward!" the old man taunted.

Ignacio clapped his hand over his mouth to stifle his giggle. He was pretending to be strong and brave, but Ignacio knew the truth. The old man was scared and hurt.

Still moving silently, Ignacio moved quicker toward him, itching to kill once again.

Greg felt something slide across the back of his neck, something cold. Maybe it was just the wind, or maybe it was that some sixth sense had activated, but either way, the feeling was there. It was like something was tipping him off that there was danger behind him.

He whirled around, raising the rifle at the same time, but there wasn't anything. All he could see were dead trees and snow coming down from the sky. The bus was a few feet away, but through the curtain of thick snowflakes and the ever-present danger, it never looked more distant.

"I know you're hiding, coward. Come out, and let's do this. You owe me." Greg taunted, sweeping the rifle left and right, waiting for any movement.

To his left, he saw some bushes moving. Without thinking, he fired two rounds in that direction, and waited. Waited to hear the cannibal screaming in pain. But nothing. There was only silence.

Silence and that feeling of being in danger.

He exhaled, both because he'd been holding his breath and out of frustration. His breath came out a thick, white cloud into the cold night.

To his right now, he heard something clattering. Like something falling out of a tree. A walnut or an acorn, or maybe the snow had been too heavy for a damaged branch.

Or maybe it's a trick. He thought, but even still, he turned in that direction and fired off two rounds. They were wild, scattered shots that would've been lucky to hit the cannibal.

The hairs on the back of his neck pricked up again—that same coldness that had touched him before slithered across his skin.

"Peek-a-boo! Behind you!" the voice was high-pitched and seemed to slice through the night like a needle.

As he turned around, finger on the trigger, ready to squeeze it, Greg felt a hot flash of pain at his side as the knife went into his abdomen.

The pain made his grip slip on the rifle. The strap kept it close to him, but even still, he knew he was at a disadvantage and could feel his chances at survival slipping away.

His chances of avenging Judy's death were slipping, too.

Ignacio grabbed the rifle from the nozzle and butt and smashed it into the man's face. There was a loud crack, like a piece of lumber being snapped in half, as Greg's nose shattered.

The man fell onto his back, still holding onto the rifle. Ignacio held onto the rifle, too, and fell with him. He collapsed on top of him, belly first, and crushed him with his weight. The man wheezed out as his lungs were deflated of all their air, and Varias Caras pulled the rifle out of his hand.

Ignacio moved the rifle up toward the man's head until the strap was up on his neck, then jumped off over his head. From this position, the strap was synched tight around the old man's neck, but there was still a bit of slack, so Ignacio turned the rifle, making the strap loop around itself and tighten up against the man's throat.

Feeling this, the old man fought harder. He reached for the holster on his hip, but the pistol wasn't there. Ignacio had already taken it out when he stabbed him and thrown it in the woods. His hands went back up to the strap, using his bloody fingers, he tried to find some space in the leash to give himself breathing room. But there was none. The strap was way too tight.

Ignacio pulled on the rifle, dragging the old man through the snow. The blood from his wounds left a wake of red in the trench in the snow his body made. Ignacio stopped in front of a tree.

There was a hefty branch about six feet off the ground that looked useful for what Ignacio had in mind. Ignacio threw the rifle over the branch, creating a pulley system with the weapon, the strap, and his victim.

He walked over to the other side of the branch and pulled on the rifle as hard as he could. The old man's body was lifted off the ground with such force that the strap snapped his neck. The sound of the bone breaking reverberated through the woods.

Ignacio watched the man's head lull to the left, then forward. The head and part of the spine completely detached from the rest of the body's skeleton.

Ignacio let the rifle go. The weight of the corpse at the other end of the pulley-system caused it to go flying up toward the branch, but the weapon got caught on this side, leaving the dead body dangling from the tree. Blood that had run down from the gash in his thigh was dripping down the front of his boot, splashing onto the disturbed snow below.

Ignacio walked around to the other side to admire his work. He poked the man's head up with one finger to see what his face had looked like moments before his death. It'd started to turn purple from the lack of oxygen, and there was an expression of desperation on it. There were tears in his eyes, too.

And for some reason, seeing these made him realize he recognized this face. He had a salt-and-pepper beard that was drenched in blood instead of a clean-shaven face, but this was the cop with the big hat who'd come talk to him back at the town. The one who'd shot at him in the junkyard, and Ignacio had let live because he'd been hurt at the time.

It was Judy's father. He'd come to kill Ignacio because of what he did to Judy.

Ignacio would've laughed if it weren't for the fact that he could hear a set of steps getting closer and closer to where he was. He had to stay focused.

Now, more than ever, he knew Papá was right. They'd come to kill him.

The other one had run away, but there was still one more coming to hunt him.

It was time to fight for his life. Ignacio pulled the knife out of the old man's stomach, then headed for a group of trees to hide behind.

CHAPTER 53

Noelle saw Mr. Olmos's body dangling from the tree at the end of her flashlight and came to a stop. The cannibal was nearby, but Noelle felt a force protecting her at the moment. She wasn't sure what it was, not right now. No, the only thing she was sure of was that it was supernatural.

Protected by this force, Noelle felt relatively safe approaching the retired sheriff. She moved her flashlight up and down, inspecting the dead body, trying to figure out what was going on. At first glance, the sight could've easily been confused for suicide, until you saw the gash in his thigh, the stab wound on the side of his stomach, and the smashed-up nose.

Then, of course, there was the rifle dangling from the other side of the branch, which made it clear someone had murdered the man. It'd gotten stuck between two smaller branches growing out from the larger branch Mr. Olmos's body dangled from.

Noelle didn't realize she was crying until a sob escaped her. Knowing this man had come out here to try to avenge his daughter's death and had died at the same man's hand broke her.

The force that was protecting her felt stronger than ever now, like she was separated from the rest of the world and not even the cannibal could harm her under this barrier. Noelle let it all out, all of the emotions and all of the sadness.

She let the gun drop to the side, heard it hit the snow on the ground with a slushy thump. And then she crumpled onto her knees, buried her face in her leather gloves, and cried. Cried harder than she ever had for a length of time that felt indeterminable.

Really, though, it felt like an eternity by the time she was tired of crying and by the time she pulled her head away from her hands.

"They're all counting on you." The voice spoke out of the darkness.

Noelle turned her head and saw Rachel standing a few feet away, a slight shine outlining her. Behind her, she could see other shapes. They looked like a group of people standing underneath a blinding white light.

Rachel was whole. There was no blood, no gashes, no broken bones. It was just her younger sister standing there, a big sweater and a long, dark red scarf wrapped around her neck.

"Rachel..." Noelle said, feeling like she was in a fevered dream. Deep down, she wondered if maybe the cannibal hadn't already killed her, and she was in the afterlife. "Rachel, you're really here?"

"I am." Rachel said, her smile growing bigger. "And so are they."

One by one, the shapes behind her began to take form. First, it was Dalton, Vanessa, and Eli. They were standing in a group to the left. Dalton gave her a small nod, Vanessa a wave of her fingers.

Next to them appeared Fred Meyers and Fletcher Duncan. Both the boys smiled and waved to her.

To their right, Mr. Olmos and Judy Olmos appeared. Mr. Olmos had his arm around Judy's shoulder, squeezing her tight, his body language saying he would never let his daughter go.

The effect of seeing him whole while his body hung as a corpse only a few feet next to her made Noelle's stomach go sour, but that feeling was wiped away when he smiled at her.

"I didn't get to thank you for giving me this chance." Mr. Olmos said, then he glanced over at his dead body before his eyes flicked back to Noelle. "Even though I messed it up, thank you. It's all up to you now."

Before Noelle could respond—and she wasn't sure she was even capable of doing so, as seeing this many ghosts at once had her stunned—the last two forms took shape. It was Gavin and Wayne Briggs standing at the edge of the group. Gavin was leaning on his little brother with his forearm, a smug look on his face. Next to him, Wayne was smiling.

Somehow, Noelle knew Wayne was smiling because he was reunited with his brother. But more than that, he was elated that his older brother had come to get revenge for him. It didn't matter to the kid that his brother had failed and been killed because his brother was his one true hero, and while he'd been dead and wandering through the woods, he'd wondered if Gavin even cared that he'd died. The fact that his brother had put himself in danger had been answer to that question. And now, at last, his soul was at ease.

Gavin took his arm off his little brother and walked toward Noelle. At first, he *floated* over the ground, his feet not leaving any prints. But as he drew nearer to Noelle and crossed the barrier between the living and the dead world, he left behind boot prints in the snow until he was standing over Noelle.

He crouched down and picked up her pistol.

"Dying fucking hurts." He said, grinning. "So don't die and kill this fucker."

Noelle smiled, then used one of her hands to wipe the tears away, but she still couldn't bring herself to talk.

"You're gonna need this." Gavin said, holding the gun out, butt facing Noelle. "Put a hole through him for me, will you?"

Noelle nodded and took the gun.

Gavin rose. "I'll see you on the flipside, Noelle. Hopefully later—way later—rather than soon."

Gavin walked back to the group and then, together, all of them except Rachel began to fade out. Getting dimmer and dimmer by the second, like a light being controlled by a sliding switch, until they winked out of existence.

"Be valiant, Noelle." Rachel said. "I know you can be."

With that, Rachel disappeared as well. Leaving Noelle by herself again. The barrier that had been protecting her—that the ghosts had been creating, she presumed—was lifted.

It was just her and the cannibal in these darkened woods.

One way or another, the end was nigh.

CHAPTER 54

Ignacio stepped out into a silver patch of moonlight, knife in hand. The moment he did that, the girl seemed to sense him. She turned to look at him.

There wasn't fear on her face. Or sadness… or anger. There wasn't any emotion on her face at all except recognition. Of course she recognized him. She'd come back here for him. For this moment.

The two of them stared at one another. The snow was dying off, so only a small flurry of flakes twirled through the air between them. This minimal stretch of time was the calm before the storm—the fate of one of them was about to be decided by this second confrontation.

At their cores, they knew this was the final moments of one of their lives.

He had a different mask on, a dark red one with a black swirl in the middle of it. It was strange and much more artistic than the one he'd had on their last encounter. It threw her off, but only for a second, because the only thing that mattered was killing him.

When she'd been imagining this moment of seeing the cannibal for a second time, she'd always imagined herself drawing first blood. And now that it was before her, she didn't intend to deviate from that.

Noelle raised her pistol, pointing it right at Varias Caras's chest—and squeezed the trigger.

Ignacio moved out of the moonlight, out of her aim, and into the darkness just in time. He heard the crack of the gun, followed by the girl letting out a frustrated groan. She'd been banking on that being the kill shot.

Ignacio ran through the woods, ducking for cover behind trees as he tried to circle around the girl. She had good aim, seeing as she'd almost just gotten him. He would have to be careful.

She heard him running through the woods. Twigs snapping underneath his weight, branches clattering as he ran through them. The problem was the sounds echoed and traveled in a way that made it difficult to pinpoint which way he was coming from.

She wasn't sure *where* he was exactly, she had to find him with her flashlight before—

Out of her peripherals, she saw a blur charging toward her. He was fast. Much, much faster than his enormous body had any right to be. His left hand was extended out, empty, fingers ready to grab onto her, while his right hand had the blood-slicked knife ready to cut her.

Noelle turned toward him on her heels and fired two rounds at him. The first one hit him at the top of his shoulder, barely doing more than nicking his skin. Even still, blood sprayed out into the air from the wound, the second one missed him completely.

Her aim had been poor, she'd known that as she'd squeezed the trigger. They'd been desperate shots she'd been hoping would stave him off and buy her more time. But no such thing happened. The cannibal pounced on her.

Noelle felt herself falling backward but kept her grip on the gun. She aimed it somewhere in his stomach and fired off a bullet as they crashed to the ground. The next thing happened so fast she barely had enough time to process it; she felt Varias Caras's weight flatten her, heard him grow in pain, then she felt the relief of his weight coming off her.

By some miracle, Noelle still had the gun in her hand. She picked herself up, aiming it in the direction he'd been, but she'd lost him again. Her flashlight revealed blood on the snow, though. Fresh blood that suggested she'd gotten him with that last round. It was spread out too erratically for her to know which direction he'd headed in, and besides, running after him blindly in the dark would be a bad idea.

He was weakened, though. Yet, strong enough to still run.

Noelle gripped the gun tighter. The advantage was hers, and a plan was beginning to formulate in her head.

Noelle started running through the woods, hoping that doing so would activate his hunting instinct and he'd chase after her.

It was a strange feeling to want a crazed cannibal to run after her, but she needed to lead him right to where she wanted him.

CHAPTER 55

He was crouched down behind some bushes, bleeding everywhere. The bullet had gone through his hip, just above the bone, and come out the other side.

He screamed, enraged. The bullet wound pulsed with hot pain, which only angered him more. Ignacio roared and squeezed his hands into fists. Every muscle in his body flexed, his skin turned red, and the veins in his neck bulged out.

He'd turned his hearing sensitivity down knowing the girl would fire the gun at some point, but now he turned it up. He could hear her running through the woods. In the map of his head, he knew she'd just ran past the vehicle the old man had been driving.

She wasn't very far. But he was hurt. The wound in his hip was going to slow him down, but if he hurried, he could catch her. He knew how to navigate through the woods better than anyone.

The only thing was, he needed to find a weapon. The knife had fallen out of his hand after getting shot and he'd thrown the chainsaw at the bus…

Now that he thought about it, there might be something useful in there. He outsized the girl by at least a hundred pounds and a whole foot of height, so he could easily kill her with his bare hands.

But the girl had hurt him badly. Twice now. And this second time had been by herself.

The innocent part of Ignacio Calderon, the naïve part of his mind that collected women to make them his playthings didn't quite understand the meaning of the word "pride." The monster inside of him, however, did. And now killing this girl was a point of pride.

This was personal now. He wanted her to feel the full extent of his brutality.

Running with a limp, he headed in the direction of the vehicle to find a weapon.

The bus was easy to find, given that its headlights were still on. The door on the driver's side was open, and the lights inside were on, too. Even though all these lights were on, the vehicle sat in silence. The chime that let the driver know its battery was being drained had shut off minutes ago, as if the bus had given up its warning.

Ignacio hit the button on the inside of the driver's side door to unlock the other doors, then made his way to the back of the vehicle. He pulled the two back doors open, and sitting right there in the middle of the bus was his chainsaw, its blade and motor covered in blood.

"It's like God is smiling down on us, Ignacio." Papá's ghost said, appearing next to him.

Ignacio reached into the vehicle and grabbed the chainsaw. He held it in his hands; the weight of it felt good. Felt *right*.

"Only two more left!" Papá announced excitedly. "Go and finish them off, mijo!"

Ignacio set the chainsaw down on the ground, placed his foot on it, then yanked on the cord. The motor came to life and the chain started spinning around the blade.

Noelle heard the chainsaw revving, heard him coming after her. The sound of the motor getting closer and closer. The bullet wound hadn't slowed him down as much as she'd hoped.

Even still, the advantage was on her side. She was unscathed—so far, anyway.

Noelle pumped her legs faster. If her sense of direction was correct, she wasn't very far from where she needed to lead him… She just hoped she could make it there in one piece.

CHAPTER 56

Up ahead, Lakewood Cabin came into view. The cabin's outside lights were like a beacon of light in the middle of the dark woods, and Noelle thought maybe this was how people lost at sea would feel when they spotted a lighthouse.

Behind her, she heard the cannibal gaining on her, the chainsaw motor roaring into the night. Noelle half turned around and fired off a wild shot in the general direction, hoping by some miracle it'd hit him and slow him.

No such thing happened, at least, she didn't think so, as the revving sounds continued to get closer and closer to her. This motivated her to pick up her pace. She was almost out of the trees and into the part that could be considered the Lakewood Cabin grounds.

Up ahead, she saw Tess running out of the cabin, katana in her left hand. The keys in her hand shined underneath the pale porchlights. They were the Jeep's keys; Tess planned to escape.

Good. Noelle thought, mentally encouraging the girl to get away safely.

Tess saw Noelle coming out of the trees and stopped at the bottom of the porch steps. Her mouth agape, for a second unable to process what she was seeing—or maybe not knowing who was approaching the cabin. But then, a second later, her face flushed with relief.

"Noelle!" Tess screamed. "You're... alive!"

"Get out of here! He's after me!" Noelle called back, trying to sound as commanding as possible.

Tess nodded to her but didn't quite comply. Instead, she ran toward her, running past the Jeep. They met near the vehicle.

"Go!" Noelle said, grabbing her by the hand and pulling her back toward the front of the vehicle. "Get out of here, Tess. Go find help."

"What about you?" Tess asked, her hand on the handle of the driver-side door.

"I'm staying to finish what we started." Noelle said. "Now, stop wasting time and get on out of here—"

It seemed as if the cannibal had materialized out of nowhere because one second it was just them two standing by the Jeep, and the next he was standing behind Tess. He pulled the chainsaw back, like someone getting ready to smash a battering ram into a door.

Noelle screamed, trying to warn Tess, but she was too late.

The cannibal drove the chainsaw into Tess's back, pushing it through her body until it came out the other side. The middle of Tess's stomach burst open as the chainsaw tore through it. Blood splattered all over Noelle like someone had thrown a paint bucket full of it at her.

If it weren't for the neck gaiter covering the lower half of her face, some of Tess's blood would've found its way into her mouth.

With the chainsaw still going through her, the cannibal picked her up into the air and gave the chainsaw some more juice. The teeth shredded up more of her insides as he did this. The momentum flung pieces of guts and intestines and more blood through the air.

Tess's legs went limp, but they jiggled around lifelessly from the vibrations of the chainsaw. Her arms fell to the side, and the katana and the Jeep keys fell from her hands.

For a second, Noelle thought about shooting her gun, but the possibility of missing and hitting Tess instead made her rethink that. Even though the girl was dead, something about putting a bullet in her felt *wrong*.

Something else, however, compelled her to grab for the katana. As if doing so would honor Tess's death, as if it were the girl's final good gesture in life to leave the sword behind for Noelle.

Noelle picked the weapon up and then whirled around. Without thinking about how dangerous it was to give her back to the cannibal given how close he was, she took off sprinting toward the back of the cabin.

There was no question in her mind now; the cannibal would follow.

Ignacio pulled the chainsaw out of the girl and let her corpse fall to the wayside. Using his forearm, he wiped some of the blood that had gotten onto his mask away, then ran after the final girl.

She was fast, and Ignacio was hurt, but he was determined. After having killed all those people and all the rage running through him, he felt like he could fight through anything.

Noelle heard the cannibal catching up to her, but she had him right where she wanted him. She craned her neck to look over her shoulder and saw he was only a few steps behind her. He was covered in blood—his own blood and his victim's blood, as well—and there was unadulterated anger in his single eye. Even from this distance and from the motion of them running, Noelle could see that. She tightened her grip on the gun and sword.

Noelle turned around, focusing her eyes on the ground, trying to remember the exact spots she'd set the beartraps. She had a good idea of where it was, but the snow was making it difficult to really be sure.

Up ahead, though, there were two mounds of snow that looked suspicious—but only suspicious if one knew what to look for. She was almost positive those were the spots…

She hoped she was right. Her guess would be the difference between life and death.

Noelle gulped as she came within two steps of one of the spots and hopped over it.

She heard the chainsaw getting closer and closer… so close she wondered if the cannibal wasn't within striking range.

And then, she heard one of the most beautiful sounds she'd ever heard in her life. The metallic squeak of the beartrap's jaw closing and its teeth clasping together. The cannibal screamed. The chainsaw revved louder.

Her plan had worked.

Noelle spun around, just in time to see the chainsaw coming right at her head. In a fit of rage, the cannibal had thrown it. Noelle sidestepped it, almost slipping in the snow. She felt the wind flip her hair as the chainsaw passed inches past her head.

Then she raised the pistol with one hand. All her preparation came down to this moment. She took in a deep breath and held it, and it felt like everything around her slowed down.

She watched the cannibal throw his arms around in the air, angry and hurt. She looked down at his trapped leg. Blood oozed out from where the metal teeth were sunk into his flesh.

The leg that had been caught happened to be on the same side as his injured hip, which was the reason he couldn't just pull the beartrap off the chain with brute strength. That side of his body seemed to have little strength left.

Noelle lined the barrel up with the cannibal, thinking about putting a bullet in his head and ending it, but she wanted him to suffer. So, instead, she aimed at his other hip and pulled the trigger.

The cannibal looked over at her, shock in his eyes, then the look converted into pain.

"NO!" He screamed, falling to his knees. The snow crunched underneath his weight.

Determined to get out of the trap, he fell back on his ass, and started reaching for the beartrap, intending to pull its jaws apart.

Knowing she'd just emptied the clip on that last shot, Noelle dropped the gun and jumped toward him, swinging the katana at his right arm. The blade sliced through his wrist like it was made of butter. Blood spurted out from the giant gash, and the cannibal drew both his arms back, screaming in agonized pain. His severed hand went flying, scuttering through the snow, leaving blotches of red as it tumbled several feet away.

Noelle saw his free leg twitching, as if he were trying his best to kick at her with it—his last stand perhaps, but the bullet wound was making it impossible. Even still, for good measure, she needed to keep it from being free.

She raised the katana over her head, holding it vertically. Then, she let out a battle cry, a deep guttural scream she didn't know she was capable of until this moment and stabbed the sword into the cannibal's leg. The sword skewered through his thigh, went through the snow, then got lodged in the earth, pinning the leg to the ground. His already blood-covered pants got soaked with even more blood from this new wound.

Noelle looked down at the cannibal. He was lying flat on his back, wheezing, no longer screaming because he didn't have the energy for it. His arm with the severed had was off to the side, lying limp like a tentacle as blood continued to pour out of the end of it. Both of his legs were still, and now that she got a good look at it, she could see the beartrap had broken his shin in a way that the bone had splintered and ripped through the front of his leg.

He reached out into the air with his only working limb, the arm that remained injured. Maybe it was him pleading for mercy, maybe it was him still trying to fight. Noelle wasn't sure, but it made no difference to her.

She kicked it down to the ground and stepped on his hand, putting all her weight on it. She felt some of the finger bones snap underneath her boot. The cannibal let out a groan. Noelle bent down, grabbed his broken hand, and pulled it toward where the second bear trap laid.

She let his hand fall into it. The weight triggered the mechanism, and the jaws snapped around his wrist. The teeth broke the bones and blood gushed out from these new wounds.

Noelle stepped back to stare at the enormous man, lying in the snow underneath the yellow glow of the cabin's backlights. His single eyes moved to meet hers. There wasn't rage or even determination in it. All she could see was acquiescence.

He knew it was over. They both did.

"Was... was Ignacio... a bad guy...?" He asked, through labored, pained breathing.

Noelle ignored the question. Instead, she stepped back, looked for the chainsaw. It was a few feet away, covered in blood and snow. Noelle walked over to it and picked it up. The weight of it made her realize how exhausted she was, but she wasn't about to let up.

Noelle shuffled back to the cannibal's side.

"I hope you're in the worst pain of your life right now," Noelle said, looking into his face but putting the chainsaw down on the ground. She planted one of her boots on its motor. "But more than anything, I hope you're terrified down to your core."

Noelle ripped on the cord. The motor revved. She pulled on the cord a few more times, the motor roaring now. She lifted the chainsaw over her head and hit the gas on it. The chains began spinning around the blade.

Noelle relished this moment for a few seconds, then dropped the chainsaw down onto the cannibal.

CHAPTER 57

Fifteen minutes later, Ignacio Calderon's body was chopped up into pieces. Noelle had used the chainsaw to tear off all four of his limbs. The wounds, where they'd once been attached to the torso, were now just holes surrounded by shredded skin, tissue, and fat. Blood pumped out from them. The warmth of the spillage melted the snow, turning it into steam that rose into the cold November air like tendrils of smoke.

Noelle stepped back, taking a second to admire her work. An action that, unbeknownst to her, was something Ignacio Calderon had done many times before in his lifetime. The chainsaw was slowing down, and she was breathing hard, but there was still one more thing for her to do. The limbs were removed from the body, reducing the torso to a lump of massive flesh, but the deed wasn't done yet.

Killing him wasn't enough. She wanted this to be overkill.

Noelle moved over to the top of his body, hearing her boots slosh through the mixture of snow and muck and blood the slaughtering of Ignacio's body had turned the ground into.

She stopped by his head. He was still wearing the red mask with the black spiral design on it, his dead eye behind it staring up into the sky. For a quick second, she thought about taking the mask off, but no.

She wanted whoever would find his dead body to know she'd killed Varias Caras, not just Ignacio Calderon.

Noelle put the chainsaw down on the ground, then stepped on it for leverage before pulling on its cord. The motor roared as it revved harder, as it pushed the chains to spin around the blade faster. Noelle gave it a few more quick tugs until it felt the chainsaw was going as fast as it would go.

Then, she willed her tired arms to lift the chainsaw over her head. She thought of everyone who'd fallen victims to him in the moment before bringing it down, of all her camping friends. Of Mr. Olmos and his daughter. Eli and Tess.

She even thought of the people she'd never met. The kids at the Halloween house party. Diana Santos. Ignacio's boss at the junkyard.

She'd killed their murderer. In some way, everything she'd done up until this point was to avenge all their deaths.

But this, what she was about to do, was entirely for herself.

Noelle swung the chainsaw down onto Ignacio's throat. The chainsaw bit and tore through the flesh and muscle as Noelle drove it into the neck. Blood and bits of human matter sputtered into the air, splashing all over Noelle's arms and hands, adding to the gristle that already covered them.

Noelle felt the resistance of the blade hitting the neckbone and put a little more force into driving the chainsaw. The chainsaw vibrated in her hands as its teeth sawed through the bone, breaking through it like it was a thick tree branch. A few seconds later, she felt the blade clear through the bone and easily tear through the rest of the flesh.

Noelle pulled the chainsaw away and let it drop to the wayside. It landed in the reddish-brown muck that the ground had turned into with a wet thud. Its blades were slowing down but very much still spinning, and the chains' teeth cut into the softened earth, sending sprinkles of the grotesque mixture through the air.

She crouched down and grabbed a fistful of the head's hair with one hand, then lifted it up into the air. She felt like Hercules lifting the Gorgon's head for all to see—except, out here, this deep in the woods, it was only her still alive.

The last one standing. Not the final girl. No, this time she hadn't just survived the cannibal. This time, she'd bested him.

This was it. The final slaughter.

The blood her clothes were soaked with had dried and was turning into a crust, making Noelle feel like she was wearing a suit of armor as she shuffled through the snow carrying Ignacio's head in her right hand. Blood dripped down from the stump where the head had once been attached to the torso, leaving a trail of blood through the snow as Noelle trudged to the front of the cabin.

She stopped at the bottom of the porch steps. The pyramidal cap on the banister posts gave her an idea. They weren't quite spikes, but with enough force…

Noelle grabbed the head with two hands, placing her palms on the sides of its temples.

Then, let out a shriek of victory as she lodged the bottom of the head onto the point of one of the post caps. There was a wet, dull sound as the head slid onto the wooden pyramid.

Now, it was truly over for her.

Noelle took her hands off the head and stepped back. A gust of wind blew by, and she was sure it would blow her away given how much weight had come off her shoulders. Of course, that didn't happen. Instead, Noelle took a deep breath and then turned toward her Jeep.

She dragged herself over to where Tess's body lay. Noelle avoided looking at the girl's body— she'd seen enough carnage for a lifetime. She found the Jeep key in the snow nearby and clicked the unlock button on it.

The Jeep chirped. Its sound almost cheerful in contrast to the events of the night. She went over to the vehicle and slumped into the driver's seat. She stuck the key in the ignition, turned it, and fired up the engine. The headlights shined on the front of Lakewood Cabin, on the cannibal's severed head.

Gravity had caused it to slump a little to the right side. Blood was dripping down the post, slowly. Ignacio's dead eye seemed to be concentrated on Noelle, but that was likely just a trick of the light.

Or a trick of the mind.

Either way, it didn't make much of a difference to her.

Noelle put the Jeep in reverse and circled around until the vehicle was facing the woods. She flicked on the high beams and then drove toward the trees.

It was time to go home. Alone.

But that was better than being dead out here.

AFTERWORD

Originally, there was supposed to be an epilogue to this book, but I somehow lost it. Maybe a demon got into my computer and ate it, or maybe I didn't hit the save button correctly. Your guess is as good as mine. Either way, the reality is, that losing the epilogue was a blessing in disguise. It gave me a chance to ponder on whether this series needed one or not.

By the time I sat down to rewrite the few hundred words and started pecking at the keys, I concluded that it was unnecessary (as you can tell… as there is no epilogue!). It didn't quite answer anything, it was more of just one last emotional bang. Ultimately, I felt it took away from the impact of Noelle's victory. I think it's best if we all have our own ideas of how she goes on living after her final showdown with Varias Caras.

Look, I know there are likely lots of questions left unresolved, but sometimes I think the best stories are the ones that remain enshrouded in mystery even after they're over. Much like the fictional location of Camp Slaughter in the series, if you think about it.

Anyway, this story is very much done. The legend has been told. If I did my job correctly, these books and these characters will live in your mind for years to come.

And if I'm lucky, maybe your heart, too.

—
3/24/2024
SG

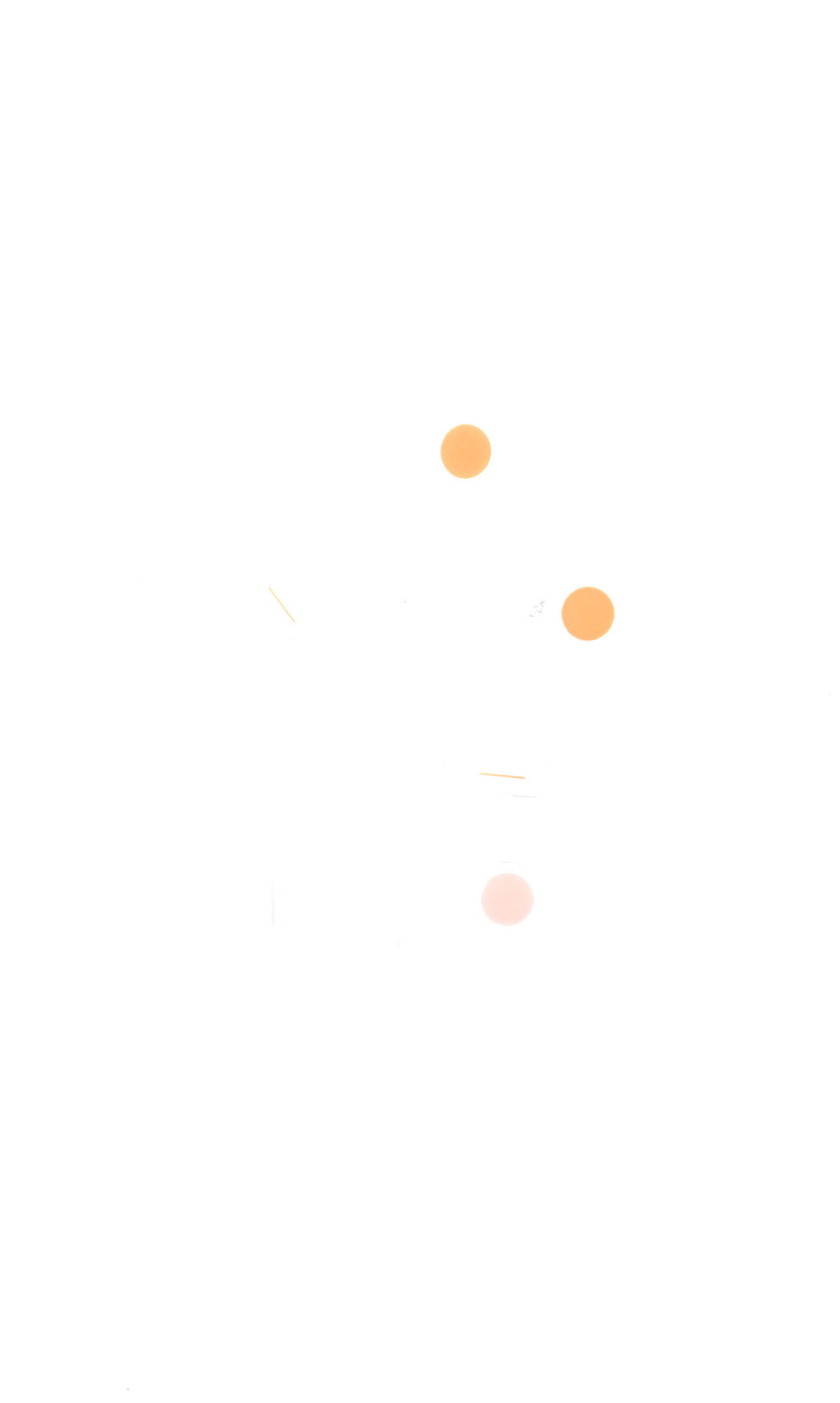

Printed in Great Britain
by Amazon